OF STARLIGHT AND MIDNIGHT

BY AMY KUIVALAINEN

THE MAGICIANS OF VENICE
The Immortal City
The Sea of the Dead
The King's Seal

THE FIREBIRD FAERIE TALES
Cry of the Firebird
Ashes of the Firebird
Rise of the Firebird

FIREBIRD FAERIE TALES SPIN-OFF NOVELS
The Exorcist and the Demon Hunter
Of Starlight and Midnight

AMY KUIVALAINEN

OF STARLIGHT

AND MIDNIGHT

A NOVEL

Livonia, Michigan

OF STARLIGHT AND MIDNIGHT

Copyright © 2024 Amy Kuivalainen

All rights reserved. No part of this publication may be reproduced, distributed, or transmitted in any form or by any means, including photocopying, recording, or other electronic or mechanical methods, without the prior written permission of the publisher, except in the case of brief quotations embodied in critical reviews and certain other noncommercial uses permitted by copyright law. For permission requests, please write to the publisher.

This book is a work of fiction. The characters, incidents, and dialogue are drawn from the author's imagination and are not to be construed as real. Any resemblance to actual events or persons, living or dead, is entirely coincidental.

Published by BHC Press

Library of Congress Control Number: 2023945946

ISBN: 978-1-64397-382-1 (Hardcover)
ISBN: 978-1-64397-383-8 (Softcover)
ISBN: 978-1-64397-384-5 (Ebook)

For information, write:
BHC Press
885 Penniman #5505
Plymouth, MI 48170

Visit the publisher:
www.bhcpress.com

For all the Thranduil girls who needed more elves.

OF STARLIGHT AND MIDNIGHT

NORNA DÓMR

THE ROOTS OF THE World Tree were the silver gray of moonlight. They were so deep down that no light ever reached them except for the luminous lanterns of the Norns as they watered its roots and sang their songs to it.

While one watered, the other wove, then it was the next sister's turn to pick up the pattern.

This is how they passed the day before drifting back to their halls, leaving their buckets next to the Well of Fate.

Urðr, the eldest, stared at her weavings of the past and frowned.

"What's wrong, sister?" Verðandi asked. Always in the present, she was the most balanced of the three.

"In the past, things have been pleasant. Perhaps they could be again," Urðr said, causing her sister to pause. Urðr, with her focus always behind her, very rarely speculated about the present, let alone a future.

Urðr tied off her stitch before stepping back from the weaving. Verðandi joined her, staring at the glossy and glowing pattern that meant Urðr had been weaving the fate of immortals.

"What are you both looking at?" demanded Skuld, the youngest of the three, as she pushed them out of the way. She was the brightest and most beautiful of the three, embodying what most people hoped for their future. "Oh, look at that."

"Quite," Verðandi acknowledged.

"Look at how beautiful it started," Urðr complained, pointing to where dark and light were interwoven in glorious complex patterns. "Now the pattern has straightened into parallel lines, separate and boring."

"I agree. It's completely screwed up now," said Verðandi, sitting down at the loom. She twisted two threads of silver in one hand and two threads of shadow in the other. Contemplating.

Skuld started laughing. "*Do it.* Do it, Verðandi. I can see it, and it's going to be *great*. Like the most fun we've had in ages."

Verðandi shrugged. "Okay, let's screw with them and see what happens."

1

SØREN STOOD OUTSIDE THE impressive facade of glass and light that was the University of Oslo Library and wondered what in the goddess Hel's name he was doing there.

He hadn't expected a university with laughing students and walkways lined with winter trees, black with rain and stripped of most of their leaves. He had expected a grand building, dripping with either dilapidation or money—that was more of the Darkness's style.

The organization known as the Darkness had been quiet since the battle in Russia two years ago. Anya—shamanitsa, honorary Álfr, and general pain in his ass—had almost wiped out the Illumination and the Darkness completely when she had combined her magic with his brother Aramis's and the Firebird's during that fateful battle.

But *almost* destroyed wasn't *completely* destroyed, and Søren still had a score to settle with the bastards who had attacked his city. He pulled out his phone and dialed a number.

"Are you there yet?" Aramis asked.

"Your dodgy tracking spell has led us to the wrong place. This is a university, not a bloody headquarters for the Darkness."

Aramis let out a long-suffering sigh. "We are looking for an artifact that has a 98 percent probability of being a book. Where better to hide it than a library?"

"I'm not an idiot, but something is…off."

"Like what?"

"I don't know. I just have this feeling. I'm going to check it out."

"Call me afterward. And Søren? Try to be polite if you talk to the humans."

Søren hung up. He was a Dauđi Dómr, a Death Judge of the Álfr. He didn't have to be *polite*. He certainly didn't have the inclination to be polite when it came to people who had plundered the artifacts of his people.

Svetilo, a mountain Álfr city in Russia, had been hit the hardest during the war with the Darkness two years ago. It was a place devoted to the knowledge and culture of the Álfr in Midgard, but it had been plundered by the Darkness and had many of its treasures stolen.

After the war, Aramis and Søren had made it their responsibility to restore Svetilo and had scouted the world for its lost books and artifacts ever since.

They had only managed to recover a third of them in the last two years.

Find the piece and get out of there, Søren prompted himself. He walked through the doors and into the warmth of the library foyer. The word "BIB-LIOTEK" was carved into a marble wall over an opening that led into the stacks.

Søren spread out dark tendrils of his magic, searching for any other magical signatures in the building. To anyone walking past him, he would simply be another person looking at their phone.

His magic jolted back to him so sharp and hot that he almost dropped his phone in surprise. He put his phone in his pocket and headed through the door. Students sat at long rows of desks, studied the timber shelves, searching for titles, and made out where they thought no one would see.

Søren followed the pulsing signal that had made his magic so excited. He halted at the end of a long row of shelves.

A woman was taking books from a trolley beside her and reshelving them. She was young, early thirties if he had to guess, with straight red-gold hair pulled back into a sensible ponytail. Even wearing high-heeled ankle boots, she barely reached five feet tall. She was dressed demurely in a knee-length black skirt and tight cream cardigan buttoned all the way up to her neck. It was almost as if she had looked up "repressed librarian" in a book and stuck to the aesthetic.

Pocket-size librarian, Søren thought. It was obviously a disguise. His magic rarely made a mistake, but here it was going crazy over this bookish mouse. She turned as if sensing that she was being watched. Large gray eyes that lifted slightly at the corners studied him behind a pair of stylish square-framed glasses. She was cute, he realized with some surprise, with her Scandinavian cheekbones and full lips.

"*Hei,*" she greeted in Norwegian. "Can I help you?"

"Do you work here?" he asked bluntly in English. Gray eyes narrowed at his tone.

"What do you think?" she replied in English. She pointed to the badge above her breast stamped with the red-and-white insignia of the university and the name "ASTA" printed in bold black letters. She had a curious accent that Søren couldn't place. A touch Scandinavian, a bit British, and a little something else. Liar, perhaps.

Be polite, Søren thought, remembering Aramis's words.

Søren smiled at her. "Thank goodness you speak English. My modern Norwegian is atrocious."

"How can I help you? You don't look like a student," Asta said cautiously, looking over his black-on-black three-piece suit and cashmere overcoat. Aramis had tried to convince him to glamour his long black hair, but he had refused. He'd pulled the top half up and away from his face in a braid and left the rest loose. It wasn't the 1920s anymore. He could have his hair as long as he wanted. Women, Søren had observed, also liked his hair and often used it as a conversation starter.

"I need a book," he replied vaguely. "I mean, an expert."

"Which one do you need more?" Asta said with the slightest smile.

"I need an expert in old books."

"How old? We have a medieval literature section. Is that old enough?"

"Yes?"

Asta folded her arms. "You aren't a student. What are you actually doing here?"

Søren pulled his magic back in. He couldn't focus while it buzzed around her, trying to reach out and stroke her.

He cleared his throat. "I'm sorry, I'm horribly jet-lagged. May I start again?"

"Only if you use your words this time. Otherwise, I'm calling security." The haughty book mouse wasn't going to give him an inch.

"I'm looking for old manuscripts and books. I have inherited one, and I'd like to see if the library has anything similar. If you know of an expert who can help me, I'd appreciate it. As you can tell, I'm not one." He gave her his winning smile that usually loosened up most people and supernaturals, but her eyes only narrowed further.

"Can I see some ID?"

"Do I look like I am some kind of thief?" He laughed.

"Don't thieves look like everyone else? We've had people try before. I want to be able to give the police a name if anything goes missing."

Asta held out a small hand impatiently. Søren took note of her black nail polish. *Interesting.* Maybe the uptight librarian's prim act was slipping. He reached inside his overcoat pocket, took a fake driver's license from his wallet, and handed it to her.

"You're from Alaska, Mr. Søren Madson? That doesn't sound like an American name," she said skeptically.

"I immigrated when I was young." He didn't say from where. "I inherited the book from my father after he died, and it sparked my interest to search out its origins here in Norway. Satisfied?"

She handed him back the laminated card. "For now."

"Are you sure *you* aren't security?"

"Worse. I'm the expert you are looking for."

Søren's smile was sharp as a blade. "Of course you are."

2

ASTA FELT THE STRANGER'S emerald-green eyes on her as she led him through the library to a reception desk in front of the sealed archives.

Her gut instinct was still to call security on the obviously rich Loki wannabe. He acted clueless, but every inch of him said otherwise. She was a sucker for a black-on-black suit and goddamn…that hair. He was attractive in a way that had made her stop dead in her tracks and stare at him like a rabbit in front of a wolf. Then he had opened his beautifully curved mouth and ruined it with his entitled tone.

Asta went behind the counter and handed him a form and a pen.

"I'll need you to fill in all of your details for the system log before I can let you in to see the collection."

Søren let out a pained sigh. "If this is a way to get my number, you should've just asked." Asta rolled her eyes before she could think better of it. Seriously, the nerve of this guy.

"Has that line ever worked?"

"More than once," he admitted.

"It's the rules."

"And you follow those often, do you?" he asked, not looking up from where he scribbled. Asta stilled. Was he on to her? He didn't look like he belonged to the university.

"In the library I most definitely do." She tried to imitate the stern, authoritative voice her mother had always used to bring people into line.

"Where are you from?" Søren asked.

"None of your business."

"It seems only fair. You just saw my license and are about to know everything about me from this invasive form of yours. You don't have much of a Norwegian accent, and your English is excellent. So where are you from?"

"Everywhere." It wasn't a lie. She'd never lived anywhere longer than six months in her entire life.

"Sounds like it." He pushed the form back across the counter. His handwriting was atrocious. Asta could barely make out what he had written but wasn't about to let him know that.

"Come on through, Mr. Madson." He joined her behind the counter and held out his arms.

"I'm ready for my full-body search. Go on. I won't move, I promise."

Heat tingled at the back of her neck, but she managed to ignore it.

"That won't be necessary."

"Afraid of what you might find?"

"I'm sure it would be as disappointing as your manners." She walked past him and swiped her card to open the medieval book room. Søren laughed under his breath, and something about it seemed to slither along her skin. She bit her lip to keep herself from smiling.

"Do you know what time period you are looking for?" Asta asked.

"No."

"What's the book about?"

"I don't know," he said with a lazy wave of his hand. "It's old. I can't read the language."

Asta pinched the bridge of her nose. This guy was going to drive her insane and blow her cover unless she dealt with him fast.

"Do you have pictures?" she said finally.

Søren looked thoughtful for a moment before pulling out his phone and dialing a number. "Brother. Can you please send me some pictures of the old book we inherited from our father?"

Asta heard the questioning tone of the person on the other end. She wondered if the brother was as mental as Søren was.

"Gods, Aramis, you *know* what book I mean. It's old, has pictures in it, odd language. It's the one we think is medieval," Søren said impatiently. "I'm with an expert who'll be able to tell me if she has anything similar. Send them through." He hung up the phone and turned to smile at Asta. "What?"

"I'm just happy to see that you talk to everyone like that and not just me."

"Like what?" He tilted his head.

"Like you're some general giving orders, and everyone is just expected to jump." Jesus, she was being rude. She couldn't help it. The guy was infuriating.

"How do you know I'm not a general?"

"I don't think I want to know what you are."

Søren's phone buzzed, and he opened the messages. Asta saw a flicker of gold bordering, and her stomach fluttered.

"This is it." He passed her the phone. "Have you seen anything like it before?"

The coffee and sandwich she had eaten for lunch threatened to come up as she squeaked, "No. Never. They look…very medieval. The detail on the borders looks similar to *The Lindisfarne Gospels*, but the designs are almost Viking."

"*The Lindisfarne Gospels* are from the eighth century. You think my book could be that old?" Søren asked curiously.

Asta carefully made her face blank. He wasn't as big of an idiot as he seemed if he not only knew the manuscript she was referring to but also knew the date of its creation.

She let out a breezy laugh. "Well, it certainly could be, Mr. Madson, but without seeing the actual book, I won't be able to tell. If you bring it in—"

"I'm not sure I'm comfortable with that. How about I email you the pictures, and you see what you can discover. If that fails, and you ask me very nicely over a drink, I will consider bringing it in for you to look at."

Asta opened her mouth to tell him what he could do with his drink offer when a crisp voice announced over the PA system that the library was closing in ten minutes.

"I'm sorry, Mr. Madson, but you need to leave. Your hunt for a similar manuscript will have to wait for another day."

"I do *love* a good hunt. Do you have a card, Asta? So I can email the photos."

"I haven't agreed to help you."

"Yes, you have. I saw your eyes light up when you saw the pictures. I have a mystery, and it'll annoy you until you help me solve it. Let's help each other, and we'll both get what we want." Søren's general voice was back again. She hated it, but not as much as the fact he was right. She *did* want to see those photos just not for the reasons he thought.

"I don't have a card," Asta said as she escorted him out of the room and back to the reception desk. Taking a pen, she wrote down an email address on a Post-it note and handed it to him.

"AstaToveJohanson@gmail.com," he read aloud. "Miss Johanson, your phone number isn't on this piece of paper."

"And it doesn't need to be. Goodnight, Mr. Madson. I'll let security know you're on your way out," Asta said, walking him toward the exit door.

"You have a safe trip home." Søren gave her a knockout smile that was ruined by the calculating look in his eyes.

"I will." Asta closed the door behind him and engaged the lock. She didn't breathe until the light turned red to indicate it had locked. He folded the note and slid it into his breast pocket before disappearing into the night.

"What the fuck, Asta?" she whispered to herself before picking up the reception desk phone and pressing the number for security.

"*Hei*, Erik, there's a man in black exiting now. Please make sure he gets out," she instructed before hanging up.

It took Asta ten minutes to get her bag and jacket from the staff room and disappear out of a side door. She needed to get home and talk to Tyra. This night had been too weird. Her phone's email tone buzzed. Glancing at the email, she saw it contained the photos of the mysterious book.

"No, I'm not looking at you before I have a beer in my hand," Asta said and closed it immediately. Her stomach clenched, and she looked behind her.

It was ten o'clock at night, and university students still mingled on the lit walkways. There was no sign of her strange visitor. Somehow she didn't think he was the type to catch public transport. Asta pulled the hood of her jacket up and tried not to run to the light-rail stop on the other side of the campus.

It took her thirty minutes to get home to her two-room apartment at Louises Gate. She still hadn't shaken the feeling of someone watching her and needed to get a locked door between her and the rest of the world. She could already hear the TV through her front door as she fumbled with her keys.

"Really, Tyra? Again?" Asta said with a laugh.

Her cousin was lying upside down on the couch in the lounge room, her huge black eyes transfixed on the TV. She was watching *The Hobbit: The Desolation of Smaug* for the third time that week. Her long black hair was woven in complicated fishtail braids that made her look like a heavy metal elf.

"Thranduil does strange things to my body. Ljósálfar have never done that to me before, so I'm fascinated. I want to meet this King of the Woodland Realm and show him what I'd like to do to him on that fancy throne of his," Tyra said with a lascivious smile as she straightened up the right way.

This was not an unusual thing for Tyra to say. As a Norse mythology nerd, her cousin was forever making strange comments on the nature of dwarves, the arrogance of Asgardians, and the treachery of the Norns. She was extremely opinionated on the Ljósálfar, the light elves from Álfheim, and the Dökkálfar, the dark elves from Svartálfaheim, and would, with the slightest provocation, launch into a great one-sided conversation about the virtues and failures of both races.

Asta sighed. "I guess I should be grateful it's not *Thor: Ragnarok* again."

"Hela is my *queen*!" Tyra shouted. "What's the matter? You look upset."

"Long day," Asta admitted. She pulled a beer from the fridge and sat down next to Tyra.

"Your mother?" Tyra asked gently. Asta swallowed another mouthful of beer.

"No. Not really," Asta lied.

It had been six months since her mother Tove had been killed in a hit-and-run in the middle of Oslo. Asta hadn't even known Tyra existed until she had shown up at the funeral and introduced herself as a long-lost Norwegian cousin. Her mother had never talked about her family, but Tyra had said that the article about the hit-and-run and the accompanying photo of Asta's mother was enough for her to track Asta down. Family was family.

They were both in their thirties and had bonded over too much vodka and grief. Asta had been surprised at how well they got along. Tyra had been raised in Norway and was the complete opposite of Asta. She was ridiculously tall, athletic, and had a sexy goth aesthetic that Asta secretly wished that she could pull off. Tyra had moved in to cover Tove's half of the rent, and Asta was glad of the company.

"Talk to me, baby cousin," Tyra insisted, slinging an arm around Asta's shoulders.

"A weird guy came into the library. You know, the super-arrogant type. He wanted to know about medieval manuscripts," said Asta, not wanting to bore Tyra with details.

"You seem pissed. What did he do?"

"Nothing. Just had a big attitude and wouldn't stop trying to flirt with me."

Tyra's black eyes lit up. "Was he good-looking?"

"Yes. Stupidly so," Asta admitted begrudgingly.

"You should've taken him up on it. You could use a good date."

"Ha! Men are the last thing I need in my life." Especially not rude, demanding ones.

"I didn't mean a man in your life. I meant a man in your pants. You don't keep them," Tyra said with a snort, and Asta laughed. They watched the end of the movie together, and it was 1:00 a.m. when Asta finally closed the door to her room.

Sitting cross-legged on her bed, Asta opened her bedside table drawer and pulled out a battered leather book as thick as a Bible. It had been in her mother's bag the day she got hit by the car. She opened the photos the enigmatic Søren had emailed her before opening the book.

"Shit," Asta muttered.

There was no mistaking it. The intricate style of the illustrations and the archaic hybrid Norse runic language were exactly the same. "What were you up to, Mama?"

3

IT WAS 3:00 A.M. when the lights in Asta's apartment turned off. Søren had spent the last four hours contemplating if he should charge up the stairs to demand she tell him all of the secrets he *knew* she was hiding.

His phone rang again, and he ignored it. Søren stared up at the dark windows, his magic humming irritably under his skin. He gripped the steering wheel hard and took three steady breaths. He knew where she was going to be. He had time to play it out. She was too naïve to be a member of the Darkness, but she had been in contact with Álfr magic recently. He could just about smell it on her.

Søren was going to have to change his tactics and return with a better plan. He smiled. He *did* love a good hunt, and stalking his prey was half the fun.

He pulled out into the quiet streets and drove back to the Radisson where he and Aramis had set up a temporary base in the penthouse suite. He'd barely stepped out of the elevator when Aramis was suddenly standing in front of him.

"Did you forget how to use your phone all of a sudden?" Aramis demanded, his blue eyes flashing with anger.

"No, I just didn't want to talk to you," Søren replied, pushing past him.

"What happened?"

"Gods, can I get a drink first?" Søren went to the kitchenette, found a bottle of vodka, and took a long, thoughtful swig.

"You have your drink. Now, did you find the book or not?" Aramis asked, leaning against the counter. Tattoos that identified him as a Dauđi Dómr, a Death Judge, for the Ljósálfar stood black and ominous across his pale skin. It had taken six months of being back amongst the Álfr for Aramis to stop hiding them. He seemed satisfied with minimizing his glamour to dimming his Ljósálfar glow and shortening his platinum hair to his shoulders when he was back amongst humans. Søren was happy that the stick that had been shoved up his brother's ass was finally coming out, but it had taken a long time for them to be comfortable with each other again.

"I didn't find the book, but I found the person who can lead us to it."

"Explain."

Søren spent the rest of the night telling his twin about the formidable, pocket-size librarian Asta and the reaction his magic had to her.

"Are you positive she isn't one of the Darkness?" Aramis insisted once he was finished. "Because if she is and she calls them—"

"I'm sure. She's like a little kitten—plenty of annoying teeth and claws but not evil. There's something strange about her though, and I mean to find out what it is. My magic doesn't like it."

Aramis watched him thoughtfully. "Is it like the way Anya's magic reacts to our magic?"

The Russian shamanitsa's magic liked to touch and dance with other power, but it was nothing like the jumpy feeling Asta caused.

"No, she's not a magic user. She's been around something though. She has a residue on her, and I'm suspicious of the reaction she had when she saw the photos you sent."

"What's your plan? Break into her apartment?"

Søren shook his head. "No, I don't want to freak her out unnecessarily."

"But that's your trademark move in these situations." Aramis tilted his head curiously. "Does this kitten have her claws in you already?"

"Shut up. She'll help us. We'll play the long game, and hopefully, she'll lead me to a nice group of thieving Darkness monsters I can kill."

Søren woke at midday with Aramis standing over him.

"What do you want?" Søren grumbled into his pillow.

"Get up. We are going to train before you go back to the university. You're moody and irritated because you haven't had a good fight in weeks."

"And you think you're going to give me a good fight?" Søren yelped when Aramis shocked him with magic.

"Get up, brother," Aramis repeated.

The lake grounds at Bogstad were icy and empty by the time Søren and Aramis arrived forty minutes later.

"I made some calls on your behalf this morning," Aramis said, pulling his sword from the back seat.

"I didn't need you to do that," growled Søren.

"Your librarian started working there two months ago. She's only been back in Norway for six months. Before that she was in Cyprus, and Melbourne prior to Cyprus. She moves a lot it would seem."

Despite his annoyance, Søren was curious. Aramis had been the head investigator for the Illumination for over five hundred years for a reason.

"What brought her back here?" Søren asked, unsheathing his sword.

"Her mother. She was some kind of activist who worked primarily with artifacts stolen from war zones and sold on the black market," explained Aramis.

"It seems like too much of a coincidence to me."

"She sounds like a woman we could've used."

"Why can't we now? We could skip the daughter altogether," said Søren.

"She's dead. About six months ago. It was a hit-and-run in the middle of the city. The daughter isn't a fool. She's still a lead," Aramis said before giving him an infuriating smile. "Besides, you like her. I don't think you've been interested in a woman in the last—"

Søren attacked with steel and fury and pent-up frustration. Aramis defended the attack easily, knowing his brother's moves almost as well as his own.

"Maybe you should let me take over. You'll just annoy the poor woman, and I'll have a better chance of winning her over. What was it Anya called you? The bogeyman? This sweet librarian doesn't need your sledgehammer of a personality when a scalpel may be more effective," said Aramis.

"I don't think you're her type. You're too vanilla." Søren grunted when Aramis managed to connect a kick to his ribs.

"She's a librarian. I'm more her type than you are. Maybe you should give up before you scare her away. How about the first one to get the other to the ground gets to go?" Aramis suggested.

"Deal." Søren knocked Aramis on his ass in three moves.

Asta was clearing books from her last PhD student tutorial session when she felt something warm run down the length of her back. With a startled yelp she collided with Søren, who was standing behind her.

"I'm sorry!" he apologized with a laugh. "I didn't mean to frighten you, Miss Johanson."

"Why the hell are you sneaking up on me then?" She adjusted her glasses on the bridge of her nose and tried to regain her composure.

"It's not my fault you have no spatial awareness."

Like yesterday, Søren was wearing a black three-piece suit, but now he had paired it with a forest-green shirt that matched his eyes. The burst of color made him only a little less intimidating. She had decided to wear flats today and now regretted it. He loomed over her from his six-foot-five height. Some days she really hated being so short.

"You found her! Excellent." Professor Anders Larson, Asta's boss, appeared through the shelving and beamed at them. "Dr. Madson will be a special guest to the library for the next two weeks while he researches his next book. You didn't tell me he dropped in yesterday, Asta!"

Asta blinked rapidly. "I'm sorry? Do you two know each other?"

"How can you call yourself an expert in medieval literature and not know who he is? Shame on you, Asta," Anders said as color stained his cheeks.

"Come now, Anders. I've only been published in America, so it doesn't surprise me that a Norwegian scholar wouldn't know who I am," Søren said good-naturedly. "I do appreciate you giving me access at the last minute. I've hit such a wall with this new book, and I knew only a trip to Oslo would fix it."

"Not at all, my friend. Asta will be able to assist you with anything you might require. She'll make herself available to you as long as you need," said Anders.

"I will? I don't remember agreeing to that." Asta crossed her arms as she looked at the two men.

"I've already arranged for Marta to take over your students and other duties while Dr. Madson is here," Anders replied with a sharp, meaningful look.

"I don't want to inconvenience—"

"Nonsense, Søren. It will be good experience for her. Happy studying!" Anders left them with a pleased smile and a promise to have drinks with Søren while he was in town.

"Hasn't this worked out well? Now you can help me with this book," Søren said with a smile.

"What the fu—hell?" Asta said through gritted teeth. "You know Larson? Why didn't you tell me you were a doctor?"

"You didn't ask. You just assumed I was what? Some bored rich guy?"

That was exactly what Asta had thought. "I don't like being lied to. If you were working on a project, you should have said so."

"I did say so. I even sent you pictures. My father knew my passion was medieval books, and he found the book I showed you but died before giving it to me. I found it amongst his things when we were going through his estate. I've been writing a book about the find which, as you know, is rare and beautiful and not at all Christian, unlike the other illuminated manuscripts of the time."

"So, you were just being a cagey scholar who's on to something and wanted to see if I knew what I was talking about?" Asta asked.

"Yes. I really was jet-lagged, and this morning I realized I didn't handle it as well as I should have. I apologize for the deception and for being…blunter… than I meant to be. Tell me how I can make it up to you."

Søren took off his cashmere coat, folding it neatly over his arm. If anything, it made her uncomfortably aware of his wide shoulders. She looked away from him, pinching the bridge of her nose and taking a deep breath. *No getting out of it now.*

Despite her better judgment, she said, "Coffee. I'm going to need caffeine before I dive into mysterious manuscripts with you."

Søren nodded his head in agreement. "Late night?"

"I'm a bit of an insomniac," she admitted. "I'll go get my coat."

"No need." Søren threw his overcoat around her shoulders. It still held his lingering warmth and hints of an aftershave that smelled like forest and spice. "What? You look like I just killed a kitten."

She shook her head. "You're a random guy."

"I'm impatient, and you need caffeine. Use the coat." Søren shrugged. "I don't need it. I run hot."

"Fine, let's go," Asta replied, hoping he didn't notice the heat in her cheeks. She gripped the lapels of the coat around her as they stepped outside into the wind. "I hope you don't mind a student café. It's the only place on campus that actually does a good espresso."

"Where you go, I'll follow," he said seriously. "Did you have a chance to look at the photos last night?"

"Yes, though I wished the resolution was a little higher," Asta replied as she pushed open the café door. It was full due to the four o'clock crowd of students, but space seemed to open up wherever Søren was. At least four women were staring openly at him, and he seemed completely unaware of the attention.

"Hey, Asta, who's your hot date?" Lisa asked from behind the counter.

"I'm Søren," he replied with a smile.

"He's *not* my date," Asta said irritably and gave her coffee order.

Søren stuck his hand inside his overcoat, brushing against the soft fabric of her sweater. "Sorry, sweetheart, I need my wallet." Asta batted his hand away, located the wallet in the breast pocket, and handed it to him. "I'm trying to win her over, Lisa. Any tips?"

Lisa's blue eyes glittered with mischief. "Try persistence. Smart girls don't fall for the usual tricks."

"Thank you, Lisa. I'll take it under advisement," he said, taking his receipt from her.

They found a table at the back of the café, and Søren took out his phone. "I'm going to get my brother to take some proper scans of the pages for you. I have printouts in my bag that I left in Anders's office, but from what I know of you, they might not be good enough."

"I don't see why you can't just bring in the bo—"

"Here you are." Lisa placed their coffees on the table and gave Søren a dazzling smile. "I love your hair. Do you braid it yourself?"

"I do. Otherwise, it becomes a mess in this wind," Søren said charmingly.

"I bet," Lisa replied, giving Asta a saucy wink when Søren wasn't looking. Asta wanted to slide under the table and hide.

"You shouldn't encourage her. She's the biggest gossip, and half the campus is going to think I'm dating you by tomorrow," Asta warned him.

"Would that be a bad thing?"

"Yes."

"Why? Are you seeing someone?" His dark brows drew together as he frowned.

"That's not the point," Asta said. God, he was annoying. "I work here. I like to be professional."

"So, you're not married?"

"Are you?" she retorted. She didn't want to talk about her dating status with someone who looked like they would be with a different woman every night.

"I was."

"She get sick of your attitude?" Asta asked and sipped her coffee.

The flirtatious glint in his eyes vanished, replaced with something dark and painful. "No. She died."

Asta's stomach plummeted. "Fuck, I…I'm sorry. I didn't mean—"

"It's okay. It was a long time ago," Søren replied, his eyes fixed on the coffee in front of him. He couldn't have been older than thirty-five, so she doubted it was as long ago as he made it sound. She recognized pain when she saw it.

"Grief is a bitch. I lost my mom about six months ago. It's the worst feeling in the world, and I don't think it's ever going to feel better," she admitted.

"I'm sorry to hear that." With surprising gentleness, Søren placed a hand over hers. "Grief changes over time, but it doesn't ever go away." His hand was so big it enclosed hers completely. Black ink showed from underneath the cuff of his jacket.

"Thanks. What's your tattoo of?" Asta pulled her hand away and picked up her coffee.

"It's a secret. If you are very good, I might show it to you one day," he replied, his teasing tone returning.

"I bet it's something embarrassing like a dolphin."

He raised a dark eyebrow. "Do I seem like the kind of person who would get a tattoo of a dolphin?"

"No, you're right." She grinned. "With that hair, you're *definitely* a unicorn guy."

"You have quite a smart mouth when you bother to relax for five minutes, don't you?"

"I use humor to get me through uncomfortable situations."

"I make you uncomfortable? Hmm, I must work on fixing that. I like your mouth when it's not angry at me."

Asta didn't like the sudden heat spreading over her. "Should we head back? I would like to see your printouts."

4

IT HAD BEEN A long time since Aramis had last worried about Søren. Oslo was meant to be a simple search and rescue mission: find the missing objects from Svetilo and go home.

It wasn't in Søren's nature to deviate from a plan or make it more complicated than it needed to be, but for the last week, he had been going to the university every day to pretend he was an academic. He claimed it was to win Asta Johanson's trust. Aramis was mystified as to why Søren thought that was important. Søren could've used his magic to force the answers out of her if he wanted to, but he was resisting.

"I don't want to screw her life up any more than we have to. She's mixed up in something she knows nothing about. I'll admit there's magic about her, but I don't know who it belongs to. I *am* going to find out, and if they are fucking with her, I'll end them," Søren said ominously.

Aramis knew his brother. Søren was protecting the girl. Aramis just didn't know why. What was even stranger was that Søren was also keeping her from Aramis. He was about to change that, and Søren would have to bear it or blow his cover completely.

Shielding his magic as much as he could, Aramis searched the university library for his brother. He wasn't surprised to hear Søren arguing, but he stopped dead when he saw a petite woman leaning over him to point at something on a laptop screen as she argued back. She had no sense of self-preservation if she was invading Søren's personal space the way she was.

Søren merely smiled at her in a relaxed and self-satisfied way that Aramis had only ever seen him use with a handful of people.

Who is this girl?

"There you are, brother! I've been wandering this place for an hour trying to track you down. You really need to answer your phone more often," Aramis said, giving Asta a warm smile. "You must be the brilliant assistant Søren keeps talking about. You never told me she was so pretty."

"I don't believe how I look has anything to do with our arrangement. I also made him turn his phone off," Asta said and held out a hand. "I'm Asta."

"Aramis." He took her small hand and let his magic touch her. Søren was right; she had magic all over her, almost like…a shield.

"What are you doing here?" Søren hissed.

"It's eight o'clock. I thought you could use a dinner break. How about you, Asta? Ready to eat?"

She looked at them and gave her head a small shake. "Wow. You really are brothers." She pulled her hand out of his grip.

"She means we are bossy," Søren said with a glance at Asta. "It's up to you. You can have dinner with my dull brother and me, or I can get rid of him, and we can keep working." She looked at the pile of printouts and the scattered pieces of translations.

"Or," Søren added quickly, "my dull brother can go and get us food, and we can keep working."

Asta smiled brightly, her large gray eyes turning to Søren before looking up at Aramis. "That one. Not that I think dinner with you would be dull, Aramis. Jesus, I have a cousin who would kill me for knocking you back right now—" She blushed prettily, and Aramis sighed in defeat.

"Are you sure? Søren is a grumpy old man when he's hungry, and you'll have to tolerate him until I get back," Aramis warned.

"I can handle him. He's not nearly as mean as he pretends to be." And then, horror of horrors, the tiny librarian gave Søren's braid a tug. Aramis flexed, ready to jump between them, but his brother just shoved her hand away playfully.

"Stop that, or I'll show you how angry I can get, missy," Søren warned.

"Oh, you have me shaking in fear," Asta said sarcastically. "Has he always been this much of a baby?"

Aramis choked on a surprised laugh. "Yes, actually. He has."

"Don't encourage her, or I'll kick your ass." Søren's eyes glittered with violence.

"I'm about as terrified as she is. Do you have a meal preference, Asta?"

"I don't care as long as it's vegetarian." She sat back down next to Søren. "Have you messed up my notes again? No wonder you're taking so long to get your book finished."

"I'll leave you to it. I'll be back soon," Aramis said, though he doubted Asta had heard him.

"Take your time," Søren replied.

Outside, Aramis took a deep breath and laughed loudly at the drizzling sky. His brother, the most terrifying Dauđi Dómr the Álfr had ever produced, had his first crush in a thousand years.

"You never told me your brother was coming in," Asta said after she watched Aramis walk away. The brothers were like night and day to look at, but they had the same killer cheekbones and expressive lips.

"He wasn't meant to. He likes to meddle."

"You might want to warn the library staff next time, so they'll know why the girls fall into a swoon." She leaned against their study table and pretended to fan herself. "That accent alone. Wait, why do you have different accents?"

"He's spent the last few years living in Britain, and I've been based in America. That's why he sounds so stuck up."

"I thought he sounded rather charming." Asta hadn't been joking about the reaction Tyra would have if she ever saw Aramis. He looked like a modern Thranduil in a suit. Forget takeout, Tyra would eat *him* for dinner.

Søren pushed a book back onto a shelf. "You think so?"

"I know so. Your brother is a stunner." Asta didn't see him move, but suddenly Søren was standing in front of her.

"He's not your type," he said firmly.

Despite her escalating heartbeat, Asta looked down at the papers she was holding and said in a bored tone, "You don't know what my type is."

Søren's hand came up and pulled gently on the top pearl button of her black cardigan. Leaning down, he whispered in her ear, "You might pretend to be a sweet, innocent librarian who likes dull men, but I know better. I know you're hiding *something*, and no matter how many of these boring little sweaters you wear, I'm not going to be fooled."

Asta looked up at him, hoping her smile was as cocky as his. "My secrets and boring little sweaters are none of your business. Now, get out of my way."

Søren backed off and went back to his laptop until Aramis returned with a bag of takeout. His sapphire-blue eyes went from her to Søren and back again.

"What's wrong, Søren? Has Asta put you in your place again?" Aramis asked.

"The library doesn't have a naughty corner that would fit his ego," Asta muttered under her breath. Søren glared at her. She ignored him. "Thank you for dinner, Aramis. I'm sure it'll help our moods. Follow me. We can't eat in here, but the staff lunchroom should be empty."

Aramis nudged his brother. "Come on. Let's eat before your temper gets out of hand." She missed what Søren said to Aramis in reply, but there was a pissed-off tone to it.

"How long are you two staying in Oslo?" Asta asked as she found clean cutlery.

"As long as we need to," said Søren, digging in the takeout bag and handing her a vegetarian laksa.

"Why? Is my brother annoying you that much?" asked Aramis.

"No, just curious. Oslo is a beautiful city, even when it's freezing," she said smoothly.

The truth was Asta needed them to leave despite the fact that working on their book was helping her understand her own. Søren's presence was causing Anders Larson to pay more attention to her, and she really needed him focused on someone else. If Anders found out she had used her mother's credentials to get her job at the university, she could be fired or worse, charged with fraud.

It all came back to her mother's stupid book and why they'd had to move to Oslo in order to get it. She needed to know *why* it was so important. The need for answers had been enough for Asta to risk lying her way into her job.

Tove had never wanted to be anywhere near her home country, yet as soon as she'd heard about the book from a dodgy antique dealer in Cyprus, they had dropped everything and gone after it. Asta was used to leaving everything and everyone behind. Some days she felt like she had been running forever.

"Asta?" Søren asked, snapping her out of her head.

"What?"

"You were a thousand miles away," Aramis commented.

"Sorry, just tired."

"Maybe you two should call it a night. I can drive you home if you like. It wouldn't be out of my way," Aramis offered.

"That's unnecessary. The public transport leads right by my place."

"It's the middle of the night. I'll take you home," Søren insisted with enough snap in his tone that she didn't want to argue with him.

Søren's mood didn't improve with food. Aramis kept the conversation easy and flowing as they talked about the places they had lived, comparing notes on favorite cities and the kind of work Asta had done. Asta was the center of attention until he escorted them to Søren's car.

Asta smiled as Aramis opened the passenger door of a black Mercedes-Benz GT Coupe. "Just when you had me believing you weren't a bored rich guy."

"We like fast cars. Have a good night, Asta. See you at home, Søren," Aramis said with a teasing gleam in his eyes.

"Die," Søren replied as he shut his door.

Asta tried to act unimpressed with the interior of the car as if she always sat in car seats that warmed her ass. A deviant part of her wanted to start pressing buttons to see what they did, but Søren was in a bad enough mood.

"You and Aramis seem close," she said tactfully as they pulled out into the wet streets.

"He thinks just because he is ten minutes older than me, it gives him the right to be an interfering prick," Søren said as they pulled up at a traffic light. He looked wild and angry under the bleak streetlights with shadows crossing his face. His hands tightened on the steering wheel. "Fuck!"

"What's wrong?" Asta asked, confused by the outburst.

"Nothing I just—" He looked at her, and his hard expression changed. "I need a drink. You live in this area. Where's the closest bar?"

"A few streets away, but you're meant to be taking me home remember?"

"You said you'd come for a drink. I'm calling it in."

"I believe you said you'd show me your book if we went for a drink. I haven't seen a book." Asta folded her arms stubbornly.

"Drinks now, book tomorrow. Deal?"

"Okay, deal. But only if you're not going to be pissed off all night."

"Fine."

Mistake, mistake, mistake, her common sense chided her, but her treacherous mouth said, "Take a left."

The first time Asta had gotten fall-down drunk was after her mother's funeral. She and Tyra had ended up at The Raven and stayed there for ten hours. Since then, it had become their local haunt whenever Tyra thought Asta was working too hard. It was still early in the night, so the music was quiet enough to talk, and the seats closest to the fireplaces were free.

"*Hei*, Asta! Where's your hot cousin?" Vidar asked from behind the bar. He was everything Asta imagined a Viking should be: muscle-bound and covered in tattoos with long golden hair and a well-trimmed blond beard. He was also good-natured, polite to women, and ensured men were kicked out for being too rude or handsy. Asta liked him immensely.

"She's teaching kickboxing tonight," she said.

"You mean I can pay her to kick my ass? Why didn't you tell me?"

"Girls only."

"Damn, what a waste. Who's your friend?" Vidar asked, casting a critical eye over Søren.

"This is Søren, my research partner. He'll have—"

"Vodka and soda. Keep them coming," Søren said before disappearing to the back of the bar.

"Friendly guy," Vidar said critically.

"Bad day," Asta replied.

"You drinking vodka too?"

"Sure. I'm only having one though."

Three drinks later, she was wondering why she didn't drink vodka all the time. Even Søren managed to smile after two.

"Why have you moved around so much?" he asked.

"You checked up on me?"

"Of course I did. I needed to make sure you weren't going to steal my research."

Asta snorted. "As if I would. I've moved a lot because my mother's work took us all over the world."

"But you're thirty-three years old. Why were you still living with your mother? Didn't you want your own life?" He seemed sincere, not judgmental, so she decided to trust him…just a little.

"Mom was brilliant but a bit paranoid. She exposed a lot of black-market antiquity rings, and that made her a target. She also had a crazy ex-husband who she didn't want to find her either," Asta said.

"Your father?"

"No. God, no. Long before she met Dad. She married super young, and the guy was an abusive psycho. She never talked about him much, but I got the impression he was a criminal of some sort. I think it's why she did the job she did. She was…fearless. I once saw her stare down a guy who held a gun in her face. She wasn't scared of anything or anyone except her ex."

Some of Asta's earliest memories were of her mother being physically sick from fear that he would find out about Asta and come after them.

"And what about your father? Is he still around?" Søren sipped his drink slowly.

"No. He drowned when I was four."

"Gods, I'm sorry."

"Don't be. I barely remember him. I have his hair color, and that's about it. He was good to my mother though, so I guess it's nice to know he wasn't an asshole."

"You get that from your mother then?"

"Fuck you," she said with a laugh, "but yes."

"That explains why you are so suspicious of everyone."

"I'm not suspicious of everyone! Only you."

"Why me?"

"Because you're so…you."

Søren gave her an incredulous look. "I am going to go and get us more drinks, Miss Johanson, and then you are going to explain what you mean by that comment."

"Oh no, I'm not," Asta told her empty glass as soon as he was out of earshot. She liked Søren a lot more when he was drinking. He seemed relaxed…well, as relaxed as he ever seemed to get. It heightened both his handsomeness and her internal argument about whether she wanted to kiss him or not.

"I know you and your brother don't get along great, but you're lucky to have him," Asta said when Søren returned with two more drinks. "If I hadn't met Tyra at Mom's funeral, I don't know what state I'd be in right now."

"He's more of a hindrance than a help sometimes. We didn't talk for a long time, and some days he drives me crazy," Søren admitted.

"I can tell by the way you wanted to claw his face off today. Seriously, all he did was bring us dinner."

"It wasn't about dinner. Aramis was spying on us. I don't like him being up in my business all the time, and he wanted to see if we were really researching," he said stubbornly.

"What else would we be doing?" she asked, but when she saw his face, she knew. "*Oh*. Really? Us?" Asta burst out laughing.

"What's so funny about that?" He bristled ever so slightly.

"Well, it's just that you're *you*, and I'm…well, *me*."

"That makes no sense."

"That's exactly my point."

"No, you drunken lunatic. Your argument about why we wouldn't be having sex makes no sense. I'm me and you're you. What kind of bullshit logic is that?"

Asta was laughing so hard she couldn't respond. When she finally stopped, she said, "You're right."

"I know."

"No. You're right that I'm drunk. I need to go home." She stood up abruptly and swayed. Søren's hand shot out to steady her.

"Okay, Miss Johanson. Let's get a cab and get you into bed," he said, picking up her bag.

"You okay, Asta?" Vidar asked, intercepting them by the door.

"Yeah, just heading home. Thanks for the drinks. I'll tell Tyra to come by," she promised.

"You will see she gets home safely," Vidar said to Søren.

"Of course I will," Søren replied coldly. Asta rolled her eyes at the pair of them.

"Okay, I'm leaving." She pushed the front door open and walked out into the freezing air. Søren followed and hailed a cab.

"I hope my car will be okay in this neighborhood for the night," he said as they climbed into the back seat of the cab.

"Vidar lives above the bar. He'll keep an eye on it," replied Asta after giving the driver her address. "Damn it, how did I let you get me so drunk?"

"You only had five. I didn't know you were such a lightweight."

"You make me nervous, so I drank more," she admitted. *Did I say that out loud?*

"I don't know why. I've been a gentleman all week."

"Don't…don't know." She tapped him on the shoulder so she could whisper loudly in his ear. "Maybe because…I don't know. Something to do with kissing, I think. I forget."

"Kissing?" he whispered back.

"Yep. Don't tell anyone." Asta watched as her fingers twisted the loose ends of his braid.

"You want to know a secret?" he asked.

"One of yours? Yeah, I do."

His emerald eyes glowed hot as he took her face gently in his warm hands and drew her close so he could whisper in her ear. "I think about kissing your smart-ass mouth all damn day."

Asta stopped breathing. "Why haven't you then?"

"Because you haven't asked, and I don't go where I'm not wanted."

"You haven't asked either."

Without hesitation, he said, "Will you kiss me so I can stop thinking about it and can research with a clearer head?"

"Um…okay." Asta leaned over and pressed her mouth over his in a quick peck. "There you go. Done."

Søren let out a long exhale as he looked at her lips and said, "Fuck it." He pulled her face back to his and kissed her so hard and long she thought she would pass out. Her hands somehow managed to get tangled up in his tie, and when they pulled apart, she looked up at him with wide eyes.

"What else do you think about?" Asta asked breathlessly. One of Søren's hands slid slowly up her stockinged thigh, while his other hand glided from her neck to the top button of her sweater.

"I think about taking my knife out and slicing every one of these maddening little buttons off one at a time and making you unravel in every way possible."

"We're here," the cab driver said.

"Are you…do you…" Asta fumbled to ask and instead pointed to her apartment.

"Tempting, but you've drunk too much, so I'm going to have to give you a rain check on the unraveling," he said, even though his hand was still on her thigh.

"Okay. Yep. Well, I'll see you tomorrow. With your book. Don't forget it." Asta hurried out of the cab and into her apartment building without looking behind her.

Inside, Asta heaved a great sigh, but she couldn't decide whether it was from relief or disappointment.

5

A RAMIS WOKE UP TO the hotel phone ringing. He fumbled for it, knocking over a glass of water in the process.

"What?" he murmured. *What time is it?*

"Good morning, Mr. Madson. I hate to wake you, but it's about your brother." The crisp voice of the hotel manager rattled through his foggy brain.

"What about Søren?"

"He's…refusing to leave the gym, sir. On the floor below you. He's threatened another visitor, sir."

"I'm so sorry for his behavior, Lars. I'll get down there now." Aramis hauled himself out of bed. "Please advise your staff to stay away from him."

"They are, sir. He has knives."

Aramis hung up the phone and ran. He shoved open the fire escape door, taking the stairs three at a time to get to the level below them. Lars, the hotel manager, was waiting outside of the glass doors with a portly middle-aged man in a tracksuit and a sweaty security guard.

"It'll be all right. I'll get him out," Aramis said, moving past them.

"Be careful, sir. I believe he has been drinking," said Lars.

"Undoubtedly," Aramis muttered, pushing open the glass door. He dodged as an empty whiskey bottle sailed past him and smashed into the wall, shattering glass everywhere.

"Fuck off, Magnus! I told you that you can't use the treadmills this morning. I don't give a shit if it helps you sleep," Søren said angrily from behind a rack of weights.

"I'm afraid Magnus has gone back to his room." Aramis looked around the gym. Equipment had been kicked over, a knife was stuck in a flickering flat-screen TV, the punching bag had been disemboweled, and another knife had pinned the speed bag to the wall. Søren was sitting against the weights rack with another half-empty bottle in his bleeding hands.

"Would you mind telling me what's going on?" Aramis asked, readying his body in case his brother explained with fists instead of words.

"Went drinking."

"With Asta?"

"Yep." Søren took another drink from the bottle. "She's got…magic over her. Hiding something. Don't know."

"The magic is shields, and she didn't make them," Aramis said carefully. "Did you…feel them out?"

"Didn't even know they were shields until I kissed her. Layers and layers of protection magic…so much she could be fucking *anything* under there. It's all locked up as tight as the rest of her. Shouldn't have kissed her."

"Who cares if you kissed her?" Aramis tried his best to sound bored. "That doesn't mean anything. You've kissed people before. Gods, you even kissed Anya."

"*Everyone* kissed Anya, even you."

Aramis ignored that particular barb. "You kissed Anya to find out what her magic would do. You did the same to Asta. It hardly warrants trashing a hotel. It's just what you do."

"I didn't kiss her because I wanted to know about the magic," Søren admitted, his drunken arrogance slipping to reveal something full of horror and fear underneath it.

Aramis sat down beside him, took the bottle from him, and had a large mouthful. "I see. How did she take it?"

"Receptive."

"And this is a bad thing?"

"Yes. I'll…fuck her life up. She won't want me if she sees what I really am."

Aramis took another drink and handed him back the bottle. "Wanting someone after all this time isn't betraying Väliä's memory, Søren."

Aramis knew the punch would come, and he didn't try to block it. His brother had needed to hear it. With blood pouring from his nose, Aramis calmly handed the bottle back to Søren.

"I fucking hate you so much sometimes," Søren snarled.

"I know. What are you going to do now?"

"I…don't know." Søren took a mouthful of whiskey, realizing too late that Aramis had slapped a spell on the bottle. "You prick—" Søren managed to say before his green eyes rolled backward, and he collapsed on the mat. Aramis took the bottle from his hand, collected the various blades from around the room, and slung Søren over his shoulder.

"Please send me the bill, Lars," he told the manager before he took his heartbroken brother back to his bed.

It was almost 7:00 p.m. when Anders came to tell Asta that Søren wouldn't be visiting the library that evening. She had known when she had woken up hungover and disoriented that there would be repercussions to their kiss. She just didn't think he'd be the type to back out of a deal even if there was a bit of awkwardness.

Asta had spent the day trying to go about her usual tasks, moving her hand to smooth her hair nervously every time she saw something black out of the corner of her eye.

By the time she got home at 11:00 p.m., her emotions had moved from nervous to pissed off. *He* had kissed *her* after all! He had no right to be upset about it.

Tyra had left a note saying she had been called in to her bartending job at the heavy metal club four blocks away, and Asta was relieved. She didn't need her too-perceptive cousin asking about her day or about what had happened the night before. After taking a quick shower to warm up and changing into a pair of striped flannel pajamas, Asta took out her notes and her mother's book.

Slowly, she thumbed through the pages, making note of the similarities it had with Søren's book. The pages felt warm under her fingers as she ran them over the words, trying to sound them out on her tongue and searching for meaning in their cadence. Asta was interrupted by the intercom buzzing angrily two hours later.

"Why can't you ever remember your keys, Tyra?" she demanded, holding the button down.

"It's not Tyra." Asta froze.

"What are you doing here?" she finally asked when she stopped swearing.

"Can I please come up and talk to you?" Søren said.

Asta went into her room and pulled on her thick robe. With trembling fingers, she pressed the intercom button again. "Stay there. I'm coming down." She didn't trust herself to be alone with Søren, not after the cab ride had left her wanting to climb into his clothes.

Søren was leaning against a wall of mailboxes. He was dressed casually in boots, dark jeans, and a black T-shirt under his overcoat instead of his impeccable suit. For some reason, it made him look tousled and undone and even more attractive. Asta opened the door and stepped out into the cold night.

"What do you want?" she asked, folding her arms tightly around her body.

"A deal is a deal." He shoved a book at her without meeting her stare.

"And you couldn't bring it to me at work because?" Asta took the book from him and carefully opened it.

"I only woke up about two hours ago. I…drank a lot more last night after I dropped you off."

"I thought you might have chickened out because you drunkenly kissed me." She didn't look up from the gilded pages. Søren made a frustrated sound at the back of his throat.

"I wasn't drunk when I kissed you, and I wasn't avoiding you."

"*Sure* you weren't. This book is beautiful." Asta touched the edges of the page with a reverence she only gave to the written word. It warmed under her hands, exactly as her book had done. They *had* to have come from the same place. She'd forgotten Søren was there until fingers touched her hair that hung to the middle of her back.

"I've never seen your hair down," he said.

"It needs a cut." Asta went back to the book.

"It's—" Søren stilled before shoving her roughly behind him.

"What are you doing?"

"Stay," he commanded. Asta was about to yell at him when she saw the group of people standing in the street. They all wore black clothing, and swords and long knives shone in their hands.

"Daudi Dómr, you have our property," one said, stepping into the glow of the streetlight. Asta froze when she saw the pointed ears, the curved eyes, and impossibly, the shadows that were wrapped around his hands. "Hand her over peacefully. We want no trouble with your people."

Søren looked over his shoulder at Asta, his expression incredulous. "It's the Dökkálfar that are after you? Fucking really, Asta? Of *all* the fucking monsters you could piss off."

"She is a fugitive from justice, and you will give her to us, or we will—"

"You come any closer, and you won't live long enough to regret it," Søren snarled.

"There are five of us, Dauđi Dómr. Just hand the girl over, and my king will thank you," the leader insisted.

Two long knives appeared in Søren's hands. "Why not? I haven't had a good fight in months." He attacked them with a blur of steel, and the wet, slick sounds of flesh being cleaved from bones filled the air.

Asta clutched the book, too afraid to move or look away as Søren, the bored rich guy who had brought her coffees all week, tore into the people that had threatened her. They moved like shadows, disappearing only to reappear behind him and try to catch him off guard with their knives. Søren was…like them. No human could move that quickly. Even with his speed, she knew some of the blades had hit him. It didn't slow him down.

"Stop this!" the leader demanded. "We don't want trouble with the Álfr!"

Dark green light emanated from Søren and swarmed over the leader. He tried to shift to shadows but couldn't. The green light held him tightly until he was scratching at his throat for air. Søren roared as one of the other attackers sank a knife into his side. Søren grabbed his attacker's head, twisted hard, and shoved the corpse away from him. He scanned the surrounding area, making sure they were all dead before turning his terrifying, blood-streaked face to Asta.

"You will tell me what shit you are involve—" Søren lost his balance, sinking to his knees and clutching at his side.

Asta ran to him. "You are bleeding everywhere." She placed her hands over his, trying to hold the wound together.

"Have to…call Aramis," he said with a wheeze.

"We need to get you off the road first—before anyone sees us," Asta snapped, anger replacing her fear. She slung his arm around her shoulders and helped him into the apartment building's elevator.

"You're so lucky Tyra is out tonight," she muttered, opening her apartment door and helping him sit on the couch. Søren fumbled in his coat pocket and brought out his phone.

"Fuck," he hissed when he saw the smashed screen.

"We need to call an ambulance," Asta said, pulling clean towels from a cupboard. She shoved his bloody hand away and placed a towel over the gushing wound.

"No. No ambulance, Asta. I'll be all right. Aramis will find me and—" Søren's eyes shut, and he fell backward on the cushions.

"Up to me then." Asta filled a mixing bowl with hot water and grabbed her first aid kit. Tove had made sure she knew how to clean and patch up a wound. Asta had just never thought she would have to do it for Søren. Asta took off his overcoat and cut his ruined shirt open.

"Fuck me," she whispered as she saw how many cuts he had. She cleaned the shallower ones, covering them with Band-Aids, and tried not to notice the black lines and branches of the tattoo across his ridiculously muscled body. Appearing before her eyes, the tattoo spread out over his neck in thick lines and reached up to the tips of his ears that were sharpening to small points.

"Don't think about it. Think about the blood," Asta hissed to herself. She lifted his hand away from the wound in his side and shifted the bloody towel.

"Holy…" She stared. The wound was already smaller than it had been minutes ago. She cleaned the edges of the oozing gash before making a patch from a folded-up bandage and sealing it with more Band-Aids.

After emptying the bloody water in the sink, she began to shake. *What the hell just happened? Who were those guys?* They were definitely professionals, which meant it probably involved Tove. Maybe the picture of her mother in the paper had finally allowed the psycho ex-husband to track them down. She had a million more questions as she stared at the injured man on her couch.

"What *are* you?" she whispered.

One thing she knew for certain. She had to run before they came back. She wouldn't risk Søren or anyone else becoming collateral in her messed-up life.

A deathly calm settled over her as she went into Tyra's room, pulled off her pajamas, and slid on some of her cousin's leather leggings and a band T-shirt. She put on two of Tyra's studded cuffs, smeared on black lipstick, and shoved her hair under a black beanie. In her own room, she stuffed clothes into a duffel bag along with her mother's laptop, both of the strange medieval books, and her research notes. She pulled on a pair of Doc Martens, but when she reached for her parka, she realized it was gone. "Fuck, Tyra. Why don't you ask first?" She would have to ditch her phone, but she shot out one last message.

```
Mom's ex found me. Needed to bail to protect
u. Will find u again. Don't hurt the guy on
couch. He helped me. Luv u. Be safe.
```

Asta made sure the message had sent to Tyra before pulling out her SIM card and snapping it in half. She looked at Søren for a long moment and pressed a kiss to his cold lips.

"I'm sorry, but I need it more," she whispered before she pulled on his overcoat. Asta took a deep breath, locked her apartment door, shoved her keys into the mailbox downstairs, and disappeared into the night.

6

TYRA'S LUNGS BURNED AS she ran from the club back to the apartment. One look at the text message had ice and fear crawling through her veins. She had vaulted over the bar, shoved aside the dancers, and bolted. Her hands went for the blades strapped under her shirt as she spotted five dark elves dead in the street.

"Fuck, fuck, fuck!" She burst through the apartment door. "Asta!" She smelled blood in the air. *Not hers.* Someone shifted on the couch. Tyra's blood ran cold when she saw the tattoos on the bloody Ljósálfar.

"Goddamn it, Asta," she hissed. Two green eyes opened and zeroed in on her.

"Dökkálfar," he hissed.

Oh, she was totally fucking fucked.

"Stay where you are." She gripped her knives tighter.

"What have you done with Asta? I swear if you've hurt her, I'll rip your spine out through your mouth," he snarled.

"You talk a big game for a guy covered in Disney Princess Band-Aids." He looked down at the bright pink plasters on his chest. He looked confused and worried, so she took pity on him.

"I'm Tyra, asshole. Asta told me not to hurt you, but if you try anything with me, Dauði Dómr, I'll fuck you up worse than you are. I haven't done anything to Asta, and I'm not your enemy. Who are you?"

"Søren."

"Odin's dick… *you're* Søren? Only freaking Asta could get a crush on a fucking Death Judge."

"Are those your friends I killed down there?" Søren asked.

"Hell no. They are the assholes I've been trying to make sure never find her."

He struggled to sit up. "Where is she?"

Tyra didn't have time to reply as the apartment door exploded into splinters, and the most devastatingly handsome Ljósálfar she had ever seen launched himself at her.

Before he could change direction, she grabbed him by the lapels of his jacket, drove her knee up into his chest, and flipped him down onto his back. She punched him once in his beautiful, stunned face before leaping over the kitchen counter to put some space between them. The platinum-haired Álfr was back on his feet in seconds with his sword drawn.

"Calm down, Thranduil. I don't want to fight you." Tyra picked up a meat cleaver from her knife block. *But goddamn it might be fun to tussle.*

"Stand down, Aramis. That's Tyra, Asta's cousin." Søren groaned, heaving himself up off the couch.

"She's Dökkálfar," Aramis said, his stunning blue eyes widening.

"Look, this situation isn't what it seems. I'm going to put this cleaver down and walk around the counter, and we can talk like grown-up Álfr, okay?" Tyra said, placing the cleaver on the counter and coming out with her hands raised. "I'll be happy to fight you another time, gorgeous, but maybe not when a bunch of pissed-off dark elves are about to swarm the building."

Aramis sheathed his sword, and she saw a flash of tattoos on his wrist. A maniacal laugh bubbled up out of her.

"You are Dauði Dómr too? Oh, gods. You are *them*, aren't you? The brothers. *Goddamn it*, Asta!" Tyra cursed.

"We need to find her," Søren said, holding his side with his hand. "Why would she just run?"

"Because that's what she was trained to do," Tyra said irritably. "We can talk about it later. For now, we need to get out of here."

"You aren't going anywhere with us, dark elf. I don't trust you or your motivations. Asta told Søren that you turned up at Asta's mother's funeral right after her mother was killed in a hit-and-run. Don't tell me that was just a coincidence," said Aramis, moving his hand to his sword hilt.

"It's not, but I can't tell you here. Look, tie me up. Take me prisoner if it will help. I don't care. We need to get out of here because more will be coming!" Aramis started to argue with her when the window shattered beside him.

"*Myrkrhata!*" Tyra shouted. When her magic hit the dark elf, he exploded into red mist. The brothers stared at her, all of them splattered in gore.

"She comes with us," said Søren as he opened a gate. Tyra stumbled back. She had never seen anyone on Midgard powerful enough to do that.

"Keep your hands where I can see them." Aramis took her by the arm, pulling her in front of him. "Thank you for your help."

"You're welcome," Tyra said before she was shoved through the gate.

Aramis stepped through the gate and into the library at Svetilo. He rounded on Søren.

"I can't believe you brought us here! She is a dark elf!" Aramis hissed.

"She's not our enemy as far as I can tell," Søren said before he leaned over and vomited up blood onto the polished stone floors.

"He's been poisoned," Tyra said matter-of-factly. "I hope you have decent healers."

"Need…need to find…"

"Asta. Yes, I heard you the first time you said it," Aramis said, hauling his brother over his shoulder. He whispered a spell, and shackles looped around Tyra's wrists. Her black eyes gleamed, but she seemed more amused than angry.

"Whatever makes you feel safer, Thranduil," she mocked.

As Aramis carried Søren through the halls, scared Álfr took one look at Tyra's black eyes and all-leather ensemble and scattered. Many would've been too young to have seen a Dökkálfar before. Those that weren't looked at their ancient enemy with fury.

"You are going to have a fun time trying to keep me safe," Tyra said with a small dark laugh.

"Please be quiet," Aramis muttered as they reached the healers' wing of the mountain. Tyra told the nervous healers of the poisons most likely running through Søren's body before Aramis grabbed the leash to her shackles.

"You're coming with me," he stated, becoming more flustered by her unsettling presence by the minute.

"I'm not trying to fight you, handsome," Tyra said sweetly. Aramis ignored her flirtatious tone. He wouldn't be able to put her in the cells, not without other Álfr treating her like some kind of novelty to scare the children with.

Dark elves in Midgard. That could be a trouble the world wasn't ready for.

Aramis ended up taking Tyra to one of the guest rooms in his apartments. The walls were the solid stone of the mountain, and the only way in or out was the main door. It was as good as a prison if he didn't drop his guard.

Aramis pushed Tyra into a chair, and the leash to the shackles fixed itself to the stone floor. Her black braid shone in the firelight, and her impossibly red lips pulled up into a smirk. Her kohl-darkened eyes ran over him in a leisurely way that made his skin itch. She was as beautiful as a quick death.

"Feel better now? Or are you going to start torturing me?" she asked finally.

Aramis bristled. "Do I *need* to torture you? Or are you going to tell me about your relationship with this human girl Asta?"

Tyra's laugh slid over him like warm silk. "Oh, honey, Asta is not human. You know that right?"

"I suspected as much." Aramis removed his dark blue overcoat and placed it on a chair. Those black eyes ran over him again as he let his human glamour fall.

"Damn, that is some beautiful silver hair. You are quite something for a light elf, aren't you?" Tyra said with a low whistle.

"Flirt as much as you like. It's not going to convince me to let you go." Aramis sat down on the bed in front of her.

Tyra's smile widened as she leaned back in the chair. "Who said I wanted to be let go? You don't think I could seduce you with these shackles on? Hell, I think you would like it better if I was tied up and helpless beneath you."

"Do I look foolish enough to ever mistake you for being helpless? Please, tell me about Asta."

"The problem isn't Asta. It's Tove, her mother. She's the reason those dark elves wanted to tear Oslo apart looking for Asta." Tyra moved to rest her elbows on her knees. "Have you ever been to Svartálfaheim?"

"No. I was young when we came to Midgard. I barely remember Álfheim," admitted Aramis.

"So you've not been home in what? Two thousand years?"

"Roughly." He never talked about it. Refused to even think of Álfheim and all the reasons why they'd had to leave.

"You weren't in any of the wars then. I guess that makes you okay," Tyra said with a decisive nod of her head.

"I was there when the Dökkálfar started to raid Álfheim and kill us," Aramis snarled softly, old wounds reopening. "We got out before the wars really started."

"I wasn't part of the raids! And what you lovely light ones didn't understand was that the wars on Svartálfaheim were so much worse than the ones kicked off with you guys. The first wave of Dökkálfar that went to Álfheim was just trying to get away. A few morons decided they wanted to start trouble by attacking villag—"

"What does this history lesson have to do with Tove?" Aramis said, wanting to close the door to his memories of Álfheim.

"Everything, gorgeous. *Everything.* The internal wars fought all over Svartálfaheim were only brought to a very temporary peace by Tove being married off to the biggest asshole in the Nine Worlds. Bláinn had started the wars because he couldn't handle being more powerful than the king but having to abide by his rules. I don't just say that for ambiance. He is literally the strongest warlord that Svartálfaheim has ever produced. They couldn't rein him in, and he started a war to try and get all the Álfr and dwarves under his thumb. Tove was given to him to ensure her people's safety."

"Then what happened? How does a Dökkálfar end up dying in a hit-and-run in the middle of an Oslo street?" Aramis pressed.

Gods, what kind of mess has my brother gotten us into?

"The worst possible thing happened. That fucking prick Bláinn became obsessed with Tove and the magical secrets her clan held. He's not the kind of person you want attention from, and Tove was in the most dangerous position of anyone in Svartálfaheim."

"How do you know all of this? Were you one of his soldiers?"

"Fuck you," she hissed with the first show of real venom. "I'd never serve that piece of shit. I was Tove's bodyguard and best friend. One of the few who was allowed to go with her when she married. It was me who stole the ring that would open a gate to Midgard. It was me who slipped it on her finger and shoved her through the gateway. It was *me* who drove a knife into my own stomach to kill myself before Bláinn found out what had happened."

She lifted the corner of her tight black singlet so Aramis could see the long scar on her abdomen. It took a special kind of courage to be willing to do something like that. His fingers twitched with the sudden alarming desire to touch her scar. He closed his fist tightly, willing the cold anger to come back.

"But you didn't die," he said.

"The Norns are bitches like that." Tyra lowered her singlet. "I told Bláinn that Tove had stabbed me because I tried to keep her from leaving. He never fully believed me, so he sold me as a slave to the dwarves instead. 'Put her in the ground so deep that she will never see the starlight again,' he told them. My people love the stars, so he thought it would break me." Her black eyes ran over Aramis again, and she rested her chin on her hand. "You look like starlight made flesh, all silver and pure light. Maybe that's why I feel like I could stare at you all night."

"You don't know me at all if you can look at me and see anything pure," Aramis said, surprised by the venom in his voice. He cleared his throat. "How did you survive down there?"

"Bláinn didn't account for me being a good slave. I took orders and kept silent."

"That's the only part of this story I find hard to believe."

"If you want my mouth silent, all you need to do is put your tongue in it," she replied so quickly that he could only stare. Her laugh was delighted. "Gods, you even blush prettily."

Aramis folded his arms. "If you were a slave, how did you escape?"

"The Svartálfaheim dwarves create the most messed-up and powerful weapons in all of the Nine Worlds. They started getting orders for weapons for a supernatural war brewing here on Midgard. Some guys calling themselves the Darkness wanted blades that would shape empires. Guess who the dwarves trusted to deliver all those items of death? Their quiet, loyal slave who was pretty enough not to scare their customers away."

Her smile grew sharp. "As soon as we hit Midgard soil, I took one of those delightful swords and killed them all. I kept a few things that I liked and dumped the rest into the sea. Midgard doesn't need the trouble that those weapons would've made. I spent the last two years here on Midgard trying to find Tove. When I finally did, she was getting lowered into the fucking ground. The Norns, as I said, are wicked old bitches. Asta was my silver lining. There was no mistaking who her mother was. I knew I had to protect her, no matter the cost. How the hell Tove managed to keep them both hidden from Bláinn I'll never know."

"Asta is shielded up so tightly we thought she was human. Tove's magic must've been powerful." Aramis shook his head, cursing himself for not exploring the magic when he'd first noticed it around her. "Do you think those men tonight were Bláinn's?"

"They would have to be. Bláinn has had agents on Midgard for the last two thousand years looking for Tove. He knew she came here. I have no idea how she managed to stay hidden for that long and was able to protect a baby as well. I can't even imagine."

"How do we find Asta now? We can't leave her out there for his men to track down again. I know my brother. As soon as Søren can move again, he will be gone."

"That's the thing. Asta? Her special talent is hiding. She might not know anything about her heritage, her mother, or magic, but Tove taught her how to disappear. When she messaged me tonight, she said she would find me again. She left to protect me, to protect Søren, because she has no idea what we are. She thinks Tove's ex is some gangster for fuck's sake! The only thing we can do is wait for her to contact me."

"Søren is the best tracker I have ever seen…"

"Two. Thousand. Years," Tyra reiterated. "He won't find her if she doesn't want to be found."

"He's not going to like that," Aramis said with a frown.

"Well, lover boy is going to have to get used to it," replied Tyra with a sigh. Aramis ran his hands through his hair in frustration.

"Don't worry," Tyra added. "Asta was sweet on him too. It might make her slip up and reach out sooner. He was covered in princess Band-Aids. He didn't do that to himself."

7

ASTA SIPPED HER TEA and looked out the window from the safety of the curtains, checking the street around her. Even after two weeks, she couldn't relax and sit still. Her mind kept playing the events in Oslo over and over again. She had been so sure that she had been doing the right thing by running. Now she had her doubts.

After leaving Søren on the couch, she had found the nearest ATM, emptied her accounts, and ditched her cards. She had booked flights to London under her two separate identities and had watched the gates from a hiding spot to see which identity had been compromised. After she had ditched Asta Johanson's passport in an airport tampon bin, she pretended to be an Australian tourist and jumped on a Busabout tour to Helsinki. From there, she had caught a ferry to Estonia and booked a month's lease of a one-bedroom apartment in the Old Town.

Her goth tourist identity worked well enough that she kept it up, visiting all the sights, buying spiced wine and nuts from the Christmas markets, and sending postcards to addresses that didn't exist. She had found Søren's wallet in one of the pockets of the overcoat, and after debating with her morals, she went through it. She had taken the euros out and added them to the wad of cash in her escape backpack before going through the cards. What she found was eerily similiar to her own wallet. He had a license in one name, three credit cards with different surnames, and receipts from four different countries.

"Who are you?" she asked the grim license photo.

In a weak moment three days ago, she had written a note, stuffed it into the wallet, and mailed it to the Alaskan address on the license. Even if Søren saw the Estonian stamps, she would be gone by the time he got it. She didn't know why she felt so guilty just…leaving him back in Oslo. Her stomach clenched whenever she thought about him bleeding under her hands.

Not having a day job had freed Asta up to study both of the books with a renewed obsession. Using her mother's laptop, she accessed university libraries and other academic databases, scrolling through thousands of articles. She hadn't been able to look at Tove's laptop before now. Whenever she'd seen it, grief, deep and sharp, had overwhelmed her. Now, her anger overwhelmed her grief. After seeing the caliber of people after her because of Tove, Asta was determined to find out every single secret her mother had hidden from her.

Her biggest challenge was coming to grips with what was chasing her. Søren had called them Dökkálfar, but all the searches came up with were references to the *Prose Edda* and various fantasy books. She struggled to say the word "magic" out loud, but that was exactly what she had seen both with the shadow guy and with Søren's dark green light that had choked him.

Asta wished she could call Tyra. She would take magic being real and the creepy men in black as evidence that Tolkien had been right all along.

Will Tyra even want to talk to me again after I bailed so completely? Asta planned on texting her over Christmas but didn't hope for a return message.

It was December 22, the winter solstice, which meant lighting a red candle as Tove had always done and trying to focus on all the things she wanted to let go of from the previous year. Asta was surprised at how short this year's list was. Things to release: grief for Tove, anger at Tove, and missing Tove. Things she wanted to keep: Tyra, medieval books, and…Søren.

Despite the questions she had, the way he had killed those people to protect her, and how pissed she was at him…Asta had *really* wanted to keep Søren.

"Don't think about it," she told herself and picked up one of the old books. She flicked through the pages until she found an illustration of a black-and-silver tree. It reminded her of the style of Søren's tattoo, and she wondered if he had been inspired by the picture.

She was still no closer to finding out what the books meant, but the task was meditative and forced her to think about something other than the spectacular way her life had imploded.

With her finger tracing over the curving words, she began the maddening task of sounding out the lines of script and letting the strange pronunciations roll over her tongue. For the first time, the words seemed to come alive in her mouth, leaving a tingling sensation she'd never felt before.

Asta jumped as her apartment door was kicked opened. Two tall figures stood in the doorway. They had the same sharp faces as her other attackers, and their black hair was shaved in elaborate undercuts with the longer tops braided.

"Hey! Get out of my apartment," she shouted. She was on her feet in seconds.

"Don't try to fight us, princess."

"Fuck off, you drunk bastards. You've got the wrong girl. Try the next apartment," Asta said, edging around the small couch.

"We don't want to hurt you, daughter of Tove, but we will not let you escape us again. He has waited too long to find you."

Asta hurled the vase from the coffee table at them before dashing into the tiny bathroom and locking the door behind her.

"You can't escape us, princess. Come peacefully." The door rattled.

"I'm really scared. You guys understand that, right? I don't know what you want from me, but my mother is dead. If you tell me what this is about, maybe I'll come out."

Asta grabbed her escape backpack from under the claw-foot tub and the coat hanging from the towel rack.

"Your mother's husband needs to talk to you, princess. There is much—"

Asta slid open the bathroom window, squeezing herself out and climbing down to the street. They wouldn't be fooled for long. She ran as fast as she could along the snow-covered footpaths, crossing over small gardens and between buildings. Pain sliced through her shoulder, and she stumbled. A small black arrow was sticking out of her.

"Fuck!" she said, sobbing. She didn't turn around, didn't stop running. She made it to the next block before whooshing sounds sped past her ears. She screamed as something sliced into her calf muscle and her right side. She pushed her way into a crowded restaurant, moving past the patrons and into the kitchens. Asta jostled a waiter and ignored his shouts as she pushed open the back door.

The alleyway was empty, but Asta knew she couldn't keep running. Hot liquid ran down her chest and legs as she heaved herself up into a cardboard recycling bin and shut the lid.

Choking on her tears, Asta huddled in Søren's coat and wrapped her hand tightly around the shaft in her shoulder.

Underneath her fear, Asta felt a warmth building inside her chest. She should have never run from Søren. He could hold his own with these assholes.

She bit into the lapel of his coat to muffle her sobs. It smelled of spring and spice. She focused on the scents, trying to distract herself from the pain seeping through her body as her adrenaline continued to pump.

"We know you're here, princess. Come out before the poison kills you," a voice called down the alley.

Poison. Asta would die in a pile of boxes. She didn't have the strength to fight. Tyra was right; the Norns really were bitches. At least she would die free.

She thought of Søren and how if she had stayed with him, he could have protected her. Heat blasted through her as her eyes closed. Her mouth tingled like it had when she had read from her book. Cold air and snow rushed around her, and she was falling.

Søren had spent the first week back in Svetilo lost in a haze of fever dreams full of pain and blood. It had taken the healers days to successfully flush the poison from his body. After that, his wounds had finally started to seal over and allow his Álfr healing to do the rest.

Aramis and Tyra had been to visit him, and Tyra explained to him how she had come to know Asta and Tove's complicated history. Aramis had kept her hands in shackles but with a long chain to give her freedom of movement.

"You know she could easily get out of those," Søren said.

"Of course I do. Tyra is keeping them on until the other Álfr trust her. You have to admit that's brave considering the years she spent as a slave."

Aramis got a weird look on his face whenever Tyra was around. His expression was often a cross between annoyance and amusement, and she seemed to enjoy exploiting his internal struggle. Søren had been too worried about Asta, even with all of Tyra's reassurances, to bother teasing his brother about the dark elf. Aramis had a surprising weakness for women with a dark streak, and Tyra was the equivalent of giving a recovering drug addict a bag of cocaine to babysit.

Søren wanted to go back to the apartment in Oslo and figure out what had allowed Bláinn's dark elves to find Asta to begin with.

"You can't help her if you are wounded, brother. Asta will contact Tyra, and then we'll be able to go get her," Aramis had said that morning, trying to console him. Søren was not in the mood to be consoled. His phone rang in his pocket, and he scrambled for it, hoping it was one of their contacts with word of Asta.

"Søren, it's Ruthann," the voice said from the other side of the world. Ruthann, the leader of the Álfr in Alaska, had finally grown the balls to call him after Søren had walked out on them all two years ago.

"What do you want?" Søren demanded. He didn't want to deal with this now.

"We received your wallet in the mail today," Ruthann said. "I thought you would want to know."

"My wallet? *Shit*. Asta. Do you still have the package it came in?"

"Yes. There was also a note tucked into it."

"What does it say?" Søren's heart thudded faster. *Please be an address. Please be an address.*

"It says, 'Sorry for stealing your coat and that the unraveling never got to happen. I hope you're not dead.' Does that make any sense to you?"

"Unfortunately. Look at the packaging. Where did it come from?" There was an interminable amount of time and rustling before Ruthann answered, "Tallin, Estonia. But, Søren, what—"

Søren hung up the phone and ran back to his apartments to strap every blade he had onto his body. Aramis and Tyra came into his rooms.

"Where do you think you're going?" Aramis demanded.

"Asta is in Tallin. Come or stay, I don't care. Don't even think about trying to stop me or I'll go through you," Søren said.

Aramis knew better than to argue. "Go and get your librarian."

"Try not to scare her too much," Tyra suggested. "She might fight you."

"She can try, but if I have to drag her back here kicking and screaming, I'm going to do it," Søren said darkly. He opened a gateway, but as he was about to step through, high-pitched alarms started blaring through the mountain fortress. Søren shut the gate instantly.

"What's that?" Tyra asked.

"The wards at the front gate. We are being attacked," Aramis said. Søren opened a new gateway, and they hurried through it. Five Álfr guards had their long blades pointed at a bundle of black on the snowy ground.

"Get back!" Søren's magic exploded out of him, knocking the guards down. He skidded to his knees in the snow. He would recognize that hair anywhere. He scooped her up in his arms, clutching her small, bleeding body to him. "It's okay, Asta. I've got you. You're safe."

8

SØREN CARRIED ASTA TO his rooms, while Tyra and Aramis hurried behind him.

"How did she even get here?" Aramis asked. "The wards should've been tripped miles back."

"She smells of magic. Maybe her own kicked in to save her," Søren said. He laid her down on his bed before he carefully took off her coat. She moaned. Her skin was already burning hot with fever.

"Aramis, please, I can help her," Tyra said, holding out her shackles to him.

Without hesitation, he made a quick gesture, and they fell away. "I'll get some clean towels," Aramis said. Tyra pulled off Asta's boots and hissed at the blood that covered her foot.

"We are going to need a healer to take this arrow out and to start purging the poison," Søren said urgently, looking at Aramis. His brother passed him the towels, and Søren pressed them onto the arrow wound.

"No time. Look at how many cuts she has! They're all laced with poison, and Ljósálfar medicine will take too long. Aramis, go and get a healer who will be able to stitch her up quickly. I'll fix the poison. Søren, give me one of your knives," instructed Tyra, holding out her hand.

Søren gave her one, not caring that she could use it to stab them. She cut away Asta's clothes until she lay only in her underwear.

"Okay, we have the arrow wound and two gashes in her leg," Tyra stated.

"There's a slash on the back of her other shoulder and side too. Gods, why would they do this to her?" Søren asked.

"They were trying to slow her down. My guess is that she gave them the slip, and whatever magic she has protected her by getting her out of there." Tyra rubbed her hands together, and purple-and-black shadows curled around her hands. "Ah, it's the winter solstice. I should've known."

"Does that make a difference?" Søren asked.

"The darkest night of the year is when Dökkálfar magic is at its strongest. That's why the magic would have worked for her even with all the shields on her. It would have risen up to protect her," Tyra explained.

Søren nodded. "That makes sense. Something similar used to happen to a shamanitsa I know. Anya's magic came to her aid more than once when she had no training at all."

"The solstice gave her magic just enough power to react." Tyra's hands glowed brighter. "Get ready to hold her down. She's going to hate this."

Søren grabbed Tyra's shadowed wrist. "What are you going to do?"

"Purge the poison using magic. If I don't do this, she'll die. Don't make the mistake of thinking you care about her more than I do," Tyra snarled. Søren let her go and stepped away.

"A healer is on their way. What else can I do?" Aramis asked.

"Pray I have enough magic built up to heal her. Thanks to your stupid dampener shackles, I may not. Now stand back." Tyra placed her hand on Asta's ruined shoulder, and her deep purple shadows poured out. Søren clasped Asta's hand as the magic covered her.

"You're going to need a towel," Tyra said to Aramis, her black eyes wide. Aramis did as he was told, and as black poison oozed out of the wounds, he wiped it away.

It was slow work, and by the time Tyra had reached the last cut, she was trembling.

"Are you okay?" Aramis asked her, but she gave him an offended look.

"Just worry about Asta. Okay, Starlight?" she snapped.

Despite Tyra's defensiveness, she was shaking from magic loss and exhaustion by the time she was done.

"Now you can clean the wounds and stitch her up," she instructed the Álfr healer.

"That was amazing," the healer said with wide eyes. "I'll see that she's well tended to."

"Thank you," Tyra said. She turned to Aramis, her haughty smile wavering as she swayed. Aramis caught her up in his arms before she could face-plant on the floor.

"Take her to the healing pools. I'll stay with Asta," Søren said.

"Let me know if she wakes up. I don't want her scared," Tyra said. Her fierceness was ruined by the way she was tucked protectively into Aramis's chest.

"I'll call for you right away," Søren assured her. "I need you to listen to Aramis and get your magic back in case Asta needs it again."

"I will. I feel so…weak," Tyra whispered, looking up at Aramis helplessly. As he cradled her closer, Tyra shot Søren a cheeky wink. He hid a smile, knowing she wasn't nearly as exhausted as she was making out. He'd let Aramis figure that out the hard way.

It took the healer another hour to finish stitching and bandaging Asta. The healer left him with an elixir in case Asta woke and instructions to keep her warm.

Søren got a clean flannel and water and carefully wiped the smeared blood and gods-awful black makeup off her until his familiar pixie librarian remained.

"You and I are going to have a long discussion when you wake up, Miss Johanson," he said to her sleeping face. "When I say discussion, I mean a lecture. About self-preservation and pissing off dark elves, but mostly about pissing *me* off and making me worry."

Asta murmured sleepily but didn't rouse, so Søren pulled up a chair, took her cold hand in his, and settled in to wait.

"Thank you for being so gallant," Tyra said sweetly to Aramis as he carried her through the hallways. A pair of shackles appeared around her wrists, and she scowled. "Spoke too soon. I'm starting to think you like me being tied up."

"It keeps you out of mischief. They won't affect your magic anymore. They are for show more than anything. Until we can get your presence accepted by the other Ljósálfar, you will wear them." He paused, then added, "Don't pretend like you can't get out of them when you want to."

Tyra studied the silver cuffs. If it weren't for the long fine chain joining them together, they would've been something she'd consider wearing for fashion. "I worked for dwarves. There aren't many locks that can hold me. These are definitely the prettiest shackles I've ever had though." Aramis flinched but didn't say anything.

Tyra couldn't remember the last time she'd been carried like a damsel, so she tried not to wriggle and just enjoyed being enclosed in the muscle-bound warmth that emanated from underneath the silvery-gray T-shirt. Aramis walked through a tunnel and down another set of stairs, and the air grew thick with warm moisture.

"Where are you taking me?" she asked.

"There are hot springs under the mountain. It will help you feel better and replenish your magic."

Tyra expected it to be a dark and damp space, but in true Ljósálfar style, the caverns were breathtaking. Globes of soft light floated near the sparkling stalagmites in front of them, and niches carved into the walls held fresh towels and glass bottles of water and wine. Even the turquoise water gave off a glow.

"This place is perfect to get naked in," she said. Aramis lowered her to her feet. "Not that I haven't minded you guarding my bathroom door every night, but still, you've been holding out on me."

"If I turn around to give you privacy, do you promise not to try to choke me to death with that chain?" Aramis asked her seriously. Tyra was tall, but she still had to tilt her head back to look him in the eye.

"If I wanted to kill you, I'd do it to your face. I'm a lady like that." She began unbuttoning her black jeans. Aramis turned his back, still scowling. Tyra pulled off her jeans and singlet, hissing as her muscles screamed.

"Are you okay, or are your pants too much of a challenge for you?" he asked. So he *could* tease after all. *Game on, Starlight.*

"My pants aren't, but can I ask you a really awkward question?"

"Nothing has stopped you before."

"Can you please unhook my bra? My arms refuse to bend backward right now." There was a long silence. "Oh, come on, keep your eyes up, and your virtue will remain intact, I promise. I don't have the energy to fight or flirt with you tonight." Tyra didn't hear him move, but then warm fingers started gently unfastening the fabric. She opened her mouth to say thank you when the fingers lightly ran a line down her shoulder.

"Who. Did. This," Aramis said through his teeth, and she flinched. He had peeked after all and seen the long red lines of burnt skin where her flesh had been torn from her by a hot whip.

"Bláinn ordered it right after Tove got out. I was almost dead from my stomach wound at the time. He had to unleash his anger somewhere. If you are going to stand there, you might as well undo my hair for me." Tyra tried to sound flippant, but his anger had struck something deep inside of her. Surprisingly, Aramis did as she asked, pulling his fingers through her braids to loosen the strands.

"I'm sorry," he whispered.

"Don't be. I knew the price for helping her escape." Tyra moved away from him and stepped down into the hot spring, not caring if he was still watching her. When she was finally in, she glanced at him over her shoulder. "Are you coming? I promise not to peek." *Much.*

Aramis had a torn look in his eyes, the anger still making them burn. It spoke of a compassion in him that would have been seen as a weakness in a dark elf. He pulled off his shirt, and she got an eyeful of pearly skin, muscles, and ink.

Freya, be praised.

"Wow, I've never seen Dauði Dómr marks before." She ran her eyes over him.

"I thought you weren't going to look."

"You saw my scars. Turn." Tyra's mouth went dry as she studied the black lines making up an intricate tree that spread across his shoulders, down his spine, and curved around his hips, disappearing into the top of his jeans.

"Satisfied?"

Gods, no. "How far do they go down?"

"Turn around." Tyra did as she was told, biting her lip to keep herself from laughing.

There was a soft splashing of water, and he said, "It's safe."

Tyra didn't feel it was safe when she saw those bare shoulders peeking out of the water. She sat on a stone seat a discreet distance away from him, not wanting to startle him away like a frightened deer.

"What?" he asked.

"I was just wondering how such an uptight guy managed to become the lover of someone as psychotic as Yanka," Tyra said. "How did you end up falling for her so hard that you let her go kick off a war?"

"You really like going for the jugular, don't you?"

"I can't help it. It's my training. Besides, I've been nothing but transparent with you. I know I'm a big scary Dökkálfar, but trust goes both ways. We might as well be friends, because you know you're not going to convince your brother to let Asta go anytime soon."

"You think so? Søren is not known for his overabundance of affection."

"Maybe not toward you, but I don't know if I'd be any different if your lover killed my pregnant wife," Tyra replied, immediately regretting her words. Aramis studied the water, looking like he had just been disemboweled. "Fuck, I'm sorry. I shouldn't have said that."

"I'm more surprised that you know about it," he said softly.

"You guys are kind of…legendary. Stories are told about you, and even though I was never involved in the wars, I heard about them. The Neutrals still talk about how you and Anya defeated Baba Yaga and Yanka. God Killers—that's what they call you. What's left of the Illumination and the Darkness is scared shitless of you and Søren. Why do you think I panicked when I found him bleeding on my favorite couch? I kept my head down on purpose, and then you notorious bastards crashed into my life."

"And as soon as we did, Bláinn's men turned up." Aramis pushed wet hands through his long hair, and Tyra tried not to giggle like an elfling. "If I had suspected what Asta was, I would've kept my brother far away. It would've been safer for all of us."

"I don't know about that. I was going to come clean with Asta sooner or later and get her out of Oslo. She was grieving so hard for Tove that I couldn't destroy her memory of her mother so soon," Tyra admitted. "I feel bitchy. Norn hands are all over this situation. Maybe we were fated to meet so I could change your mind about how pleasant dark elf females can be."

"I can't say I've had much success with women who have a dark side," admitted Aramis with the smallest of smiles.

"It's because you've been doing it all wrong."

"Obviously. You know about Yanka, so you know how terrible my choice of women is. Last time I did something out of love she tried to destroy two worlds."

"That's nothing! The last time I did something out of love, I tore apart a peace treaty that escalated to civil unrest and plunged Svartálfaheim and Álfheim into a never-ending war. I think we both have our fair share of fuckups."

Aramis's laugh was humorless. "You win. How can one woman cause so much chaos?"

"It's my winning personality." Tyra enjoyed the way his mouth twitched when he tried not to smile at her. "As I was saying, we Álfr are naturally drawn to each other. Your light calls to our dark and vice versa. Before the wars and everything went to hell, we actually used to interbreed quite a bit. There's a difference between darkness and evil. Anya, your adopted shamanitsa sister, is proof of that. I only know rumors, but it sounds to me like Yanka took advantage of your feelings and exploited you. You can't be faulted for that."

"I still should've known better than to set her free. I thought I was repaying a debt. I had a fool's hope that Anya might be able to keep her from doing anything unwise and finally stop Yanka's game with Baba Yaga. I was a fool, and the people of this city paid the price for it," Aramis said.

The guilt and pain emanating from Aramis made a part of Tyra want to comfort him. He wasn't ready to welcome it, so she said, "Yanka was the fool, Starlight. If she weren't already dead, I'd kick her ass for hurting you."

"Why? You don't know me."

"I know enough to think she was mad, as well as dumb, to blow her chances with you." Tyra gave him a wicked smile. "I can't complain. It means I'm free to flirt with you as much as possible."

"You certainly do like to flirt. I can't quite figure out if you're serious or if you are trying to get a reaction out of me."

"Can't it be both? I was trapped with nothing but dwarves to look at for nearly two thousand years. Can you blame me for wanting to flirt with you?"

"You've been in Midgard for years. You've had more than dwarves to look at."

"But you are…" Tyra shook her head. "You're very bashful about the attention. I'm surprised you don't have an Álfr harem or two."

"I'm a Dauði Dómr. I abandoned the position during the years I worked for the Illumination. I tried to stop a war but caused one instead. I'm supposed to be Anya's guardian, to teach her our ways and foster her magic, but she left for Skazki after the war. I haven't heard from her since, which goes to show how good of a guardian I am. Even amongst the Álfr, I'm an outcast, and I'm too damaged for anyone to want to pursue." Aramis's voice held no bitterness, and that surprised Tyra most of all. It was the plain matter-of-fact tone of someone who had accepted their fate. It made her want to shake him.

"At least the damage makes you interesting. Speaking of damage, is it true you only have one real hand?"

Aramis held his hands up. "What do you think?"

"I think one is made of wood. The craftsmanship is something next level, and that's high praise coming from someone who saw what dwarves can do." Tyra drifted closer to him. "May I have a look?"

Aramis hesitated before holding it out. "Just another way I'm broken."

"You're so full of shit." Tyra shook her head. She had seen broken, and if the Ljósálfar put someone as beautiful as Aramis in that category, they'd clearly forgotten what a dwarf looked like. She took his hand and studied it, twisting it around in hers. The wood was pale and pearlescent, and the light gray grain was so fine it was barely noticeable. Where the wood attached to flesh, there were silver scars like fine roots.

"It was made by magic—strong magic. Even the wood has an essence of magic. It almost has a different energy vibration than the rest of you. And it functions like a real hand?" Tyra moved his fingers, observing that there were no joints in the wood, nothing. Just fine carved lines across his knuckles and his nail beds.

"It took me some time to get used to casting magic with it and to regain weapon dexterity, but yes, it functions like a real hand."

"And touch? Is that different?" she pressed, not wanting to let it go just yet.

"It's different in that it's hypersensitive a-and—" Aramis stammered as she lifted one finger to her mouth and sucked it.

"You don't seem to be as broken as you think." Tyra let his hand go and moved away to the other side of the pool. Aramis stared at his hand for a moment before he put it quickly under the water. He looked like he didn't know whether to be outraged or aroused. *Perfect.*

"I suppose you're right," Aramis said, clearing his throat.

"You are like the best god and my namesake, one-handed Tyr, god of war and justice." She smiled. "Maybe it is another sign that our fates have been woven together. You certainly have me bound." She jingled her wet silver shackles at him.

"If you hate them so much, you can always unlock them." A challenging glint shone in his deep blue eyes.

Tyra stretched them above her head, letting the chain rest over the back of her neck. "I know, but I'm rather enjoying being bound to you, Starlight."

9

ASTA WOKE WITH A dry mouth and Søren frowning at her. He looked like he had been at it for a while. She wondered what he was doing here until the memory of what happened before she blacked out came screaming back to her. Her body gave a hard jerk, and she gasped as pain screamed through her wounds.

"Drink this," he said irritably and handed her a small glass vial.

"What is it?"

"Something to stop the pain." She downed it and then gagged violently.

"That tastes like hot garbage," she complained.

"Better than dying of poisoning." He handed her a glass of water, and she drank it greedily.

"Thanks. Where am I? How did you find me?" Warm fuzziness was seeping into her arms and legs, and she sighed with relief.

"You found me…here in Russia," Søren said slowly.

"Russia! But…that's not possible… I was in a garbage bin!" Asta tried to sit up. Søren placed a heavy hand on her shoulder, gently but firmly keeping her in place.

"Stay still, or you'll pull your stitches. I won't be putting you back together again," he warned. Asta stopped struggling, and he stepped back.

"Those things that were chasing me… Did you kill them?"

"Not yet," he said, green eyes full of violent promise. He paced slowly around the room, and Asta could see a change in him. He held himself differently, like a ball of tightly bound energy held soldier straight. In a tight black T-shirt, leather pants with knives tucked into special pockets down the sides, and black boots, Søren looked like a warrior waiting to kill something. He stopped pacing and ran his hands over his face.

"Can you please help me understand why you ran away in Oslo? Seriously, what the fuck, Asta? You *knew* people were after you, and you just ran."

"If this is because I took your book, I—"

"It's not about the fucking book!" he shouted. "You could've been killed or taken. You should've stayed where I—*we*—could've protected you."

"You were half-dead on my couch and couldn't protect yourself!" Asta yelled back. "I only knew you for a week, so you don't get to tell me what I should or shouldn't have done! For all I know, you could be working with them. You are like them—"

"I am *nothing* like them!" he snarled.

The door to the room opened, and a familiar voice said, "Move, or I'll make you."

"Tyra?" Asta choked out. Her cousin pushed around the solid wall of Søren. She looked unscathed with a half-mocking smile on her face.

"Hey, little one, nice to see you're feeling good enough to yell at this loser," Tyra said.

"What are you doing here? And why are you in shackles?" Asta said as she held her hand out to Tyra.

"It's because I'm a prisoner of love, right, gorgeous?" Tyra turned and winked at the man behind her.

"If you say so," said Aramis dryly. He touched her wrist lightly, and the chain disappeared. Tyra climbed into the bed beside Asta and wrapped her in a hug.

"It's about time you woke up. I've been going nuts for the last two days waiting for you." Tyra kissed her temple.

"Nothing has ever stopped you from waking me up before," Asta replied.

"You've never had a big scary Ljósálfar guarding you before." Tyra shot Søren an irritated look. He shrugged, unrepentant.

"We will leave these two ladies to talk," Aramis said, resting a hand on his brother's shoulder. "Tell her the truth, Tyra."

"Don't tell me what to do," Tyra said stubbornly. "You should go get some sleep, Søren. I've got her from here." He gave Asta a long look full of frustration and want before he let Aramis steer him out.

"Behave, or the chain will go back on," Aramis said to Tyra. She blew him a kiss as he shut the door.

"Tyra, what is going on? What are you doing here?"

"Let's start with you. What's up with you running off without saying goodbye? I know tall, dark, and angry has no reason to be upset that you took off, but I freaking do."

"I sent you a text," Asta said weakly. "I was trying to protect you."

"Haha! *You* protect *me*. You're adorable."

"Screw you. How did you get here?"

"I got into a scuffle with the boys after I discovered you had gone. I promise I'll explain everything, but tell me where you have been and how the hell did they find you again?" Tyra said. Shoving down her confusion and frustration, Asta told her of the night she was attacked and how it ended with her hiding and bleeding in a dumpster.

"I think they are after Mom's book," Asta said.

"What book?"

"It's like the one Søren has had me looking at. Mom was carrying it the day she died." Asta told Tyra about finding the book, the strange way it heated under her hands, and the beautiful, illuminated pictures. Tyra's face went cold and hard.

"Wait one moment," Tyra said and disappeared out the door. Asta couldn't make out the content of what was being said outside, but Søren's voice soon joined Tyra's as they shouted at each other.

Asta had had enough. She pulled herself out of bed and went into the small bathroom. After washing the sleep from her eyes and using some mouthwash, she took stock of her surroundings.

How did I get here? How is any of this possible?

The walls in the bathroom were made of solid stone, and there were neat bottles lined up on the basin. She opened one and sniffed. The strong scent of spice and spring hit her nose. *This is Søren's room.* She hobbled to the nearest wardrobe and pulled on a dark green button-up shirt that fell to her knees. He would probably get pissy about her taking it, but she wouldn't hang around in her underwear while they argued.

Asta shoved open the door. Aramis was standing between Tyra and Søren as they argued in a language she'd never heard before. All three turned to her at once.

"Tell me what is going on, you insufferable jerks," Asta said. "I'm sore, I'm scared, and I'm done with all this secrecy crap. Who is after me? Why do they keep calling me 'princess' like I'm some freaking five-year-old girl?"

"Go on then, Tyra. Tell her what we are," Søren snapped. Despite his angry expression, he still held out a hand to Asta to steady her as she walked slowly to a couch.

"What are you?" Asta said.

Tyra let out a groan. "Might be easier to show her." She looked at Aramis pleadingly. He gave her an encouraging nod. Something like a heat wave shivered over them, and suddenly everything about them seemed sharper, clearer, and infinitely more frightening. Aramis and Søren glowed softly. The color of their eyes grew brighter, and the tips of their ears sharpened to small points.

"You guys are…what?"

"The word you're looking for is Ljósálfar—light elves," said Tyra. She lifted her head, and Asta's world shook beneath her. Her cousin, who she had been living so closely with the last few months, had also changed. She had the same pointed ears and slightly upturned eyes as her attackers, but dark purple shadows curled around her feet and legs. "I…I'm Dökkálfar. Dark elf."

"And so are you," Søren said coldly. "Surprise."

Aramis didn't envy Tyra as she tried to explain her history to Asta. All the cocky confidence that usually emanated from her had abandoned her. She was sincere and exposed, and the love she had for Asta was obvious and intense.

Aramis kept his face calm, but he was still rattled by their arrival in his and Søren's lives. He scratched at his finger gently, trying to remove the feel of Tyra's lips on it. It had been annoying him for two days, and the sensation grew stronger whenever he looked at her for too long.

Aramis never should have gone into the pool with her, never should have stared at the torn-up scars on her back, and never should have wanted to know what they felt like, what *she* felt like. He had barely slept that night, knowing his room was only one over from hers. Tyra couldn't escape her room, not with all the warding he had put on it, but it hadn't stopped him from locking his bedroom door for fear of…something he couldn't quite define. She had gotten under his skin as quick as a switchblade. He was starting to understand how Søren had felt when he'd first seen Asta. There was an undefinable curiosity, an itch across his skin that he couldn't scratch.

It must be a dark elf glamour.

To Asta's credit, she didn't cry or react poorly when Tyra told her about her mother. She must know that being half dark elf wasn't the worst thing in the world that could happen to her. She would've been in real trouble if Bláinn had found her instead of Søren. Asta wasn't one for hysterics even though she must have been in pain from her wounds and had a confusing couple of weeks.

Aramis tried to be unobtrusive as he slipped out of the room. Asta needed food, they all needed wine, and Søren wasn't about to leave the two women alone. His brother looked like he couldn't decide whether he wanted to kiss or kill the tiny woman. Aramis was becoming intimately acquainted with that feeling himself. *Damn dark elves.*

After twenty minutes of breathing space, Aramis returned to Søren's rooms with vegetable soup for Asta and wine for the rest of them.

"Here, eat something. It'll make you feel better," he said to Asta.

"Thank you, Aramis," she replied, her voice small. Tyra took the wine with a thankful wink. Tyra was telling Asta about how she had found the newspaper article and had known that she wouldn't be the only one to see it. She had done her best to make sure she would be around to protect Asta.

"You should've told me the truth," Asta said angrily. "My *mother* should've told me the truth."

"She was trying to protect you. It might've been the reason she risked coming back to Norway. Maybe she thought the book held information that would help her defend herself against Bláinn's spies."

"Ah, so you did have a book after all," Aramis said, looking to Søren. "I told you my magic wasn't playing up."

"You…you knew I had a book?" Asta demanded.

"We suspected. This citadel was plundered two years ago, and we've been trying to get back what belongs to us," Aramis explained. "We were in Oslo trying to find some items the Darkness had sold on the illegal markets. Your mother must've learned about the book from one of her underworld contacts and recognized it for what it really was—a book about Álfr magic."

"If that was the case, why didn't you just ask me?" Asta said to Søren, her large gray eyes narrowing in anger.

"I didn't want to disrupt your world any more than what was necessary," Søren replied, folding his arms. Asta threw her spoon at him, and he only just managed to dodge it.

"Disrupt my world? You *lied* to me. You put on a whole show to get my help when you knew what the book was all along!"

"I could've torn the memories straight from your head. I was trying to win your trust, so you'd tell me what you knew instead of forcing me to take it."

"You tried to win my trust by *lying* to me!" Asta pulled herself to her feet with as much dignity as her wounds would allow. "I have to say well done. It takes a lot to fool someone who's been on the run her entire life, but you succeeded. I hope you had a great laugh over it, you complete and utter prick." She turned on her heel and headed back to the bedroom, slamming the door behind her. Søren hissed out a long breath of profanities and stood up to go after her. Aramis grabbed him by the arm.

"Leave her alone. Tyra? Make sure she eats something. We'll be back later." He steered Søren toward the door.

Thank you, Tyra mouthed at him.

"Come on, brother. We need to train," Aramis suggested.

"I don't want to train."

"Well, pouting at Asta isn't an option. You've been doing that for days. No wonder those dark elves cut you down so easily," Aramis said, deliberately provoking his brother. Søren swung at him. Aramis moved, grabbing Søren's arms and using his momentum to slam Søren into a wall with his arms pinned behind his back.

"See what I mean? That was sloppy, not to mention bad manners. If I let you up, are you going to remember to act your age?"

"Let me go," Søren demanded. Aramis released him with a light shove.

"You are exhausted and frustrated, and that's not a good combination when you are dealing with a woman whose world has crashed and burned. Work out, sleep, and begin again tomorrow."

"And you're an expert on women now?" Søren snorted.

"Forgetting Anya so soon? You have no idea how hard it was for me to win her over and get her to trust me."

"I lied to Asta, Aramis. I should've just taken the fucking book and left." Søren pushed his hands through his tangled hair. "This whole situation has been the worst mistake."

"Or the best. We haven't had any contact with the dark elves for centuries. It might be time to bury prejudices and work on building bridges," Aramis said, as they passed through corridors, heading for the training rooms.

"Just because you want to do some burying into Tyra doesn't mean the other Álfr are going to feel the same way."

"That was a low blow even for you."

"Doesn't make it less true," Søren replied as they walked onto the cushioned training mats. "She's just your type—violent and completely fucked u—"

Aramis tackled his brother to the ground, getting in two hard body blows before Søren managed to throw him off.

"Hit a nerve did I, *Starlight?*" Søren mocked.

Aramis threw a knife at him. "I'm not the one who sat on my ass like a moon-eyed idiot for weeks on end. Was it nice playing human? To have a woman look at you and not see the bitter man who's only happy when he's killing something?"

"You are one to talk! You bathed in blood for years when you were a trained dog for the Illumination. Should I tell your little dark elf how much your loyalty is worth? The Dauði Dómr bond couldn't hold you when you had to choose between it and Yanka. You threw the Illumination away for Anya. I wonder if you'll throw Svetilo away for Tyra as soon as you get your dick—" A bolt of battle magic threw Søren across the room into a rack of wooden spears.

"We are both horrible and undeserving, and you know it." Aramis was panting, and his ribs burned. "Did you ever stop to think that maybe Asta reacted so badly because she was getting feelings for you?"

The confused look on Søren's face said he hadn't. Søren climbed back to his feet, tossing a wooden spear at him. Aramis twisted, catching it in midair just in time to block Søren's follow-up blow.

"Don't be an idiot. We had one drunken kiss that meant nothing," Søren said, locking his spear around Aramis's.

"You weren't drunk, and it meant enough that you destroyed a hotel gym."

"Doesn't matter what it meant. We get Asta better, get our books back, and send them on their way."

Aramis knocked him to the ground. "If you say so, little brother."

10

TYRA WAS THE ONLY person Asta had allowed to visit her for the last three days. She claimed she had to rest, but Tyra knew the truth. Søren had embarrassed her, and it was up to him to figure out how to fix it. Tyra said as much to Aramis as they sat drinking wine in his rooms. He hadn't locked her up in his guest room, so she was taking advantage of his couch.

"Should I even ask what you are doing?" Aramis said when he returned with another bottle of wine. Tyra was sitting backward with her head upside down as she stared at the stone wall in front of her.

"It helps me think," Tyra said. "I'll have another glass of wine if you're pouring."

"What's on your mind?" He sat a careful distance from her. Even upside down, he was a juxtaposition of silver-and-gray loveliness. It really wasn't fair.

"The obvious problems. Asta is sulking. I wonder how close Bláinn is and hope those bastards didn't find my stash of blades in the apartment. I have no idea how we are going to get the shields off Asta and train her to use magic, or what I'm going to wear after you get tired of me cutting up your T-shirts," Tyra answered. The last one didn't bother her much at all, but from the pained look on his face when he'd found her in his kitchen using scissors to cut up one of his shirts, it wasn't a long-term option.

"Apart from the sulking, how is Asta?"

"Healing fast. She should be up and about, but she's sticking to her room to mope as long as she can. She has questions about the magic she used. I tried to show her a basic spell, but since the solstice has passed, there's no way for her to touch her magic again with the shields on her. Also, Søren needs to think of something to win her over again, because I don't know how much more of her sad face I can handle."

"I don't think he knows how." Aramis leaned forward and rested his elbows on his knees. "They need to be forced together even if it's just to fight it out. Svetilo is the repository of Álfr knowledge, story, art, and history. She likes books. It would be a good way to bribe her out of the room at least."

Tyra righted herself and reached for her wine. "If I didn't know better, I would think you're trying to matchmake."

"I haven't seen Søren even remotely interested in another woman since his wife died. He needs a friend if nothing else."

"Asta *would* be tempted by a library, but she would still try to make me take her."

"You won't be able to because you and I will be in Oslo getting your weapons. We can't just leave Svartálfaheim blades lying around for anyone to find, and it will be a good chance to retrieve the books from Tallin and investigate if Bláinn has more people in the area," Aramis replied. "That is…if you would like to accompany me."

Tyra drained her wine. "Getting blades and hunting bastards? Sounds like my kind of date." She gave her wrists a hard flick, and the shackles fell to the couch. Aramis looked at them and burst out laughing. It was infectious and open, and she couldn't help joining in.

"You really are the most surprising creature." He shook his head. "And it's not a date."

"Whatever you need to tell yourself, Starlight."

Aramis knew Tyra would welcome the opportunity to get out, but he underestimated the intensity of her enthusiasm. She was almost hopping from foot to foot as he put a holster of blades over his shoulders and pulled on his coat.

"You know, I used to test blades for the dwarves. If you want me to give your smiths some pointers, I'd be happy to," she said, turning a knife over in her hand.

"How did you get that? Give it back." Gods, she was fast. He hadn't even felt the movement of the air. "When did you steal that?"

"After you put them on and before you got your coat around your shoulders. It's not my fault you're too slow to realize when someone is stealing from you." Tyra flipped the knife between her hands a few times before pressing up against him and reaching slowly into his coat to slide it back into its sheath. "Slow enough for you?"

"Keep misbehaving, and I'll leave you behind." Aramis tried to keep his voice steady and ignore her warm body against his. "What did you say your job with Tove was? Bodyguard?" He had never seen a bodyguard move like her before. She didn't move like a soldier either but as something much more.

"Something like that." She stepped back from him.

"You're something all right."

"Try not to break your brain figuring out what that is," she advised, picking up her coat.

Søren glared at them suspiciously as they entered his rooms. He was trying to look like he was reading, and Aramis knew he'd been waiting for Asta to venture out of his bedroom. Much to Aramis's amusement, Søren hadn't demanded she move in with Tyra but had taken to sleeping on his couch—ready to pounce as soon as the door opened an inch.

"What are you two up to?" Søren asked suspiciously.

"We need to go to the Oslo apartment and the place Asta stayed in Tallin to collect some things and our books," said Aramis.

"If they are still there," Søren replied. "I'm on gates duty then?"

"Gates and Asta." Aramis nodded at Tyra, and she disappeared into the bedroom.

"Asta won't even leave the room."

"I have it on excellent authority that you'll be able to lure her out with the promise of the library. She must have questions about the dark elves. I'm sure Tirith will have something for her to read."

Søren raised a black brow. "Tirith—who threatened to use my skin for vellum should I go rummaging in his shelves without permission—that Tirith?"

"He and Asta will get along, and he won't begrudge your presence if you don't say too much. He has a right to be upset and protective. His books have been scattered gods know where." Aramis tried his best to sound convincing. The door opened before Søren could reply, and the two women were looking at them.

The color had returned to Asta's pale cheeks, and she was wearing a pair of leather training pants and one of Søren's shirts with the sleeves pushed up to her elbows. Søren seemed to be struggling to form words and was avoiding her eyes.

"Bring me back some clean clothes, would you?" Asta said to Tyra before fixing a bored expression on her face as she looked toward Søren. "I hear you've organized a trip for me to meet your head librarian."

"That's right," said Søren calmly. "Tirith could use an expert's eye and suggestions about how to repair the books that were damaged by the fire."

"What fire?"

"I'll tell you on the way." Søren straightened. "Unless you want to stay in bed longer."

"No, I'll come. I'm interested to see more of this place in case I need to leave," Asta replied. Søren's jaw worked, but he managed to keep his mouth shut.

"It's good to see you on your feet again, Asta," Aramis said with a smile. "Søren? Send us to Oslo first. I'll text you when we need to come back."

"Watch your backs." Søren looked over at Tyra and then back to Aramis. "Watch your front too."

"Don't worry. I'll take good care of him," said Tyra. "Come on, gorgeous, let's go hunting."

"Gods, she really is your type," Søren muttered as he pulled the gate open.

"Play nice," Aramis replied before Tyra grabbed his hand and pulled him through the gate.

The apartment looked remarkably untouched considering Søren had left five dead dark elves outside. As the gate closed, Tyra's hand shot out to keep Aramis from stepping forward.

"Wait," she warned. Picking up an abandoned mug from the coffee table, she tossed it at the open bedroom door. It hit an invisible wall and exploded, sending ceramic shards in every direction.

"Amateur hour," she muttered, holding out her hand toward it. *"Vísa."* Twisted silver lines appeared, a web of knots and magic.

"Do you know how to undo them?" Aramis asked as he leaned closer to study them.

Tyra gave him a cynical look and stuck her hand into the web to pluck a knot. The silver web unraveled inward before vanishing altogether.

"As I said, amateurs." Tyra went into her bedroom. "If they weren't, they would've been able to feel out my babies."

Tyra pulled back a woven rug and drew a symbol on the floorboards. Aramis's ears popped as the protection spell vanished. She knocked on a board that popped up, and she moved it aside.

"I'm trying very hard not to be impressed right now," Aramis admitted.

Her smile was dazzling. "Be impressed all you like. You haven't seen anything yet."

From the tiny space, she pulled out two long daggers that she buckled around her thighs and a sword as long as she was tall. Aramis could feel its energy hum along his skin.

"May I have a look?" he asked, and she passed it to him without hesitation. He pulled the sword from its sheath and admired its dark and deadly beauty. The metal of the gently curved blade was black, and a tracing of small stars inlaid with silver stretched down it.

"Are these your personal touch?" Aramis pointed to the stars. She looked a little guilty. "They are lovely, Tyra. It's a gorgeous weapon built for war. It seems only fitting it belongs to a woman with fire in her eyes and death in her smile." He sheathed the blade and held it out to her. He couldn't have been certain, but there might have been the faintest of blushes along the top of her cheeks.

Tyra strapped it to her back, the long blade almost touching the back of her knees. Aramis had never seen a woman wield a blade that big, but he was looking forward to it. She packed her clothes into a large duffel bag, and they did the same in Asta's room.

"That's all?" he asked. Two bags seemed inadequate.

"When you've never belonged anywhere, you travel light," she said matter-of-factly. "Bláinn is always going to be hunting Asta and me, so it's best not to get too attached to things we don't need."

Aramis texted Søren to open a gate back to Svetilo. "Is there anything we can do to get Bláinn to stop?" he asked as they waited.

"You mean apart from driving a sword through his head? Probably not."

"Why go after Asta? She's not his child, and Tove isn't alive to make her useful as a bargaining chip, so why bother?"

"Because Tove has embarrassed him for centuries, and if she can't pay, someone else will. I won't let Asta suffer like I did for the sake of his pride. I was prepared to die for Tove. Don't think I won't do the same for Asta."

Knowing it might cost him another hand, Aramis rested his hand on Tyra's back where her scars lay. "You've paid *enough*. We aren't going to roll over for some dark elf monster who threatens those we care about."

"You're very sweet, but you just don't get it." Tyra's black eyes were sad.

Green light filled the room, and they carried the gear through to Svetilo. Asta was eager and ready to take hers and headed for a shower.

"Is she talking to you yet?" Tyra asked.

"Enough to say she wants to look around," Søren replied. His green eyes darted to where she'd disappeared. "Tallin next? Asta gave me an address but without having seen it…"

"Drop us as close as you can," Aramis said, looking down at his watch. It was nearly 9:00 p.m., and he wanted to give Søren a chance to mend his friendship without interruption. "I'll call you for a pickup in a few hours." Tyra gave him a curious look but didn't argue.

"Fine. Just make sure you find those books," Søren said, opening another gate for them.

It was snowing on the streets of Tallin, and Tyra slid awkwardly as they hit the cobblestone streets. Aramis reached to catch her by the elbow before she could fall on her face.

"Of course it would be snowing," she said as she righted herself. With a shake, a glamour slid over her, hiding her weapons. She left the tips of her ears in their pierced points, and the small star studs winked at Aramis, teasing him as much as the rest of her did.

"We are close." He offered her his arm. "I wouldn't want you to slip again."

"Aren't you the gentleman?" Tyra wrapped her arm around his. With the snow catching in her inky hair and her cheeks flushed with cold, Aramis suddenly wished he wasn't such a gentleman.

"Some days more than others," he admitted.

"Come see me when it's an off day." Tyra pulled a piece of paper from her pocket. "This is the address Asta gave me."

They walked through the streets in an easy silence, both of them stretching their senses and magic around them, searching for anyone lying in wait.

When they found Asta's apartment, Tyra checked for traps, disabling a magical alert as Aramis picked the lock.

"Look at our excellent teamwork," Tyra said as the door swung open. Unlike the apartment in Oslo, this one was trashed. The broken furniture and the holes in the walls made it look like there had been a brawl. "Shit, do you smell that?"

"Bodies." Aramis pulled out his knives. Tyra cast more revealing magic, but nothing registered.

"Okay, let's find these books and get out of here. I can feel Bláinn's magic everywhere."

Aramis sent out his own magic and found the book Søren had given to Asta under an overturned couch. "I'm surprised they didn't find this."

"They wouldn't have been looking for anything magical except for Asta. They are too stupid to know what Ljósálfar magic feels like." She stepped into the bedroom. "Oh, fuck."

Aramis was beside her in a second, and his mind struggled to make sense of what he was seeing. The remains of three dark Álfr had been pinned to the walls with shards of living shadow. Someone had written a message on the walls in bloody runes: *Tovesdóttir, stop running or pay the price.*

"We can't tell Asta about this," Tyra whispered. "She'll blame herself."

"They were trying to kill her! Why would he do this to his own soldiers?"

"They failed him. They had Asta and hesitated instead of just taking her. Find the other book, Aramis. I'll take care of this," Tyra instructed.

Careful not to touch any of the blood spray, Aramis searched the room until he found the second book, wedged in between the mattresses.

"No wonder Tove wanted this so badly," he said. "It has some of the best shielding spells I've ever known in it. Bláinn might not have known or bothered to track this kind of Ljósálfar magic. I wonder what kind of magic the signature would have if a dark elf cast light elf magic."

"We can try it if you like." Tyra's power spiked, and shadows spilled out of her. She held out a hand and whispered, "*Gufanár*." The shadows searched out the bodies on the walls and the blood around the room, disintegrating the evidence until there was nothing left.

Outside the apartment, Tyra took a deep breath. Her hands were clenched tightly by her sides as she stared at the night sky. Aramis wrapped his hand over hers, loosening her fist.

"Let's get a drink," he said, gently pulling her away. The fury in her eyes simmered as she looked up at him. He held her gaze until it softened ever so slightly.

"Your hair looks better when it is long." She pulled a piece that only just grazed his shoulders.

"I'm less noticeable when it's shorter."

"Who told you that lie?" she teased as they walked. When they reached a large historical square, they found one of the less crowded restaurants and ordered spiced wines.

"Do you think Bláinn made that mess in the apartment?" asked Aramis softly, conscious of the human ears around them.

"Bláinn or one of his generals." Tyra took a sip of her steaming drink. "It definitely held his signature."

"I didn't think he would be stupid enough to leave Svartálfaheim for such a thing. I know how draining gate magic can be, and I know it would take even more to open something between worlds. I've only ever seen it done once, and it nearly killed the Álfr who did it," Aramis said. The memory of the night he and Søren had left Álfheim would be seared into his mind forever.

"Bláinn knows his generals will keep his throne safe. His inner circle has always been deathly loyal to him. Half of Svartálfaheim looks at him like he's some kind of god, and the other half fear him enough not to step out of line. The dwarves don't give a shit who's on the throne or who the Álfr make war with. They are war profiteers, and they are never going to be out of work."

"They sound charming," Aramis said dryly.

"They are okay, I guess. Their culture hasn't changed for a thousand millennia, and they don't care what happens above ground. They aren't cruel, just busy. After they realized I wasn't going to run away, they let me work like everyone else. I was used to test weapons, because I had the skills and knew what weights would be better for an Álfr."

"You didn't think about settling down with a nice dwarf and having hybrid babies?" he asked, hoping to make her laugh. Tyra snorted her wine up her nose in shock.

"Oh, gods, no!" She coughed. "Have you seen a dwarf recently?"

"Explains why you flirt with everyone you meet."

"I don't flirt with everyone. I flirt with *you*. There's a very big difference," Tyra said, clarifying. "Even if I had wanted to hook up with a dwarf, they wouldn't have been interested in looking at my vagina unless it turned into a diamond." The waiter who had been delivering a fresh round of drinks nearly dropped his tray.

"Don't mind her. She plays too much *World of Warcraft*," Aramis said, trying to hold in his laughter as he ordered food.

It wasn't until he was settling the bill two hours later that Aramis realized that despite his initial protests, their night *had* turned into a date of sorts. Tyra seemed to already know it as she waited for him outside, her smile smug.

They reached the place Søren's gate had dropped them, and Aramis pulled out his phone.

"What are the chances that they are being pleasant and teasing each other again?" he asked.

"I hope Asta is giving him a hard time. He's so straight it'll be good for her to bend him out of shape," Tyra said maliciously.

"You would have to be the only person I've met that thinks Søren is the straight one. That's me. Straight, boring, well-behaved."

"You have really fooled them all, haven't you? You act like you have to be the responsible one, the calm one, but I can see it inside of you." She leaned close to whisper in his ear. "Everyone knows the heart of a star burns with the fires of creation. I've seen enough forges in my life to know when one is being smothered. All it would take is one hard blow of air, and you would burn and burn and burn." His hands were suddenly on her hips, bringing her close, her thighs pressing into his.

"Are you going to be this almighty gust?" Aramis asked curiously. "Or are you only interested in teasing my ashes?"

"I *do* love to tease." She smiled wickedly. "I know you're going to take a bit of coaxing, but I'd settle for a taste."

She rose on tiptoes, and for a moment, Aramis thought she was going to kiss him. At the last second, her hot gaze changed. She shoved him backward as a dagger flew past his face. Her sword was in her hands, quicker than a blink.

"You're surrounded, *Draeimi*. Lay down your weapon," a dark elf said, appearing in an alleyway entrance.

"Scared you can't take it from me yourself, Thrynn?" Tyra said, strengthening her stance. Aramis's magic pounded in his veins, begging to be released.

"Your taste in company has certainly fallen. Is there no depth you won't sink to? Fucking a Ljósálfar," Thrynn spat. "Disgusting."

"Are you still upset that I'm not fucking you? I'd rather have a troll inside of me."

Thrynn's smile darkened. "Perhaps I'll arrange that when I drag you back to Svartálfaheim by your hair."

"Not if I have anything to do about it," Aramis growled. He drew his long knives, ready to kill the dark elves stepping from the shadows around them.

"You're trying to defend my honor? Gods, that makes me so hot," Tyra said as they positioned themselves back-to-back. "After I kill these assholes, I'm getting that taste, Starlight."

Søren had tried to warn Aramis about how the dark elves moved, but nothing could have prepared him for seeing it himself. It was like fighting shadows and smoke. He trusted Tyra to take care of Thrynn as he kept the other three away from her. The blood on his blades told him that he'd hit flesh more than once, but the elves disappeared only to appear again, keeping him on the defensive.

With a frustrated shout, he unleashed his magic in a roar of light and heat. His three attackers appeared in different positions with their burnt skin blackened. Aramis sliced his blade sideways, and they exploded into ash. He turned to search for Tyra and was struck dumb by the sight of her.

Aramis's heart pounded as he watched her move, cutting down her enemies with her massive sword like they were nothing but annoying insects. In that terrifying glorious moment, he knew she would never need his protection, never need him to train her, and never need him to make sure she didn't succumb to darkness. He wouldn't have to pretend to be better than he was to set an example for her. He didn't have to be anything he wasn't with her, and she didn't need him for one damn thing. Tyra was darkness and death, and he wanted her so badly his bones ached.

When Tyra was done with his warriors, Thrynn finally gathered the courage to face her. He was twice her size and weight, but she more than held her ground against him. She wielded the huge sword as if it were an extension of herself, moving to block every attack with an almost-bored ease.

"You still make the same moves. What have you done in the last two thousand years apart from kiss your master's ass?" she said, knocking Thrynn aside.

"It doesn't matter what you do to me. Bláinn will get Tovesdóttir and make you watch as he peels the flesh—" Purple shadows threw him up against the wall of the nearest building, pinning him there.

"You tell Bláinn that he's lost. If he comes near me or mine again, I'll burn his world to the ground," Tyra said, her voice cold and clear.

"You think this Ljósálfar will protect you against him? Bláinn will come for you both. The Ljósálfar won't risk sacrificing their people for two disgraced dark elf bitches."

Thrynn screamed as Aramis's dagger buried deep into his stomach.

"She's got her claws in you already you poor dumb bastard. It took a whip to get them out of me. Think about trading them to Bláinn, before she betrays you too," Thrynn hissed, managing a laugh through the pain.

Aramis rang Søren. "Get us out of here," he said and hung up. He wanted to carve Thrynn to pieces, but it wasn't his revenge to take. Tyra pulled his dagger from Thrynn's stomach with a jerk as the green aurora of Søren's magic opened a gate on the street.

"Give Bláinn my message," Tyra said, pulling her shadows away to free Thrynn before the gate shut behind them.

11

ONCE SHE WAS CLEAN and dressed in her own clothes, Asta finally began to feel steady again. She took her time getting ready, knowing Søren would be waiting patiently outside the door. He hadn't tried to talk to her since she had yelled at him. He had let her be, even though she was in his room, and hadn't tried to force his way in to argue with her.

Like all things concerning Søren, she was torn between wishing he had and being glad he hadn't. Tyra, Tove, elves, pissed-off kings, the fact she had magic and it had transported her from Estonia to Russia in the blink of an eye—it had all been too much. As much as she had tried to deny what she had been told, her past had also started to make sense. Her mother's overprotectiveness, the type of work she'd chosen to do, and why she had moved them so often.

Asta had been so caught up in her feelings about Tove's death that she had dismissed Tyra's wildness, her struggle to understand basic references, and the way she was fascinated by simple things like toasters and TVs. She had taken Tyra's constant fixation on Norse mythology for obsession. Now Asta was recalling every odd thing that had happened, including the way Tyra had reacted to *Thor: The Dark World* by complaining about misrepresentation and then staying drunk continually for a week. That had seemed like completely normal Tyra behavior at the time. She supposed it *was* normal for Tyra. Not her cousin, but a sworn protector. *What has my life turned into?*

"Books. Focus on books," Asta said firmly. Books were the one thing she could find a middle ground on. They were the only thing she understood in her new reality.

Søren was waiting for her, and his eyes quickly took in her neat attire.

"You are looking back to normal," he said. "Where are your glasses?"

"I don't need them. I only wore them at the university," Asta admitted.

"Why?"

"To help suit the role I was playing there. Mom used to wear them, and I was…kind of using her credentials." Why had she told him that? It wasn't like she would ever be able to go back and work there again.

Søren got to his feet. "You lied to them?"

"I needed the job." She folded her arms. "Are you seriously going to try to lecture me about lying? Because—"

"I wouldn't dream of it. Are you ready? I don't want Tirith to wait too long. He doesn't like me very much as is."

"How's he going to feel about a dark elf in his stacks?" Asta asked as she followed him to the door.

"I'm going to let it be a surprise." Søren shot her a smile over his shoulder. "I'm sure you'll get along fine with him, little librarian. You both love books and are angry with me."

"Should I have shackles on like Tyra?" Søren's apartments were in a hallway of stone, and as they walked, she grew more and more nervous about seeing other Álfr.

"If anyone tries to put shackles on you, I'll break their fucking arms. Tyra is considered a threat because she threw Aramis across a room. If not for that, she wouldn't be wearing them at all. Not that he thinks she's a threat now, but they seem to be having too much fun with the pretense to stop."

"I kind of noticed that, though I'm really not surprised she's crushing on him considering her Thranduil obsession. They seem to be getting along well." That was an understatement. Tyra was eye-fucking Aramis whenever they were in the same room. Asta had seen her with men before, but she seemed almost bored with them compared to the hawklike attention she paid to Søren's brother.

"He's hopelessly weak for dangerous women. They'll tear each other apart one way or another. I'm staying out of it, and I suggest you do the same."

"You don't have to warn me. I know better than to mess with Tyra when she's obsessing. If he were my brother, I'd be worried."

"I've had more important things to concern myself with." Søren pushed open a door, and she stepped nervously into a vaulted hall of stone full of Álfr moving about carrying books, talking in groups, and going about their business.

"This is the main hall that connects all of Svetilo," Søren explained.

"And we are inside a mountain?" Asta stared at the ceiling hundreds of feet above her.

"A mountain in northern Russia, about three hours from Arkhangelsk. When the Ljósálfar left Álfheim, this is the first place they built. Now it's mostly where scholars, artists, and healers work and train. Our histories and records are kept here along with books of magic."

When they neared the middle of the hall, the carved stone was warped and blackened. At its center was a fountain shaped like a tree with water tinkling from its metal leaves and branches. The fountain looked new compared to everything else.

"It's a memorial," said Søren as they stopped to look at it.

"You said there was a fire?"

"Two years ago. Svetilo was attacked by the Darkness. Did Tyra tell you about them?"

"Yes. She said that 'they are a bunch of evil bastards.' The Illumination was supposed to be their balance, but she said they were just as bad."

"In some ways, yes. The Darkness wanted anything that would give them an edge in the last war, so they attacked the Álfr here. A lot of people died. My men and I… We arrived too late to stop them."

"I'm sorry." Søren's voice was filled with a loss she couldn't understand, and she knew any attempt to comfort him would fall short. "Is that why you and Aramis have been searching for your relics?"

"Yes. I permanently left our compound in Alaska to stay here and help rebuild Svetilo, to recover what was stolen, and to make sure they are never left undefended again."

"What kind of awful bastards would attack a library?" Asta shook her head.

They followed a small crowd through beautifully carved wooden doors and into a library of stone archways, shelves, and so many books. At the sight of it all, Asta's legs wobbled.

"Are you okay?" Søren's hand moved under her elbow to steady her.

"I'm just wondering if I died from my wounds and went to heaven, that's all." She took a deep breath.

"Dauði Dómr, I thought I made myself clear the last time you stepped over this threshold that you weren't welcome to do it again." The curt voice echoed through the citadel, and the hushed noise vanished.

An impressively tall Black Álfr with long gray hair was striding toward them, his silver-and-blue robes streaming out behind him.

"I thought I told you that you can't keep me from doing what I like, Tirith," said Søren. "Keep your dress on. I'm just showing our guest around. She's a librarian and a medieval literature and manuscript expert."

"Is that so?" Tirith looked her over carefully.

Asta stepped forward, unable to look him in the eye. "It's an honor to meet you, sir. I'm very sorry to hear of the losses you have suffered recently. If there is anything I can do to help you with restoration, please let me know."

There was a long silence before Tirith said, "At least she is more polite than you." He lifted her chin and gave her the full weight of his gray eyes. "What brings you here, child? What is this magic I can feel locking you in?"

"Asta found one of your books but was attacked before she could bring it here herself. Aramis has gone to collect it," Søren answered for her.

"She has her own mouth, Søren," Tirith replied, and Asta grinned despite the close inspection she was getting.

"I don't know about the magic inside of me. Perhaps you could help me understand it a little better? Søren has been very quiet about it, but it's what brought me to this place during the winter solstice," Asta said. Søren hadn't told her anything because she had been refusing to talk to him, but Tirith didn't need to know that.

"He isn't smart enough to know what he's looking at when it comes to such binding magic and would most likely not be bothered to learn." Tirith sighed, letting her chin go. As mad as she was at Søren, Tirith's comments still grated her.

"Søren protected me when I needed it, so if you would allow him to show me around, I'd appreciate it. I don't want to disrupt you."

"Nonsense! I'd be happy to take you on a tour of the library, and maybe we can see what's keeping your magic locked u—"

"Where she goes, I follow," Søren said.

"Do you think because she's half dark elf that she would cause trouble if you weren't dogging her heels? You should know better than to judge a race over the actions of a few," Tirith chastised.

"It's not because she's Dökkálfar. It's because I said so. She's my guest after all," Søren said coolly.

"Let him come," Asta said, giving Tirith her sweetest smile.

"Just as long as he doesn't say anything." Tirith threw his hands up in defeat. He offered Asta his arm, and she took it.

"Unbelievable," Søren muttered softly.

✦

For as long as Søren had known him, Tirith had been a bastard. Søren hadn't taken it personally, because Tirith was a bastard to everyone. Watching the ancient Álfr melt under the intensity of Asta's smile and her curious questions was in equal parts disturbing and glorious. Was that how he had looked to Anders Larson and the students while he'd worked with Asta? He hadn't stood a chance.

"Do you have any books about…about my people?" Asta asked nervously.

"Of course we do. Let me show you," Tirith said, escorting her through the long stone aisles.

Søren wandered after them, giving them space to talk so Asta could ask any question she needed to. He wanted her to feel comfortable with her nature even if it might take a while for everyone else. Dark elf. How had he not seen it to begin with?

He had been so blinded by her innocent librarian persona and those goddamn adorable little cardigans she wore—today's was the color of peaches—that he hadn't questioned her further. She looked nothing like the dark elves that haunted his childhood memories, and Tyra was such a force of nature that he didn't connect either of them with the horror stories he'd heard.

By the time they left the library two hours later, Søren's and Asta's arms were full of books for her to read. Tirith had invited her back to look over damaged vellum, and Asta seemed to have some of the spring back in her step. She hadn't berated him again, but that didn't mean he was dumb enough to think he'd been forgiven.

"Do you think Tyra and Aramis are okay? I thought they'd be back by now," Asta said, biting her lip.

"They will be fine. Aramis will want to make sure the dark elves that attacked you are gone, or if not, he'll try to question one of them. Tyra wants to figure out how they found you in the first place." Søren opened the door to his apartments for her.

"I was talking to Tirith about that, and I think *I* called them to me. They would have sensed me using my magic without realizing it." Asta placed the books down on a small coffee table.

"What do you mean?"

"I was trying to make sense of the language in your books. I was reading aloud, and even though I didn't understand the words and the protections were over me—"

"You were casting the magic because of the solstice, and they could track it." Søren placed his books next to her and sat down on a couch. "Damn. Why didn't I think of that?"

"I had no idea what I was doing. I still don't. Tyra tried to help me use magic again, but it's completely buried." She sat down in a chair across from him. She looked very young and overwhelmed, and Søren hated it.

"Can I just…say something?" he asked nervously. "You don't have to do anything, just listen for a moment. I've had many days to think things over, and I need to get this out before you go back to hiding from me."

Asta folded her arms protectively over her chest. "Okay."

"I'm sorry for the deception when we first met. I went about everything entirely the wrong way. At the time I thought I was protecting you. The first day I went to the library, I was there for a fight. I thought someone from the Darkness was hiding there, and I was ready to tear them apart.

"The magic led me to you, and I couldn't do it. I couldn't threaten you or hurt you to get what I needed. I scrambled, and the lie was bad. I made up the whole persona of being a doctor and planted memories in Anders Larson's head so he would allow me to work with you. I thought some asshole had put magic on you for some malicious purpose, and the thought of anyone hurting you filled me with rage. If I stuck close to you, they would reveal themselves, and I'd be able to save you, kill the asshole, and get our book back. Those were the lies and reasons why I told them. Everything else was *me*. I didn't take you out for a drink that night because I was working some kind of an angle. I did it because I really do like your company. I don't do"—he waved his hands about impatiently—"*friendships* well. Or at all. It's been a long time since my wife died and I haven't wanted to spend time with another woman until now. I don't know how to make it up to you. I don't know how to win your trust back or change your opinion of me so that we can learn to be friends again. I'm sorry I lied and for hurting you."

Asta was staring at him like he had two heads. *Fuck, I knew none of it would come out right.*

"We both lied," she said finally. "I wasn't who I said I was either. My mother lied to me about who she was, and Tyra lied to me for months. I get it. We can't just share what we are with people. I was like that even before I knew about the blood and magic in my veins. Now that everything is out in the open, how about we make a deal? No more lies, no more angles. If you want to know something about me, don't go behind my back. Come to me. I'll respect you by doing the same. I know your reputation is pretty terrifying. It's not something I've seen, except to protect me. I won't listen to gossipy Álfr or Tirith's warnings without getting the truth from you. Deal?" She held out her hand just as his phone rang.

"Shit, I need to take this. It's Aramis." Søren answered it. "What?"

"Get us out of here," Aramis demanded, and the line went dead.

"Something has gone wrong," Søren said. The gate's magic tugged at him, but he still knelt down to take her hand and kiss it. "Deal. And thank you, Asta. Now do me a favor and get behind me." Then he pulled out his knives and summoned the gate.

Aramis and Tyra appeared through the green light, bloody and with weapons drawn. Søren closed the gate quickly after them.

"What happened? Are you okay?" Asta was beside Tyra in a second, ready to hug her. Tyra stopped her with one look.

"Don't. I'm covered in dark elf," Tyra said. She went to the kitchen and placed her gore-slicked blades on the sink and washed her hands. "Gods, I need a drink."

"There are spirits in the cupboard above your head," said Søren.

Tyra pulled out a bottle of vodka, opened it, and had a long swig. "Better." She had another drink before handing it to Aramis. He took a large mouthful and passed it back to her.

"Are you hurt?" Asta asked.

"Don't worry. None of the blood is mine." Tyra shot a glance at Aramis. "They get you anywhere before you cooked them, Starlight?"

"No," Aramis said.

"Cool spell by the way. The sneaky bastards didn't expect to get turned to ash."

"Anya taught it to me," Aramis replied with a fond smile.

"She's a psychopath. You'd like her, Tyra," Søren said. "You want to fill us in on what happened?"

"A bastard called Thrynn was there. He's one of Bláinn's generals. Damn prick bastard," Tyra muttered. Aramis pulled one of the books out of his coat pocket and offered it to Asta. Søren saw the title and did a double take.

"No wonder Tove went back to Norway for it," Søren muttered.

"Why? What's in it?" Asta asked, turning the book over in her hands.

"Protection spells. Wards. You name it," Søren told her. "This general—he was waiting at the apartment?"

Tyra slid down the cupboards and sat on the kitchen floor. Søren had seen that look before; the past had just smacked her in the gut.

"Thrynn made lots of threats, but it didn't work out well for him," said Aramis. He turned the tap on and calmly washed Tyra's blades and his own. Søren didn't know what had passed between them, but he knew what it looked like when Aramis was trying to be caring. Aramis and Tyra described the bodies in the apartment and recounted everything that had happened afterward.

"I'm going to have to train you two to fight dark elves," Tyra said, her eyes already glazing over from the alcohol. "You both had your asses handed to you, and I can't have that happen if these skirmishes escalate."

"But they won't be able to find us here, right?" Asta asked. Her hand twitched with the top button of her cardigan.

"They saw Aramis. He's unforgettable. They will figure out where we are hiding sooner or later," Tyra said miserably. "We need a plan and some training and some—"

"Tomorrow," Aramis told her. He held out a hand to her. "Tonight, we sleep. Tomorrow, we train." Tyra placed her hand in his, and Aramis hauled her to her feet. She sheathed her clean knives and picked up her sword.

"Don't look so worried. Bláinn isn't hiding under your bed, and Søren will protect you," Tyra said to Asta. With a sigh, she kissed Asta's forehead. "You are worth every sleepless night, little one." After they had gone back to their rooms next door, Asta turned to Søren.

"I can't be the only useless one here," she said, her small chin rising. "Will you help me figure out how to remove the shields Tove put on me so I can use my magic?"

"You'll let me be your study buddy again?" he asked. Her teasing smile hit him like a blow.

"Well, you *were* pretty good at it," she replied as she turned toward the bedroom.

"Enjoy my comfortable bed while I'm still feeling generous, princess."

"Suffering develops character," she called as the door shut behind her.

Despite enemies closing in around them and the chunks of dark elf clogging up his sink, Søren smiled for the first time in weeks.

12

THIS WAS NOT HOW Tyra had wanted to end the night. A part of her mind was still standing in the street in Old Town, watching the snow stick stars to Aramis's dark blue coat like he was a celestial god who had torn a strip of the night sky to clothe himself. There were warm fairy lights tied around street lanterns and the smell of smoke and spice and sugar in the air.

It had been the perfect moment for a first kiss…and it had been ruined by that bastard Thrynn.

Standing naked in her small bathroom, Tyra looked at the smears of blood on her face, the ash and darkness burning in her eyes. *Draeimi. Draeimi. Draeimi.* She could hear the whispers around her, the ones that used to follow her wherever she walked, the whispers that turned to a chant before a battle.

Tyra took another large swig of vodka and got into the steaming shower. She lathered herself all over twice, washing her hair until her scalp ached. She took the time to dry and braid her long black hair, hoping the action would calm her. When she was with the dwarves, she had felt she would never be clean again, and now there were few things she loved more than the slippery feeling of clean hair.

Climbing into her bed, she curled up into a tight ball and pulled the soft fur blanket over her.

Tyra covered her ears with her hands, hoping, praying to whatever gods would listen, that the nightmares wouldn't come.

No matter how many centuries passed, she would never forget the sick look of joy and hatred in Thrynn's eyes when she was dragged out of the filthy cell, taken into the yard, and whipped bloody in front of Bláinn's entire court. No one tried to defend her, no one tried to stop Thrynn or speak against Bláinn. No one was brave enough to look away, but none of the hollow eyes ever really saw her in the bloody mud.

The gods didn't listen, and she fell into the darkness and violence of her nightmares to scream with pain and madness.

Aramis hadn't known what to say to Tyra when they made it back to Svetilo. She hadn't wanted to talk, and he had let her disappear into the guest rooms. Lying on his bed now, staring at the ceiling, he thought that had been a mistake.

Despite her bravado, seeing Thrynn had affected her. Tyra had closed in on herself and her own thoughts, and her usual flirty banter was nowhere to be seen. *Draeimi*. The word reverberated through him. It was a title that held a weight he didn't understand, and as soon as Thrynn had said it, Tyra had been dragged down.

Maybe I should have killed him and been done with it, Aramis thought as he rolled over and got out of bed. He needed to walk or pace or...something. Despite it being only a few hours before dawn, the tense coil of adrenaline in him wouldn't loosen. He was in the kitchen when he heard the first scream. The cup in his hand smashed across the ground as he raced to Tyra's room. As he opened the door, a pulse of shadow pushed him back roughly.

"Tyra!" he called, trying to push through the magic to reach her. She was crouched on the floor, shaking and screaming in pain but completely asleep. He reached out with his magic and touched hers, a brief flicker to let her magic know that he wasn't an enemy it needed to fight. The pressure lifted, and he hurried to her side.

"Tyra, wake up. You're having a night terror." Aramis reached out to touch her lightly on the back, and she roared, knocking him to his back and striking out at him. He wrestled in her grip, grabbing her hands and pressing them tightly together.

"Wake up, Tyra!" he shouted, and her body jerked as her eyes finally opened.

"Aramis?" Her voice was tiny as she stared down at him underneath her. "D-did I hurt you?"

"No, I'm fine. I heard you cry out and tried to wake you." Aramis let her hands go. Her breath dragged in with a ragged gasp as she pushed herself off him.

"I-I'm sorry. I can't...can't breathe. Buried alive! I'm being buried alive." Tyra looked around the stone walls like a trapped animal. She gripped the stone floor as the panic attack overtook her.

"Easy, I have you. Let me help," Aramis said urgently. He tossed a blanket over her shivering body and scooped her up. He kicked open a door carved with a moon and hurried up a steep flight of steps. The temperature dropped rapidly as he neared the top and pulled back another heavy door. An icy wind blew in on them as he settled her down on the stone viewing platform that had been carved into the mountain.

"Open your eyes, Tyra. You're not trapped. You're in the stars." She opened her weeping eyes to look at the sky, blazing above the valley stretched out in front of them.

"What is this place?" she asked, looking at the sheer drop only meters from her.

"My rooms used to belong to an astronomer. This is the platform she had shaped from the mountain so she could chart the night skies. I would've shown you sooner, but I didn't know if you would try to escape." Aramis sat beside her.

"It's so… Gods, I can't breathe it's so beautiful." She stared at the expanse above her, and her hand clutched gently at her throat.

"You'd better start. I don't want the first time I kiss you to be CPR." She managed a choked laugh. She must have realized he was shivering, because she crawled into his lap and tossed the fur blanket around them both. Aramis couldn't remember the last time he'd had a woman come to him in such an affectionate manner. Tyra had a way of laughing at his emotional defenses right before she bulldozed through them whether he objected to it or not. With every day that passed, those objections seemed to be disappearing.

"Much better. I don't want you to freeze to death on my behalf." Tyra turned her eyes back to the stars. "Tell me what they're called."

With her warm body tightly curled in his arms, Aramis pointed out every constellation he knew the name of one by one while she repeated the names back to him and asked him questions until her heart stopped racing and her breathing leveled out.

"Thank you for this, Starlight," she whispered softly as the sun began to rise. "I can't actually remember the last time anyone did something so kind for me. *And* you defended me last night, also a first."

"I don't think you needed my help with that last one. If you ever looked at me like you looked at those dark elves, I'd probably soil myself," Aramis admitted. She'd been elemental. The way she'd moved was burned into his brain forever.

"I'm going to have to teach you to fight them. They will be back, you know. All we did was piss them off." Tyra fiddled with the edge of the blanket. "Thrynn was right. You can't let them threaten the lives of the Ljósálfar because of me and Asta."

"I'm not trading you to some dark elf warlord with a grudge," Aramis said as simply and nonpossessively as he could manage. "We aren't going to argue about it. If they turn up here and make their threats, we'll deal with it. Søren and I aren't Álfr they will want to start a war with if they can help it. You're under our protection, which means you're one of ours. It doesn't matter what blood is in your veins. Understand?"

"Yes," Tyra answered softly, nestling farther into him.

They watched the sun come up in silence, and when he heard a soft snore from Tyra, he gently picked her up and carried her back to bed.

13

IT WAS MIDDAY WHEN Tyra burst into Asta's room and launched herself at her with uncontrolled enthusiasm. Tyra scattered the neat piles of books Asta had created on Søren's couch as she wrapped her arms around Asta.

"Oof! What's the matter with you, psycho?" Asta complained, looking to Søren for help. He sat in an armchair opposite her with a book in his lap and an amused expression on his face.

"I'm sorry. You know there's no stopping her," Aramis said, coming in behind Tyra.

"My little one, let's go train before your brain melts from reading all of these *books*. Do you even know what half of these say?" Tyra demanded, pulling one out from under her butt.

"Søren has been helping me with the translations," Asta explained, placing a new notebook on the table in front of her. Søren had surprised her that morning with it, as well as a new fountain pen to write with.

"I bet he has." Tyra fluttered her eyelashes rapidly at him. "You trying to *tutor* my charge, naughty little light elf?"

"You are one to talk. I'm quite sure you are grooming my brother for some nefarious purpose," Søren replied, placing his books down.

Tyra stretched herself out across Asta's lap like a cat. "He loves it."

"He loves you trying your hardest," Aramis said indulgently as he looked down at her Led Zeppelin T-shirt and her black leather leggings.

Asta rolled her eyes at them and looked to Søren. "What are they going on about?"

"She wants to train. She's bored," Søren said, getting to his feet. "They did rescue the books last night. Maybe we should indulge them?"

Asta held out her hand to him. "Fine. I could do with a walk."

"Hurray!" Tyra exclaimed, throwing herself off Asta, disappearing in a cloud of shadows, and reappearing behind Aramis. She gave him a quick slap on the ass before disappearing and turning up perched on the bench.

"Behave yourself," Aramis said.

"Or what? You're going to spank me? You will have to catch me first." She waggled her tongue at him.

"You're asking for it, dark elf," Aramis warned.

"You're asking for it, dark elf," Tyra mocked in a terrible imitation of Aramis's deep voice.

"Enough! Let's go," Asta demanded as Søren helped her up. "Have they been this bad the whole time?"

"Since she kicked his ass the first night in your apartment," Søren whispered to her. "I don't think they can help themselves."

Asta didn't think she was expected to train, but seeing the banter flowing between Tyra and the two brothers made her smile. There was an unspoken warrior thing between them that she didn't think she could ever understand, and it was amusing as hell to watch.

Aramis led them to the training areas with Tyra disappearing and reappearing on his back before disappearing and turning up several meters in front of them.

"You show off!" Asta called, laughing despite herself.

"He likes her. I haven't seen my brother smile like that in centuries," Søren commented as he watched them tease each other.

"You're not worried?" Asta whispered to him. Søren's smile was sweet in a way that she hadn't seen before.

"No, she's kind of perfect for him." As they watched Tyra dance around Aramis, he shook his head. "Although I'm pretty sure she's going to break his heart."

"Or he'll break hers," Asta said.

Tyra was waiting for them by the time they reached the training halls. She was inspecting her nails as she sat lazily on one of the high windowsills.

"You guys are going to have to learn how to move a lot quicker if you are going to have a chance against Dökkálfar," Tyra said critically.

"Come down from there, and I'll give you a fair fight," Søren said. Tyra's smile was wide and sharp enough for Asta to take his hand.

"Søren—"

"I'll be fine. Stand out of the way. I have a feeling she's going to make us work for it," Søren said.

Asta sat down on a weight bench and watched as Tyra reappeared between the two brothers.

"Okay, let me see what you have got first. I won't disappear, for now. I just want to see where you are at," Tyra said, becoming the teacher Asta had seen at her kickboxing classes.

"Who do you want to go first?" Aramis asked.

Tyra's chuckle was deep and filthy. "Both of you at the same time. One-on-one will be too boring…for me."

Søren and Aramis shared a look, the latter lifting his shoulders in a shrug. Then they moved together, and Asta had to put her hand over her mouth to keep from shouting a warning to Tyra. But Tyra didn't need a warning. She moved between their attack like she was liquid, and the brothers almost collided with each other. They kicked, swung, dodged, rolled, and did it all again, so fast Asta couldn't get over their stamina. Would she be able to move like that if her shields were removed? Tyra wore the same amused expression the whole time.

"Stop dicking about, you two! I'm not going to break if you hit me," Tyra shouted at them, and impossibly, the speed and ferocity of the attacks increased. Asta watched Søren move with a flexibility and grace that changed her thoughts from worry to positively carnal in some moments.

The night they'd been attacked in Oslo she had been too focused on patching up his wounds to admire the way he was built. Now he was only dressed in loose training pants and a black singlet, and it was still too much clothing in her opinion. Gods, Søren was deadly. She had seen him fight against the dark elves and had been stunned by his ferocity. Now that there were no pretenses between them, Asta saw that this was who he was—a warrior, a killing machine just like Tyra.

"You would be wise to guard your heart against the Dauði Dómr," Tirith had warned the previous day.

"Why is that?" Asta had asked, trying to keep the blush from her face. She struggled to articulate how she felt where Søren was concerned. They had fallen quickly back into a comfortable pattern of research, light banter, and arguing with the occasional touch. Only a few days at Svetilo had shown her that Søren wasn't like that in anyone else's company. Everyone carefully avoided him and Aramis, but whether it was from awe or fear, she couldn't figure out.

"Do you know what a Dauði Dómr is? It is a Death Judge. He's an assassin and an executioner, so he has more ghosts than memories. Be aware that you'd be lying down with a wolf and not a lamb," Tirith said.

"Can I ask why you hate him so much?" Asta said. There was an undercurrent when he spoke of Søren that felt too personal.

Tirith rubbed at his eyes. "I don't hate him. I'm…disappointed in him. Did you know he used to be married?"

"Yes, he said that she died."

"Väliä was my stepdaughter. She was killed by Yanka, who was Aramis's consort at the time. Väliä was also pregnant, and Álfr children are impossibly rare. He was meant to protect them first, to put them first, and when he didn't, they both died. I can't find it in me to forgive him for it, and when I see him, I am reminded of what I lost."

A sharp twist of pain had pierced through Asta's chest. She hadn't known Väliä had been pregnant. No wonder Søren and Aramis didn't speak for years. To lose a wife and a baby in one day… She couldn't imagine the depth of Søren's grief.

Watching Søren laugh and train on the mat in front of her, she wondered how he was still as functional as he was. Søren was next-level damaged, yet she liked his company. As for his ferocious side, she had only seen that when he was protecting her. And the one time he'd kissed her—a memory she'd tried to put out of her mind to keep her sane.

"Okay, Aramis, put the shackles back on me to make this a fair fight," Tyra demanded. He made a strangled sound of frustration before he launched forward to tackle her and hit air before slamming down into the mat. Tyra reappeared, sitting on his back and pressing her knees down into his shoulders to pin him.

"Someone is a sore loser," Tyra purred before leaning down and giving his face an impetuous lick. Asta squealed in disgust as Søren laughed at the horrified look on his brother's face.

"You are so dead, elfling," Aramis growled.

"Catch me if you can, gorgeous." Tyra moved off him and came back to Søren. "You are quicker than he is, but Aramis is better at improvisation. I understand you are both proficient in battle magic, which will give you an edge but only if you are quick enough to locate your targets. I'm going to have to teach you to sense the shifts in magic that will help you track their movements when they aren't visible."

Asta did her best to follow Tyra's instructions as she explained the disappearing magic dark elves used. Tyra let both brothers reach out with their own magic and touch hers to understand the feel and shape of it, so they'd know how to sense it.

Tyra schooling two Dauði Dómr on fighting and magic was a glorious thing to behold. Søren listened patiently while Aramis kept staring at her like he wanted to get his hands around her neck. Tyra—being Tyra—goaded him whenever she could, just to see his tension rise. Søren's prediction about them destroying each other could come about after all.

After two hours of watching them sweat and fight and argue, Asta declared she was going to the library.

"If it's okay with Tyra, I can take you," Søren insisted.

"We aren't done training," Aramis said irritably.

"No, *you* aren't done training," Søren replied. "Give him hell, Tyra. Someone needs to beat that pout off his face."

"Is it really wise to provoke him? He looks angry," Asta whispered.

Aramis, the generally stable and good-natured brother, looked like he was ready to start throwing lightning bolts at Tyra.

"That's not anger on his face." Søren shook his head. He must have seen confusion on her face, because he added, "Unraveling."

Asta's face burned red. He'd used *that* word. His dark green eyes glittered with knowing mischief.

"Thank you for posting my wallet back to me while you were hiding out. I'm going to have to insist that next time you write me a cryptic note you make sure you provide your address," Søren said casually as they left the training rooms.

Oh no, he's seen the note. He knows about my regret that we didn't…that he hadn't…

"I wrote that to a Søren who doesn't exist," she replied stubbornly.

"My title didn't exist, but that Søren is this Søren whether you're ready to deal with that or not."

"Whatever you say. I'll admit you still have terrible manners."

"I can prove there's only one Søren." His smile grew wider.

"What are you going to do? Act like an entitled rich guy? Get your bossy—"

Søren pulled her gently into a dark corner off the walkway, and giving her plenty of time to protest, he bent down and kissed her. Asta had managed to convince herself that their kiss in the taxi hadn't been as good as her drunken mind had remembered. Holy gods, did he blow that theory sky-high now. Her free hand tangled in his hair, pulling him closer to her as she stood on tiptoes.

Søren's hot mouth moved from her lips and kissed her jawline to her neck, leaving fire burning under her skin wherever he touched. Finally, he lifted his head, his fingers lightly running over her cheekbones, and pressed two more gentle kisses on her lips.

"I told you there was only one Søren, and he likes kissing you," he said, with a ridiculously smug smile on his face.

"You had to go and ruin it by talking." Asta sighed as she pushed at his chest with her free hand. She could feel the curves and dips of hard muscle underneath the singlet, and she almost lost her nerve.

"It was worth it." He stepped back and released her. Asta pulled her sweater down primly where it had ridden up. Søren watched her as if her disheveled state and burning cheeks pleased him.

"You really are insufferable," she muttered. She tried to remind herself of Tirith's warning about lying down with wolves, but she realized that he had it so wrong. Søren was no wolf; he was a goddamn panther. *And one hell of a kisser.*

On the winter solstice, she had lit a red candle and made a wish to keep Søren, but now she was wondering if she could survive it coming true.

Tyra was trying hard not to show how much fun she was having throwing Aramis around the mat.

"I knew you were good, but you are killing me," he complained.

"Better me kill you on the mat than another dark elf on the street." She hadn't planned on working him so hard, but the truth was she wanted him to be prepared. If the conflict came to a head, she wouldn't be able to protect both Asta and him, and Asta would always come first. Aramis grabbed a water bottle, and she took a moment to watch him drink. Really it was disgusting how attractive he was even flushed and gleaming from exertion.

"I think you like beating me up. You get this naughty little smile right before you drop me," Aramis said, before offering the bottle to her.

"Maybe I like it when you're all hot and bothered." She took a long drink before putting the bottle down. "Break time is over."

"Aren't you worried that if you teach us how to track you in a fight you'll be giving us a huge advantage if we ever disagree?"

"Do you really think it would help you stand a chance?"

"What does *Draeimi* mean?" Aramis said, blindsiding her. "It's a title, isn't it?"

"It is." A small flutter of panic ran through her. He was Dauđi Dómr, so maybe he'd be able to understand. He was watching her carefully with those huge sapphire eyes that made her common sense disappear every time. Between that and the sexy sweating, she was really done for. She turned away from the view in self-defense. "How about if you catch me, just once, I'll tell—"

Aramis slammed into her, dragging her to the mat and pinning her down. His body was so big that she felt closed in and caged and utterly vulnerable. His long silver hair curtained around them, and her heart thudded painfully as he smiled down at her.

"That was cheating," she said stubbornly.

"You've had me on my back all day, but now I'm the one cheating?" He laughed, and the vibration of it rocked through his body and into hers. *Oh, Freya, kill me now, so I may die happy.*

"If you wanted to get me on my back, all you had to do was ask," she said.

"Stop trying to distract me with your wicked tongue."

"You don't know how distracting my wicked tongue can be." She tried to wiggle out of his grip, but he held her firm.

"Just tell me what it means, or I'll make this more difficult for you." His mouth moved into his catlike smile.

"Sounds like fore—" She forgot what she was saying as his tongue licked up her neck.

"Now we are even," he said hotly in her ear. "You taste nice, little elfling."

Tyra exploded into dark purple shadows, knocking him backward and reappearing with a training spear aimed at his crotch.

"*Draeimi* means 'Killing Smoke,'" she replied. "It is my title alone, one that I earned and deserved. I was loved until I was feared. After they made me this way, and I became too powerful, they tossed me aside."

"Their loss is my gain," Aramis said softly, his hands in the air in surrender. "Hopefully. One day…if you'll let me."

Tyra shook her head and lowered the spear. "You don't know half of the horrible things I've done—"

"I know that if we hadn't been interrupted by Thrynn, I would've kissed you." His catlike smile was back along with the heat in his eyes.

"I'm sure it would've been a great first kiss." Tyra walked off the mat. "I'm done training for the day." She hesitated by the door and turned as he climbed back to his feet. "Starlight?"

"Yes, Tyra?"

"I still want that taste." She disappeared out the door before she could do something really stupid like tear his clothes off in the middle of a public space.

"You are such a chickenshit. You should've just kissed Aramis while he was on top of you. That's two perfect moments you've walked away from," Tyra whispered to the foggy full-length mirror of her bathroom twenty minutes later. She'd taken a long shower and wrapped herself in a robe, but her body refused to relax.

She'd never been nervous around men, so what made Aramis so different? Because he was.

Aramis looked at her and treated her like she mattered instead of a one-night stand. He wasn't afraid of her or what she might have done in her past. If she started something with him, it would never be casual.

"It's already gone past casual," she said aloud.

The door to the bathroom opened, and Aramis stood in the fog like an avenging angel.

"Do you mind? What are you doing here?" Tyra demanded.

"I want that taste," he growled. Before Tyra had time to think, he grabbed her around the waist, pulled her tight against him, and kissed her hard. Her hands gripped his shirt, pulling him closer, opening her mouth, and letting her tongue dart against his.

Tyra had kissed a lot of people since she had escaped slavery, but she'd never had someone make her body and magic hum as much as Aramis did. He wrapped his fingers tightly around her braid.

"I dream about this hair," he hissed against her lips.

"Is that all?" He spun her around, so her back was against him.

"No." Using his other hand, he untied the belt of her robe, loosening it so that it came off her shoulders. His hot mouth bent down and licked a long burn scar across her back.

Tyra shuddered, her body breaking out in goose bumps as he continued to attend to her scars. She'd never been ashamed of her scars, but he was loving them like every kiss could brush the ugliness of their memory away. He pulled her braid back gently, exposing her neck so he could kiss her from shoulder to ear.

"Had enough?" he asked.

"No," she said. *Not nearly enough.* Aramis pushed her up against the smooth stone wall. His hands held her arms above her head as he kissed her again. She wrapped one leg around his hips, and a sound like a whimper came from his mouth. No man had made a sound like that because of her before. He murmured a filthy curse in elvish against her lips, before releasing one of her hands so she could grip his silver hair.

More, her brain demanded. She kissed Aramis hard, biting his bottom lip, wanting him naked and pressed up against her. He slowly released her and took a step back.

"Wait…where are you going?" Tyra asked.

"You said you only wanted a taste," Aramis replied simply, kissing her cheek and shutting the door behind him.

14

ASTA KNEW TYRA WASN'T someone who was fully operational before midday, but when Tyra came to breakfast the next morning, her presence was like simmering fire and thunderclouds.

"What's wrong?" Asta whispered as she fixed her coffee.

"Nothing important." Tyra picked up an apple and started tossing it lightly into the air.

"I was worried when you didn't come to dinner after training. Did something happen with Aramis?"

Tyra slammed the apple down hard on the table, scattering smashed pieces of pulp across it.

"No."

"Bullshit," Asta said.

"It's nothing I can't handle."

"Yeah, it looks like you're handling it." Asta wiped up the pieces of apple and dumped them into the bin.

"I just need a run. I'm cooped up in a fucking mountain. I did nearly two thousand years of that." Tyra bit into one of the larger broken pieces of apple.

"If you want to run, there's a good mountain path. You'll have to deal with snow, but it's there." Søren had appeared in the doorway behind Asta.

"Sounds great. The snow doesn't bother me," Tyra said, relief in her eyes.

"Excellent. I'll get Aramis to escort you after breakfast," Søren said.

"*Great*," said Tyra, forcing the word out through gritted teeth.

Søren had a gleam of mischief in his green eyes when he winked at Asta behind Tyra's back. He was going to get a knife in his throat if he pushed Tyra too far.

"You seem a bit upset. Sad that you kicked our asses so thoroughly?" Søren asked.

"I expected more from you both. I can work with what's there though." Tyra sniffed. "What are you doing today, Asta?"

"Tirith found some books for me on dark elf genealogies and other histories," Asta replied, with a bright smile. She'd nearly bounced with excitement when she got the message.

"Dark elf histories written by light elves no doubt. You think they are going to be honest?"

"Well, you aren't exactly forthcoming, so I'm going to have to take what I can get. I'm not an idiot. I know biased commentary when I read it," snapped Asta, hands on her hips. "Go for your damn run and take your bad mood with you." Tyra snarled at her, and Søren moved between them as fast as lightning.

"I don't know what my brother did to piss you off last night, but I suggest you take your dark elf territorial growling bullshit out on him."

"And what about *your* territorial bullshit? Hmm? I'm the only family Asta has, so remember that when you're pissing and scratching around her," Tyra replied. She pulled open the door and almost collided with Aramis. The sweet smile of surprise on his face melted as she glared at him.

"What's going on?" he asked uncertainly.

"You're taking the beast for a run," Søren said, folding his arms. "A long one in the snow. Try not to push her off a cliff."

Tyra stuck her middle finger up at him before pushing past Aramis. "Going to get changed," she muttered. Asta let out a small sigh of frustration.

"Søren, what did you do to her?" Aramis asked.

"I might ask you the same thing," Asta said.

"Oh." Aramis's confused expression changed into the face of a man who has been kicked in the balls. *Tyra, what did you do to this poor guy?* Asta had seen firsthand the way Tyra shut men down. It didn't seem right, considering how obsessed with Aramis Tyra had been acting. *None of your business, Asta. You have bigger problems, remember? Magical shields around your body and the fact you don't know how you feel about having kissed Søren again.*

"I don't want to know. Just make it up to her if you're the one who upset her," Søren muttered.

Asta reached for her coffee. "Tyra is not upset. She's embarrassed and doesn't know how to process it except by getting pissy. You should've seen her when I had to show her how to use a microwave." It was another thing that had seemed strange at the time, and Asta had completely ignored it.

"I'll fix it," Aramis said firmly, "or I'll dump her in the snow until she cools off."

"Don't forget she can kick your ass, brother. Gird your loins," Søren advised as Aramis headed out the door.

Søren turned to her. "Genealogies, hmm? I think Tirith is going to do his best to unravel the mystery that is you, Asta."

"Something Tyra said the other day has me thinking. She said Bláinn had started to experiment on Tove and had mentioned something about wanting to exploit the gifts that her family had."

"And Tyra didn't elaborate?"

"No, and I haven't wanted to push her because talking about it seemed to really upset her. She was powerless to stop it, and as you can tell, Tyra hates not being in control of a situation. I thought I'd try to find out for myself before I had to ask her."

"Are you worried about what will happen when we do break the shields?"

"Not particularly. You all keep telling me that magic is innate with the elves, and I will be able to learn to use it. Why? Are you worried?"

Søren hid a smile. "As long as you don't end up like Tyra, I think we'll be fine. Besides, I like your cute little librarian act."

"Shut up," she said without any real venom. She had spent most of the past few months wishing she was *more* like Tyra instead of such a dork. To be wanted the way she was… She shut the idea down.

"If Tove went to the trouble she did to protect you, you must be something else magic-wise. It's the only reason I can think of, especially if her shitty husband was trying to unlock something magically in her. No matter what, remember that you'll still be Asta. All the magic in the world won't change that," Søren said seriously.

Asta turned and put her cup in the sink, so he wouldn't see the effect his words had on her. "Thanks. We should get moving. Tirith doesn't strike me as a patient guy."

"He's patient with you. It's me he barely tolerates." There was a touch of hurt in his tone, and Asta now knew why. She wanted to tell him she was sorry about his wife and the baby but didn't think he would like that Tirith had told her about them. Instead, she stood on tiptoes and kissed his cheek.

"*I* tolerate you, so he'll have to just put up with it." She moved away to grab her things before Søren had time to react. "Let's go."

Just focus on the run, Tyra prompted herself as she pulled on her sneakers and retied her braid.

"Are you ready?" Aramis asked. When she nodded, her shackles appeared.

"Seriously?" She groaned.

"I'll get rid of the chain once we get outside. It's for show, and you know it."

Tyra followed Aramis out into the common areas and shared walkways. It *was* a beautiful stronghold, with every part of the rock carved in some intricate pattern, and there was light everywhere. Living in a dwarf mountain for so long, she had gotten used to the darkness and the blocky geometric shapes the dwarves favored when they felt the need to carve at all. The natural lines and rough dips of the mountain were beautiful as they were to the dwarves.

But they were still stone walls no matter how lovely. Tyra needed air and open spaces before she screamed.

"You're very quiet today," said Aramis as he walked ahead of her.

"Thinking." *Of all the ways I'm going to kill you.* Aramis's frown deepened as if he could guess exactly what she was thinking.

Good.

Aramis opened a wooden door, reinforced with steel, and the winter day unfolded in front of her. She was struck dumb by the cold air, the gray-and-white landscape, and the mist on the range of mountains in the distance.

"I'll take you down and through the forest," Aramis said, knocking her out of her enthrallment. She gave him a sharp nod. The path was easy to follow, and when they reached the tree line, he pointed to where the main thoroughfare veered off into a path barely two feet wide.

"That way. You can go first, so I'll know if you try to escape," Aramis said, and as promised, the chain that bound her cuffs together disappeared.

"Only if you can keep up." Tyra rolled her shoulders. "Don't look at my ass either."

Aramis only pointed to the path. Tyra shoved down the urge to knock him down with her magic and took off at a run.

Tyra did her best to forget about her Ljósálfar shadow and whatever the fuck had passed between them the night before. She breathed in deeply, revelling in the cold air around her. Two years out of the mines and she still worshiped winter. Every time it snowed, she was jolted by its frozen, clean beauty, and the sharp lick of cold against her skin was as seductive as a lover's kiss after so many years of sweat, grime, and darkness.

There must've been some kind of magic keeping the little path clear, and if she weren't so pissed off, she would've liked to stop and enjoy the heavy snow-laden trees. As it was, all she wanted to do was slam Aramis into one. She felt a tremble of magic, and the snow in front of her rose up in a wall. She only managed to slice it down with her own power right before she collided with it. She was showered with snowflakes as it came down. A deep masculine laugh echoed behind her.

"Cool you down a bit?" Aramis called.

Tyra would *not* turn around. She ignored him and kept running. She was on to him now, knew the feeling of his magic from their training session the day before, and every time he threw an obstacle of ice toward her, she was ready for it. He was trying to play with her, and she was fighting hard to stay pissed off at him.

They came to a large clearing, and Tyra realized too late that he hadn't followed her. She skidded to a halt and turned just in time to see the walls of ice building around her, caging her in. Her body reacted to protect herself, and dark purple power exploded out of her, whipping around her in a fury that destroyed the threat, demolishing the walls of ice. Panicked that her power would hurt Aramis, she called it back inside of her before it could reach the forest and start tearing it apart.

As the snow showered down around her, Tyra spotted Aramis still standing on the other side of the glade. Mesmerized. He seemed to shake it off, then he was striding toward her through the falling ice, looking like a silver-haired god of winter. *Freya, save me.* She hated wanting him so much.

"So that is why Thrynn and Bláinn were so afraid of you that they put you in an inescapable hole," Aramis said, his blue eyes wide.

Tyra's hands clenched by her side. "I'm sorry, I didn't think. I pulled it back when I realized."

"You were holding back?" Aramis looked around at the decimated, melting glade.

"Yeah. This was a very small reaction." Tyra knew what he was processing behind his calculating blue eyes. He was thinking about what she'd do on a battlefield and realizing *exactly* how she'd earned her title. She waited for his expression to change to fear or disgust. This Ljósálfar had no idea who he had been touching the night before. He still didn't.

Tyra straightened her spine. She didn't care what some pretty Ljósálfar thought of her. She had been the most feared battle commander in Svartálfaheim history, and she wouldn't be made to feel ashamed of that.

"You are...incredible," Aramis said.

"Yeah? If I'm so incredible, why did you leave last night?" The hurt words slipped out so fast, Tyra cringed.

"Is *that* what you're so angry and embarrassed about?" He folded his arms, staring down at her. "If you didn't want me kissing you, you should've said something."

He thinks I regret it? She stared at him dumbfounded. "You really are an idiot." When he continued to stare at her like a clueless elfling, she growled, "I'm not embarrassed because it happened. I'm angry that you just left me standing there high and dry."

"*You* were the one who said you only wanted a taste," Aramis said with a smirk, and Tyra swung her leg around and knocked him on his ass. Ice snaked around her feet, and he pounced on her, bringing her down in a cloud of snow. He pinned her arms above her head and held on until she stopped struggling.

"Listen closely, you tempestuous, little Dökkálfar." Aramis leaned down to whisper in her ear, "I don't know what *boys* you have fooled around with since you came to Midgard but do *not* mistake me for one of them. I am an immortal, and I've waited a long time for someone to make me feel this way. If you think I'm going to spend you all in one night, you have another thing coming. I could drag this out for *centuries*, because I intend to keep you interested in this game, and me, for as long as I can. Understand?"

Tyra had to wait for her brain and hormones to catch up with her tongue before she managed to whisper, "Yes."

"Good." Aramis rocked back. It was enough momentum for Tyra to shift a knee between them and roll him over. He grinned up at her, and gods grant her patience, she could have cried for want.

"Don't make me wait centuries, or I'll make your life hell." Tyra fed the hunger in her by bending over him and kissing him. She gave his bottom lip a hard nip before she disappeared into shadows, moving herself to the other side of the glade before her self-control was gone altogether.

"You *better* run," he shouted. She made a rude gesture at him.

"You're going to have to move a lot faster if you think you can catch me, Starlight," she called back and bolted.

15

TWO HOURS LATER, ASTA had a pile of books in front of her almost as tall as she was.

"Wow, I never thought you'd have so many," she said to Tirith. She was a little intimidated by the pile.

"To be honest, neither did I. Once I started looking, I seemed to find more and more," he replied with an excited smile.

"I thought you guys hated dark elves." Asta looked at Søren.

"Not all of them. We left Álfheim because some of the tribes began raiding, which led to a war," Søren said vaguely.

"There was a time long ago when both species used to coexist. Here, I'll show you." Tirith took out one of the books and began flicking through it. "This is one of the more interesting volumes I found. It seems to be a shared history of the Álfr." He held out the book, showing more of the illuminated illustrations Asta had fallen in love with.

"This is a story of how we came to be. We lived in peace for centuries," Tirith continued as he turned to another page.

"I wish I could read it," Asta lamented as she reached out to trace the twisting patterns in the borders.

"Once we get the shields off you, I might be able to help with some translation magic. Without them off, I won't be able to tailor the magic to work for you," said Tirith.

"Never mind. I have Søren to translate for me, and when he gets sick of it, I'll make Tyra do it," Asta replied.

"That is if Aramis hasn't strangled her in the woods," Søren said, a wicked gleam in his eyes.

"It would be the other way around," Asta protested, defending her cousin. She had seen Tyra the day before. Søren and Aramis didn't stand a chance of defeating her mighty cousin. "Besides, I think he has a crush on her."

"Undoubtedly. I could have told you that from the moment Tyra tried to kill him." Søren laughed.

"Poor, dear Aramis," Tirith murmured as he placed the book back on the pile. "It would be useful if Tyra were here. I have a lot of questions she could answer for me."

"We won't have to wait long. Tyra panics if she doesn't check on Asta on the hour," Søren said, not looking up from the page he was reading.

"She's only been like that since I met you," Asta replied. Søren had a predatory gleam in his eye when he grinned back at her. Asta ignored the heat flaring at the back of her neck and straightened the sleeves of her sweater.

She glared at him. *Stop it.*

He looked at her innocently. *Stop what?*

"This book is referencing another of genealogy. I'll try to find it for you, Asta, that way when Tyra returns, we can search through the royal bloodlines for your family," Tirith said, getting to his feet and shuffling off between the shelves.

"I think he's more excited about that prospect than I am," Asta commented, once he was out of earshot.

"You don't want to know what made your mother so special that her ex-husband is still hunting her after all these years?" Søren asked.

"Bláinn sounds like he can't stand losing. You know what made my mother special? Everything. She was good at *everything*. No one becomes interested in something and is able to master it in a week, but she could. It was hard to be her daughter and be so average," snapped Asta. She put her hand over her mouth in shock. She'd never said those words aloud despite all the times she had thought them. It was the truth though. Tove could make paranoia seem exciting and eccentric. Every new place was another adventure. It was Asta who was sick of moving around and not belonging anywhere.

"Clearly you have a warped perception of yourself. Your mother *kept* you average on purpose. Made you seem like everyone else. Even wrapped up in shields, my magic knew you were special," Søren said matter-of-factly.

"Really?"

"Why do you think I was so ineloquent when we first met? My magic was going haywire."

"I thought you were jet-lagged and possibly a little drunk."

"I wasn't *that* bad."

Asta raised a brow. "And I quote, 'I need a book…I mean, an expert. I need an expert in old books.'"

"Keep it up, and I'll bend you over my knee," Søren threatened. Asta's laugh died on her lips as Tyra appeared out of the air behind him, placing him in a headlock.

"Raise a hand to my baby cousin, and I'll cut out your throat in your sleep," Tyra said with a chilling coldness. Then she kissed his cheek loudly and let him go. "Unless she asks for a spanking first, and then I guess it's okay."

"I *hate* that you can do that," Søren said slowly, his eyes narrowed.

"I *know*, isn't it great?" Tyra pulled up a chair and sat on it backward. "How's the studying going, nerd?"

"Good. Tirith has questions for you so stick around," said Asta, showing Tyra the book about their beginnings. "Do you know this story?"

"I have a question first. What did you do with my brother?" Søren asked.

"I didn't do anything to darling Starlight. He's gone to get me food because I was starving after my run," said Tyra, taking the book from Asta and browsing through it. "Oh, I remember this one. I was telling the hot brother about this the other night. We all used to get along and have babies together."

Søren snorted. "You told me no such thing."

"I said the *hot* brother." Tyra smiled sweetly. Asta prayed to all the gods for mercy.

"Ah, Tyra, you are here. Excellent," Tirith said, saving Asta from having to separate them.

"It's cool that you have a copy of this." Tyra looked through the pages with a nostalgic smile. "I haven't seen this since I was a girl."

"And when was that?" asked Tirith.

"A long time ago," Tyra replied with a mysterious smile.

"You said you didn't raid with the Dökkálfar when they started invading Álfheim. I was a boy then, so you must be how old?" Søren asked.

"Older than you."

Asta winked at her. "You chasing Aramis makes you a bit of a cradle robber."

Tyra laughed. "I haven't even *rocked* his cradle, let alone robbed it."

"Don't be gross," complained Søren.

"Who's being gross?" Aramis asked as he came around the stacks. Tirith saw the plate of food he was holding and uttered a small cry of distress.

"I promise not to spill any. Asta said you wanted to ask me something?" said Tyra, moving her chair far back from the table and taking the plate from Aramis. She gave him a smile that had the points of his ears turning pink.

"You're lucky I need answers. Keep it away from the books," muttered Tirith, putting down the oversized tome he was carrying. "I found this record of genealogies. If Asta's family is royal, we should have them listed in here."

"Asta's family is just as bad as Bláinn. They sold Tove off," grumbled Tyra.

"They are all on Svartálfaheim and are no threat to us. Just tell me who they are," said Asta.

Tyra seemed to fight an internal struggle before she muttered, "Drekiónd."

"What did you just call me?" Asta demanded, her eyes narrowing.

"She wasn't cursing at you. It's your family name. It means 'dragon soul,'" Tirith said, opening the book up.

"Oh. Sorry, Tyra," said Asta. Tyra gave her a nod as she demolished a small bread roll. The happy mood she'd come in with had vanished.

"Here. This is your family." Tirith showed her a sprawling family tree of names. A strange sensation passed through Asta as she traced the names with her fingers until she reached the bottom.

"My mother isn't here." She looked at Tyra.

"It probably wasn't updated once the wars kicked off. That's Siv and Steinar, Tove's parents, and this is Daimar and Hagen, your uncles." Tyra pointed at the bottom runes. "Steinar is okay, but Siv is a total bitch who I could absolutely believe has dragon blood. She's got poor Steinar by the balls."

"Dragon blood? Are you serious?" asked Asta.

Tyra let out a humorless laugh. "Oh, yeah. That's where the name Drekiónd comes from. There's a story about your family's line. The legend goes that a dragon from Múspellsheim spied Svartálfaheim in her flames and decided she wished to see it for herself. She flew from her home of ash and flame, following the blackened root of Yggdrasil until she made it. Knowing she would frighten the small, gentle Álfr of the soft green land, she wrought a spell to bind her in the form of Dökkálfar and took the name Alvida. She fell in love with a dark elf—who can blame her because we are so attractive—and their babies started your line. It's the reason why your family and its powerful magic is so feared."

Asta thought she was going to be sick. It had to be a story, right? She couldn't believe she was part dragon.

Søren sniggered beside her. "Dragon blood would explain your temper."

Asta threw a pencil at him. "Shut. Up. I'm having an identity crisis, and I don't need your input."

"My point exactly," Søren whispered to Aramis.

"Would this powerful magic you mentioned be what Bláinn was trying to pull out of Tove?" Aramis asked, ignoring his brother.

Tyra flinched. "As I said, it is a legend. Bláinn thought he could unlock the magic somehow and use it to rule all Svartálfaheim. Tove's parents gave her to him as a peace offering, even though I tried to warn them that Bláinn believed the stories."

"You still haven't mentioned what the magic actually does," Asta said. She gave her cousin a hard poke in the shoulder. "Out with it."

"Bláinn thought the magic would be wild, elemental, dragon magic. Fire, destruction…maybe even shapeshifting," Tyra said, relenting.

"Shapeshifting?" asked Asta.

"Yeah, Bláinn thought that because Alvida could take an elf form, the magic might allow an elf to change into a dragon. Like I said, the guy is fucked in the head. He tortured Tove for it, trying to make the magic manifest to protect her. He burnt her. He—" Tyra was shaking, her hands clenched tightly into fists as she tried to contain her fury. Aramis very gently rested his hands against her shoulders, and she stilled. Asta couldn't believe her eyes. Even she wasn't stupid enough to go near Tyra when she was angry.

"Don't forget, you got her out," Aramis reminded her gently.

"I did, and now he knows about Asta, which is even worse," said Tyra.

"If he couldn't get a full-blooded dark elf to manifest magic, I'm going to be of no use to him unless he wants me to curate a book collection," Asta said, trying to soothe Tyra.

Tyra reached out and took her hands. "I love you, but you don't know what you're talking about. You must have something unique magic wise, or Tove wouldn't have worked so hard to convince you that you're human. Bláinn knows that, so he won't stop looking for you."

"If he sends more Dökkálfar, I'll deal with them like I dealt with the last group he sent after her. Bláinn will never lay a single finger on Asta," Søren said, his tone so cold it raised the hair on Asta's arms. She would never forget what he'd done that night to protect her. His face promised death, and if she hadn't seen the kinder side of him, she would've run faster from him than the dark elves.

"There won't be enough Disney Princess Band-Aids in all of Midgard to patch up what he'll do to you," Tyra said without any real venom.

"We can worry about Bláinn when and if he draws near. At the moment the most pressing matter is removing Asta's shields, and then we will know what we are dealing with," Tirith said before the inevitable argument broke out.

"Should we even bother? Maybe it is better if I stay like this," Asta asked, her voice small. She didn't want anyone getting hurt trying to defend her.

"That's not going to make him stop trying to get to you. It's not just about the magic. Bláinn could ransom you back to your grandparents, he could marry you to keep the treaty, or he could kill you out of spite. I've seen him do a lot worse for slighter offenses."

"Stop trying to frighten her," said Søren.

"She *should* be frightened of Bláinn. We all should be. You really think the dwarves haven't reported that I've run off with their merchandise? That he hasn't heard about how I kicked Thrynn's ass in Estonia? Bláinn is coming. It's just a matter of time, and he's not going to stop until I'm dead."

"Asta isn't the only one under our protection," Aramis reminded her. Instead of ripping his head off, Tyra leaned back against him ever so slightly.

What happened between them? Asta wondered. She could never calm Tyra down like that. She had tried. *That* was a bigger mystery than whatever magic Asta might have.

Asta looked back at the family tree, tracing the lines and feeling the hum under her skin the way she did when she touched Tove's book. *Drekiónd.* She had always wanted to know where she belonged, to have a family. She missed Tove. No matter how angry Asta was with her for hiding so much, Asta wished she could talk it out with her.

"With the shields off, Asta may be able to protect herself better. Her magic helped her on the winter solstice even with the shields. Without them? Gods know what she will be capable of," Tirith replied.

Asta could barely remember what happened that night after she'd climbed into the huge recycle bin, bloody and afraid. She had no memories of the magic coming out of her, only that she'd been thinking of Søren. There had been heat and a falling sensation, then he was suddenly there, striding through the snow and holding her close. She risked looking up at him and saw the same worry in his green eyes that she'd seen that night.

"It doesn't matter how good of an idea you all think it is to take the protections off her. It's Asta's choice. If she doesn't want them removed, you won't be touching her," Søren said slowly, not looking away from her.

"This is all a lot to take in. I don't even know where to begin, and I can't think straight," admitted Asta, hugging her arms around her.

"Why don't you take Asta down to the gardens for a break, Søren? I need to talk through some things with Tyra," Tirith suggested, and Asta gave him a grateful smile. A walk would be good.

"Only if you want to," Asta said to Søren, but he was already on his feet.

"Make sure Tyra behaves," Søren said to Aramis.

"Make sure you keep your hands to yourself, or I'll cut them off," Tyra threatened him in reply.

16

SØREN COULDN'T REMEMBER THE last time he'd been in Svetilo's subterranean gardens. He *did* remember how much Väliä had loved them, which made him question Tirith's motives for suggesting this visit. Asta was quiet beside him, a small crease forming between her brows as her mind focused on faraway things. He didn't blame her. If he'd been told his blood might contain a bit of dragon magic, he'd be thoughtful too.

"Stop staring at me," Asta said, making him focus back on the walkway in front of him.

"I was only checking that you were still there. I don't think I've ever seen you this quiet."

"Whatever. I was thinking about Tyra's massive crush on Aramis and hoping he knows what he's doing."

"Knowing my brother, I can honestly say he has no fucking idea." Søren opened a set of doors to reveal a twisting flight of stone stairs. The air grew warm, humid, and rich with the smell of tilled earth. As they stepped out onto a garden path, Asta let out a small gasp of surprise.

"This is incredible." Her gray eyes were wide as she looked at the carefully tended gardens around her, before glancing up at the small balls of light that floated above them. "What are those?"

"Captured pockets of sunlight. The gardeners use magic to store sunlight from outside, then they bring it down here to help the plants grow."

"They didn't think it might be easier to just…plant food outside?"

"I forget you haven't seen where we actually are. That will be our next stop. To answer your question, it would be too cold to grow all of this outside." Søren led her through the orchards and the flower beds to the nursery where Álfr were potting seedlings and washing, sorting, and storing the harvested vegetables. They gave Søren a few curious glances but didn't seem concerned to see them.

"Do you think I should take the shields off? I was becoming okay with the idea, but now I'm hesitant again."

"You don't really believe your ancestor was a dragon, do you?"

"Of course not! Tyra did have a point about my mother shielding me though. What if…if I am dangerous?" Asta bit her bottom lip.

"Magic is neutral. It's only dangerous if you are untrained or you use it for dangerous purposes. I don't know why Tove did what she did. Maybe she thought it would isolate you more if you knew. I believe it's because the Illumination, the Darkness, and bastards like them would have sensed your magic and tried to kidnap or recruit you."

When Asta gave him a blank look, he gave her an abbreviated version of the conflict that had always existed between the two organizations that had sought to control the supernatural community for so long and explained how they had made creatures and magic users pick sides. It had all changed two years ago when Anya, Aramis, and Yvan, with the help of a neutral army, had put an end to the organizations' feud forever. The remnants remaining were too weak to reform again.

"As I said, your mother strikes me as someone who would have a good reason for doing what she did to protect you."

"What if the magic comes out, and I can't control it? What if I hurt someone?" Asta said as she paced.

"You really think Tyra and I would let that happen? We can train you. Even Aramis helped Anya wrangle her power under control, and she was a far bigger mess than you are." Søren saw he wasn't convincing her and knew he had to try a different tact. "Can I show you something?" Asta nodded, and he picked up a small clay pot filled with earth.

"This contains a seed," he said, putting it on the table and moving her in front of it.

"Okay?" Asta gave him a blank look. He moved behind her, placing his arms and hands over hers. He ignored her small intake of breath as he moved her hands to rest on the small pot.

"We want the seed to grow, so we focus on it, on what it will become, and how big it needs to be," Søren said into her ear. Very slowly he released some of his magic, so it curled around her fingers like shimmering emerald smoke. As it had the first time Søren had seen her, his power purred around her like it had a mind of its own. Asta trembled ever so slightly, and he tried not to think of why.

"Magic is a part of the Álfr as much as our breath," he whispered. "To deny it is like denying our own heartbeat. Are you focusing on the seed, Asta?"

"Yes."

"Can you feel my magic under your skin?"

"Yes, it's like a warm tingling sensation." Asta nodded as her fingers twined in his. Channeling his magic through her fingers, he let her control it.

"Imagine the seed growing and push that warm tingle toward it."

"Okay." Asta focused, and Søren felt a tug on the power right before the small pot exploded in her hands, making her squeal in fright.

Søren burst out laughing as he wrapped his arms around her. "You're okay."

"Stop laughing. You could've warned me!"

"You were meant to be focusing on the seed growing, not breaking the place."

Asta loosened herself from his grip and picked up another pot, before wriggling back in the circle of his arms. "Let me try again."

Smiling, he took her hands once more. "Slowly, *drékisma*. Think of a seedling, not a tree."

"Less talking, more giving me your magic," she said, gripping his hands. He didn't mind her bossy tone or that he was now leaning flush against her warm back, his arms around her tightly. He let the magic curl around her fingers and seep into her skin.

"I can feel all of your lovely dark green magic inside of me," she whispered in surprise.

"Focus on the seed," he said a little sharper than he meant to. His self-control frayed around the edges as she tugged on his magic.

"Shh, let me do it." Asta breathed deeply, her fingers letting go of his so she could stroke his hands. The magic curled between them. Søren groaned softly. His magic had always acted strangely around her, and now it was as if her small pale fingers were touching him in his very core, moving his magic and desire around like chess pieces. *This was a very dumb idea…*

"Look!" Asta said, forcing him to focus on the plant. A small shoot had sprouted out of the earth. She turned in his arms, almost bouncing in excitement until she saw his face and stilled. His hands gripped the table hard on either side of her, caging her in. "Are you angry at me? Because you gave me your magic and told me to try to use it."

Søren wanted to weep. "No. I just didn't think it would feel like that to let you…" He didn't have the words.

Understanding slowly danced over Asta's face, but instead of being embarrassed or horrified, she looked downright devious.

"Well now, isn't that interesting?" Her head tilted to one side. "What did it feel like?"

The wood splintered into Søren's hands as he leaned down to run his lips up the side of her neck, breathing in the smell of her warm skin and feeling her pulse jump.

"Like that," he growled.

"O-oh. I see," Asta said, not nearly as cocky as she had been a second before. "And does using magic always make you feel…this way?"

"Sometimes. It might be different when your own magic is released, and it touches mine," Søren explained, his mouth on her collarbone.

"Really? I wonder what that is going to feel like."

"Like dying probably," he admitted, and she laughed. Her hands rested on his chest as he lifted his head.

"Getting these shields off is starting to sound better and better," Asta said with a teasing smile. "You better get out of my personal space before one of these gardeners comes in and sees you acting inappropriately."

"I haven't even begun to be inappropriate with you," he argued. Oh no, inappropriate was the fantasies that were currently running through his brain of pushing the pots off the table and taking her on it.

"Is that so? Can you tell me when you start, so I don't miss it?"

"That depends entirely on you. I've already kissed you. The next move is on you, so I know my efforts are welcome and won't go to waste."

Asta frowned. "You seem pretty confident in the quality of said efforts. How do *I* know that they are going to be worth it?"

"There's only one way to find out."

"You know what? You're absolutely right." Asta stood up on her tiptoes and kissed him. Søren let go of the table and lifted her up on it, so they were at the same height. He shuddered when her hands went under his shirt to explore his bare skin and to pull him closer so she could wrap her legs around him and grind her core against him. *Gods, help me.*

Asta's hands moved from under his shirt to trace his neck and burrow into his hair. He couldn't believe he'd ever seen her as a sweet and innocent librarian.

She was setting him on fire. Whatever she'd done with his magic had made him feel unhinged and mad with want. He was going to tear her clothes off and—

"Well, I'm glad we got the question of wasted efforts out of the way," Asta said, breaking the embrace, unlocking her legs, and sliding back to her feet before he had the sense to stop her. "Let's see what else is around here to explore."

So aroused he couldn't move, Søren watched her walk out of the nursery like nothing had happened. He cursed dark elf females under his ragged breath and followed her.

17

ASTA THOUGHT NOTHING COULD compare to the beauty of Svetilo's gardens, but she had to drastically reevaluate that stance when she stepped into the healing spring caves that evening.

"Are you going to tell me why Søren looked like you had kicked him in the balls when you came back from the gardens this afternoon?" Tyra asked as she pulled off her shirt.

"I have no idea what you are talking about." Asta looked around in case other Álfr were listening. Tyra had suggested that she be allowed to take Asta to the springs for a girls' chat and Aramis, who had looked suspicious about what Tyra's idea of a girls' chat would be, had allowed it on the condition that they use one of the more private pools.

"I'll be back in an hour, and you better be here," he had said. Tyra had merely smirked at him until he'd become flustered and let them be.

Tyra produced a bottle of wine she had smuggled out of Aramis's rooms and opened it. "Don't lie to me, Asta. You looked like a smug cat, and Søren looked like he was about to spontaneously combust."

Asta laughed as she kicked off her boots and pulled off her knit sweater. She wasn't comfortable getting naked in front of other people, a terrible trait for a Scandinavian, but Tyra had promised to turn her back when the time came.

"Who knows what Søren's problem was? He was probably terrified you were about to jump him again. Although we both know he's not the brother you'd like to jump."

Tyra took a big mouthful of wine from the bottle. "True. Stop trying to distract me. You know if you don't tell me, I'll start making things up in my head, and they'll be at least twice as bad as what actually happened." She offered the bottle to Asta, who took it and had a mouthful of her own.

"I wonder how they get wine to taste so good. I have always hated it, but this stuff I could get used to."

"You better look away in case my bare tits frighten you," Tyra teased.

"Shut up." Asta turned around. "It's not my fault I'm a lady."

"That's right, you are. Which means we have the same parts, you prude." There was a splash, and Asta risked turning around. Tyra was already swimming in the luminescent blue waters, her naked body hidden beneath. Asta took the opportunity to step out of the rest of her clothes and climb in. The warmth of the water closed around her body, and she groaned happily.

"This was the best idea. How did you find out about this place?" Asta asked as she placed the bottle of wine on the smooth rock ledge beside her.

"Aramis brought me here after I healed you." Tyra swam back to join her.

"You got in here with Aramis…naked?" Asta raised an eyebrow. Her cousin hadn't said a *word* about this.

"Very platonic naked swimming. Sadly." Tyra reached for the bottle of wine. "The view was nice though."

"I bet it was. Seriously, what *do* they make these Álfr out of to make them so good-looking?"

"Starlight and sex and muscle. My favorite combination." Tyra grinned.

"You have it *so* bad," Asta said, taking another mouthful of wine.

"I can't help it. Kinda like *you* can't help it. I keep saying that Dökkálfar and Ljósálfar are designed to be irresistible to each other, and everyone keeps ignoring me. Come *on*, Asta. You have to tell me. You both came back, and Søren handed you off, made a lame excuse about needing a run, and never came back. He's either outside sitting in the snow or masturbating furiously somewhere."

Asta snorted her wine with surprised, embarrassed laughter. "Gods, Tyra, don't say stuff like that when I'm drinking."

"Why not? It's the only time you loosen up to tell me delicious secrets."

"Okay, okay, but it's not what you think. It was actually about magic, not sex." Asta congratulated herself on getting through the entire story about Søren giving her his magic and teaching her to use it without sliding under the water with embarrassment. She wasn't ashamed of what had happened, but she'd never had a girlfriend to talk about boys with before. Tyra had been slowly working on Asta for months to get her to finally open up, and now she did with ease. Asta expected Tyra to tease her senseless, but instead, she looked thoughtful.

"You know how I hate to burst your bubble? Well, you're wrong if you think today was all about magic and not sex."

"We made out. Clothes were on. It was sexy, but it wasn't sex," Asta argued.

"You don't get it, because your magic is locked up. Søren put his magic in you—he gave it to you to use and to control. It wasn't just about teaching you something. He let you take parts of him inside of you and move them about. What he did, in Álfr terms, was actually more personal than sex."

"You touched magic with them the other day when you were training! That's the same thing."

"Ah, not even *close* to the same thing. They felt out my signature. They didn't mix their magic all up inside mine and let me take it from them and use it. That is personal. I've *never* trusted someone enough to join magic with them, let alone given them control over it," said Tyra with a shake of her head. "You did that, made out with him, and just walked off? No wonder he looked so fucked up when you came back. He's gone up ten points in my respect book for his self-control."

"I didn't think it was a huge deal. Must mean Søren likes me a bit, right?" Asta laughed nervously.

"Girl, you have no idea of the fire you're playing with. He acts like a pussycat with you, but I know all the stories about him. The supernatural community thinks he's from the goddess Hel herself. I don't know why you couldn't just fall in love with a sweet lecturer at the university."

"Blame my dragon blood." Asta took another drink. "I'm not like you, Tyra. I really don't know what I'm doing when it comes to feelings and relationships. I don't know how I'd keep him interested even if I managed to catch him." Søren intimidated and intrigued her and made her wonder if she would survive it if he touched her for longer than the few brief caresses they'd already had.

"Oh, sure. Because clearly I know what I'm doing." Tyra rolled her eyes. "No one knows what to do when the attraction starts to build. You have to run with it and see where it goes. Just be yourself, and believe me, he's not about to lose interest. I've seen the way he looks at you. You should've seen him when you ran off. He was half-crazed that he couldn't find you and protect you. He might have a scary-ass reputation, but at least I know he's always going to look after you."

Asta tucked her hair behind her ear and voiced her other major concern. "What if when the shields come off, I become a different person?"

"Magic won't change who you are. Magic *is* who you are. You are Álfr. You will be *more* you. Magic is innate and intuitive for us. Søren was right that we aren't going to let you go through this on your own. You'll have all the training and support you need."

"I don't know if I ever thanked you for coming to find me at Tove's funeral. Despite the circumstances, I'm really glad you're in my life, Tyra, and that you hung around."

"Aw, honey. If it wouldn't weird you out when my breasts touched your breasts, I'd hug you right now."

Asta splashed her instead, and Tyra dodged it, her laughter echoing around the stalactites above them. "Okay, I'm tired of talking about me. What's going on with you and Aramis? You are moon-eyed and lusty around him."

Tyra blew out a breath. "You've seen him, right? I'm pretty shallow."

"Stop bullshitting me. Just tell me, or I'll ask *him* what's going on." Tyra looked almost bashful which disturbed Asta even more than the account of Aramis turning up in Tyra's bathroom to make out with her. *So much for being the gentlemanly, subdued brother.*

"Wow. I'm really surprised you let Aramis get away with that," Asta said when Tyra finally stopped talking.

"What do you mean? I didn't want him to stop."

"*That's* what I mean. You're just letting him tease you with no retaliation."

"I'm trying to behave, so we don't get kicked out of this nice mountain fortress we've found ourselves in."

"The Tyra I know would've torn his clothes, or his head, off by now."

"Maybe your good influence is rubbing off on me. Maybe I'm just patient," said the most impatient person Asta had ever met in her life.

"Cousin, you're trying to date him. Like proper I-want-to-be-your-girl-friend-and-have-sexy-dates-at-the-Christmas-markets-in-Estonia dating." Asta fluttered her eyelashes at her.

"Shut up, or I'll drown you. Estonia wasn't a date. We were getting the books and kicking Thrynn's ass."

Asta rolled her eyes. "Yeah, okay. I don't know why you're so worried about it. I think it's nice that you have actually found someone you're interested in that isn't Thranduil. I mean, Aramis is pretty damn close though."

"You're right. I *definitely* have to find a way to pay him back," Tyra said with a firm nod.

"No, that's not what I said at all," Asta said, but Tyra's eyes had already glazed over with mischief. Asta really needed to change the subject.

"Do you really think Bláinn will try to find us here?"

"Yes, but I don't want you to worry about it. I won't ever let him take you. I'd die first, and trust me, I won't go down easy." Tyra took her hand and squeezed it.

"If he turns up, this place is protected, right? I mean, after the attack two years ago, they had to make sure no one could get in without permission. The Álfr here will be safe."

"I won't lie to you, so I'm going to say I honestly don't know. I don't trust easily, but I trust Aramis and Søren. They are the ones in charge of the safety of this place, and they have promised to protect us."

"They couldn't lay a single punch on you the other day. How are they going to protect all of us?"

Tyra gave her a gentle smile. "I'm not a normal dark elf. They are…amazing warriors, Asta. Don't doubt their skill. They are kind of legendary. Fuck, Aramis helped kill Baba Yaga and Yanka, and Søren killed Vasilli in single combat. They were all gods. The supernatural community actually calls Aramis and Søren 'The God Killers.'"

"If they are god killers and still can't lay a hand on you, what does that make you?" Asta had never been scared of Tyra, but she felt like there was a well of secrets inside of Tyra that she had no idea about.

"I am the person who loves you most in all the Nine Worlds, and if anyone tries to take you away from me, they are going to regret it. That's the only thing you need to know." Tyra's black eyes were angry and haunted, so Asta tried to think of something to make her laugh.

"Okay, but if you're some kind of special creature with teeth in her vagina, you really should give Aramis a heads-up."

It worked. Tyra's mood lifted and her laugh was filthy as she said, "Where would the fun in that be?"

18

TYRA HAD TRIED TO shake off her worry in front of Asta, but it still sat at the bottom of her stomach long after they had returned from the pools. Søren hadn't come back from wherever he was hiding when she had dropped Asta off in Søren's apartments. A part of Tyra wanted to interfere, convince Asta that she should move in with her and let Søren have his room back. The less protective part of her wanted Asta to act on whatever she was feeling for the scary bastard.

"I'm sure he's not far away," Aramis had said when a small frown had appeared between Asta's eyes.

"I kissed him today without permission. He might not have liked that," Asta had replied.

Aramis had struggled not to smile. "That won't be the problem. You want my advice? The more you kiss him, the better. Rattle his cage, as Tyra would say."

"I would not say that! I'd say climb him like a tree," Tyra had added, and Aramis had rewarded her with the kind of grin that made her want to take her own advice.

"Okay, I'm not going to listen to either of you. I'm going to bed with a book. I don't need Søren watching my door, because I don't plan on running."

Now, Tyra was pacing her room, mulling over what Thrynn had said about what Bláinn had done to the dark elves in Estonia and about Asta's hidden magic and what it could mean. Bláinn wouldn't be the only one who wanted Asta. As soon as the Drekiónds knew Tove's fate, they would do anything they could to secure their granddaughter. Vigdis, that fucking witch, was probably already scrying for them. That gave Tyra an idea.

Digging about in her duffel bag of gear she pulled out the velvet bag that contained her rune stones. Every now and again the Norns threw her a bone and gave her a warning. Tyra sat down on her bed and tried to focus.

Tyra had encountered many surprises since she'd come to Midgard. One of them had been finding rune-reading books readily available. Such things couldn't be learned by just anyone. The humans viewed them as fortune-telling tools which was the opposite of what they were. Rune stones were used to view the past and present threads of fate, and by looking at the patterns, it might be possible to determine the future if you stayed on the same path. The future was not woven yet, and there were many threads one could follow.

One of Tyra's gifts was being able to see other people's paths and receive murky glimpses of their next steps. Vigdis, the royal family's Seiðr, had resented Tyra for having the gift. Tyra's mother had no such ability, so it must've come from her father's side. That had worried Vigdis most of all.

Focus on Bláinn and worry about Vigdis later. Tyra shut her eyes, reached into the velvet bag, and began to draw the black stones out one at a time. She had intended to draw three, but something in the back of her mind tingled, and she kept drawing.

When all the stones were gone, she opened her eyes. Rage and fear and disgust hammered through her as she studied the pattern. She knew it wasn't going to be a pleasant experience, digging around in the wyrd of Bláinn, the sick prick, but her stomach still churned. With a hiss of anger, she swiped at the stones, sending them scattering around the room. Darkness crept over her, overwhelming her with the tight, hot, choking fear of being stuck under the mountain, shackled to a forge, and dying from her wounds and fever. Tyra pushed her hands through her hair. She needed light *now*, before the nightmare of her own memories dragged her down.

Aramis hadn't warded his room, which was his first mistake. He was so trusting. Tyra didn't knock as she opened the heavy wooden door. Aramis was sitting up in bed reading, and he looked up in surprise as Tyra's purple shadows covered his mouth and wrists and tied his arms to his carved wooden headboard.

"You thought that quick kiss in the snow made everything square between us, Starlight?" she asked, her eyes running along his bare, tattooed torso. She'd only seen his bare back the night at the pools, and she was delighted to find his front just as pleasant. He mumbled something angrily against his magical gag, his strong arms straining against the bonds that held him made Tyra's womb clench. She could've come just from looking at him too long.

"My, my, you really are lovely, aren't you?" Tyra murmured as she took a step toward him. Her hands loosened the tie of her black satin robe. Aramis stilled as his deep blue eyes focused on what her hands were doing. His gaze became so intense that Tyra almost lost her nerve. *What was it about this Ljósálfar that made her feel like she was a nervous virgin again?*

"Would you like to see what's underneath?" she asked him. He nodded very slowly. Tyra knew she'd packed the indigo lingerie for a reason. When she'd bought it, its deep blue color and small diamantés had reminded her of the night sky. Aramis took one look at it and strained against his smoky bonds again.

"You might as well stop that. You won't be able to loosen them without knowing what holds them," Tyra said as she came next to the bed and drew back the blanket that covered the rest of his torso. She leaned down close and ran her tongue over the point of his ear. "And I don't feel like telling you what that is just yet."

Gods, he smelled good. She'd planned to only tease him, but her self-control was becoming more frayed by the second. A growl reverberated through him as her loose black hair brushed against his chest.

"You are right. This tasting business is *so* much fun," Tyra said as she climbed on top of him. His waist and hips were hot between her thighs, and a tremble passed through her. Aramis must have felt it, because his silvery brows lifted in surprise.

"Oh, like you don't know that you're fucking gorgeous," she snapped, her nails gliding down his chest. He shuddered as she leaned down and brushed her mouth over one of his nipples. Aramis's hot skin tasted as good as it looked. He smelled like the sea and snow and fir trees that reminded Tyra of the way she felt during her first winter on Midgard, watching the snowstorm blow over the ocean. It was the scent of freedom, and she slid farther down his body until she felt the band of his tight dark gray boxers.

"Underwear to bed? How disappointing." Tyra enjoyed the way his eyes fluttered when she ground her hips against him. It was probably a good thing he wasn't naked, or she really wouldn't have been able to stop herself. Her fingers traced the silvery trail of hair from his navel, and he bucked underneath her as she ran a hand over him. *Holy shit, that was a bad idea.* Tyra's smiled widened as she looked back at his burning eyes.

"So, you *are* happy to see me after all," she said. Aramis's words were muffled as he yelled something at her that sounded an awful lot like curses. Her hand massaged him gently as she leaned forward, her breasts straining against her bra. "Are you having fun yet, Starlight?" He bucked again, hard enough for her to slip back down until she was over him. Feeling him hard through her panties made her lose her nerve for a second, and she felt her entire body blush. *Gods.*

"Did you just maneuver me?" she asked with mock surprise, trying to regain her composure. He shrugged, unapologetic.

Tyra moved against him, and the cockiness was wiped clean from his face. With her hips grinding against him, she trailed her hair down his body and sank her teeth into him hard enough to leave a mark. He whimpered. Tyra's legs were trembling again. She needed to stop this before she came just by dry humping him. She climbed off him, and he cursed again behind his gag.

"Yeah, you're right. We should make this go on for *centuries*," Tyra said, giving his ear a final nip. "The ties are bound by your arousal, so they'll disappear when it does…or when you break the headboard." Aramis's eyes were round as she slipped off her panties and dropped them on his chest. "Sleep well, Starlight." Then she walked from the room, shutting the door on his cries of outrage.

An hour later Tyra heard wood splinter in the room beside hers. The door to his room followed, and she saw his shadow outside of her door. He didn't come in, but she had to turn her face to her pillow to smother her laughter as she felt him place another fourteen different wards on her bedroom door to keep her locked in.

19

"SHOULD I EVEN ASK what happened?" Søren said when he spied the broken pieces of headboard through Aramis's bedroom door.

"I had an accident last night."

"An accident involving a dark elf with big black eyes who could murder us all without breaking a sweat?"

"I broke it. Tyra wasn't there," Aramis replied as neutrally as he could. He was still *furious* about it. So much so he couldn't look Tyra in the eye this morning. When Asta came to get her to go to the library, he'd given them permission to go on their own, because he wasn't sure he could handle Tyra's perpetual smirk or control his desire to yell at her for the torment of the previous evening.

Søren sat down at the breakfast island and poured himself a cup of coffee. "I'm starting to think the reason why we stopped interbreeding is because they drive us crazy enough to want to kill them."

"I noticed you disappeared last night. Are you and Asta fighting again?" asked Aramis, tearing his eyes away from the broken bed and joining Søren at the island. His brother didn't just disappear or come visit him early in the morning. Aramis could've sworn Søren was still drunk from the previous evening.

"We aren't fighting," Søren said with a small shake of his head.

"She thinks you are angry because she kissed you, which I can't believe she'd want to do but here we are."

"You know what happened the first time I kissed her. It was like that but worse. Yesterday caught me off guard that's all. I didn't expect her to kiss me, not when I—" Søren looked away.

"What did you do, Søren?" Aramis asked carefully. Søren was worried about something. If he had hurt Asta, even by accident, he would never forgive himself.

"I didn't know how to convince her that having magic once her shields are off would be a good thing, so I let her use some of my magic. It's left me feeling all"—he made a dramatic hand gesture—"fucked up."

Aramis took a deep breath. "What do you mean you let her use some of your magic? You gave it to her?" Søren explained what had happened in the nursery, stunning Aramis completely.

"Don't you get all fucking righteous on me, Aramis. Not after you gave Anya a piece of your magic permanently," Søren finished defensively.

Anya had been different. He hadn't given her his magic; *her* magic had siphoned it from him, and then they'd had to deal with it the best they could. It was the wrong time to argue that Anya's magic had once tried to do the same thing to Søren too. His brother had been reckless to the point of suicidal when he'd tried to provoke Anya's magic from her all those years ago. He wasn't that person anymore—neither of them was.

Søren had offered something to Asta, and she'd been able to play around with the very heart of him—all to try to grow a plant. *Gods, how did I end up with such a brother?*

"How did it feel?" Aramis asked instead. Søren gave him a long, pointed look.

"How do you think it felt? Even shielded up so tight she passes for human, Asta played around with it like she knew what she was doing. She was a complete natural. It was like pieces of my soul were twisting around her fingertips. I only meant to use her hands like a puppet, so she could see it and maybe feel it enough to inspire a bit of wonder. It curled around her like it belonged to her. She *used* it like it belonged to her." Søren's usual cool eyes glowed with expression and wonder.

"Have you never shared magic like that before, not even with Väliä?"

"No. Not like that. Väliä was the complete opposite of Asta. I don't remember ever being this messed up over a woman before. It must be a dark elf thing, right?"

Aramis looked at the broken pieces of his bed. "You might be right."

"All I wanted was to find a lost book," Søren said helplessly.

Aramis poured him more coffee. "You were the one who made me bring them home."

"And now we might have a psychotic dark elf warlord on our doorstep any day. We don't have a standing army. I could call in some warriors from Alaska if I need to, but they might not be able to get here in time."

Aramis reached out and placed a hand on his brother's forearm. "We'll keep Asta safe, Søren. One step at a time."

"*How* are we going to keep her safe? When those shields come off, who knows what magical signatures she could broadcast out? And it's not just Bláinn looking for her."

"If they come, I'm sure Tyra will have a plan. We will shore up our defenses and wards, set watches with the warriors we already have. I don't want people to panic, not after what happened last time."

"Aramis, Tyra is one dark elf. Granted she can kick our asses, but what happens if Bláinn brings an army?"

Aramis had seen a small glimpse of Tyra's dark magic. *Draeimi*. Killing Smoke. She was hiding herself and her abilities for a good reason.

"I think Tyra *is* an army," Aramis admitted slowly.

"An army of attitude perhaps"—Søren snorted before pointing at the broken bed—"and whatever happened there."

"That was me. I had a nightmare." It wasn't exactly a lie. Almost losing his mind like an untried elfling over a girl in lingerie was definitely nightmare territory.

Søren raised a dark brow. "You think she's an army, and you still think it's a good idea to encourage her the way you do? Your choice of women hasn't been exactly stellar."

"Tyra isn't anything like Yanka or even Anya. She might be a weapon, but she's got more joy in her than I've seen in anyone in years. She's infectious."

"So is the clap, just saying."

Aramis laughed. "Maybe dark elves do make you crazy. After everything that's happened, maybe we deserve to have a bit of good crazy in our lives. I know you do."

Søren rubbed at his face irritably. "I don't know how to make any of this work. I never thought I'd go through this again after Väliä. Feeling all churned up like this all the time is too hard."

"Asta is worth it though. She's one of the good ones and is disturbed enough to find you attractive." While Aramis didn't relish seeing his brother in pain, he couldn't help but enjoy seeing him fretting over a woman.

"Die." Søren looked as if something had just occurred to him. "Where are they anyway?"

"Tirith has taken them to the healers to study the shields."

"You let them go on their own?"

"The Álfr aren't worried about Tyra now that Tirith has vouched for her, and nearly all of the citadel's librarians are in love with Asta."

Søren's eyes narrowed. "Which librarians?"

"They will be fine. I can't keep Tyra shackled and under guard forever." *Even if I want to.*

"I still think we should've put her in the dungeon."

"She wants Asta to move into the other spare room," Aramis said, hoping the alcohol in his brother's system would soften the blow.

Søren scowled. "This is exactly why Tyra should be in the dungeon. I haven't laid a finger on Asta, so Tyra should leave her where she is."

"Come now, Søren. The mountain is full of gossip already. It's one apartment over, and both Tyra and I will be able to watch over her."

"What does Asta think?"

"Asta thinks you're angry at her, so she's agreed to it."

"Damn it."

"Sorry, it's for the best. It will make it more amusing for me to see you two sneaking in and out though." Søren's scowl deepened.

"I need to talk to her."

"You need to go sleep it off first, so you don't say anything stupider than normal. Maybe you should be honest and tell her that letting her use your magic affected you."

Søren's laugh was bitter. "Oh yeah, it had an effect. Probably a similar effect to whatever caused you and Tyra to do that to your bed."

Aramis sighed. "I told you she wasn't there."

"Tell that to the pair of panties hanging off the side of your mattress."

20

THAT AFTERNOON, TYRA ANNOUNCED that Aramis needed to take her on a tour to review the security wards around Svetilo. She had seen enough of libraries and healers' towers. She needed air and exercise.

Asta strongly suspected Tyra wanted a quiet place to make out with Aramis, but that was neither here nor there. Asta hadn't seen Søren all day and was doing her best to ignore her growing unease.

"With any luck he's still asleep. He was drunk when I saw him this morning," Aramis said when he came alone to collect them.

"Do you want to come for a run in the snow instead?" asked Tyra and Asta laughed.

"Oh God no. I'll follow up with some reading Tirith gave me and let the hungover elfling keep sleeping." Asta was not one for runs in the snow, and besides, Aramis looked like he was about to leap out of his skin at the chance to talk to Tyra alone. Asta had a strong suspicion Tyra had acted on a few of those mischievous ideas she'd had when they were at the hot springs.

"If he's awake, make him talk to you. He's not angry at you," Aramis added softly as she reached the apartment door.

"Don't care if he is," Asta replied primly, and Aramis's smile widened.

It was dark inside Søren's rooms, and if it weren't for the fire burning, Asta would've tripped over the empty bottle of scotch in the middle of the walkway. A jacket, shirt, and weapons had been discarded on the couch, and Asta followed a trail of boots and socks to the bedroom.

"Søren?" she whispered as she pushed the door open a little farther. He was sprawled across her bed half-naked and sleeping softly. His long black hair was a messy tumble across the pillows. Asta bit her lip, fighting an internal struggle about waking him up. It was his bed after all, and the view was worth taking a moment to admire. His Dauđi Dómr tattoos were on full display. The intricate designs that formed the tree made her fingers itch to trace over them, exactly the way the illustrations in the books did. It would mean touching all of those warm muscles, and Asta was sure once she started, she wouldn't stop.

"What are you staring at, *drékisma*?" Søren asked sleepily, making her jump.

"You are in my bed."

"You mean *my* bed. I thought you were moving."

"Is that why all my stuff is still in here?" Asta asked as she pulled her pajamas out from under his leg. "If you don't want me here, you should just say so."

"Do you always have to turn everything into an argument?"

"Only when you're being a grumpy dick face. Now that you mention it, yeah, that is all the time," snapped Asta.

Søren opened his green eyes. "What did you just call me?"

"Did I stutter? You know I really don't get you at all. You kissed me first, but when I try and kiss you back, you go get drunk and angry. You should stop giving me mixed signals all the fucking—"

Søren pounced, pulling her onto the mattress and pinning her down. "I don't think my signals are mixed."

"Only because they are *your* signals." Asta was doing her best to sound pissed, but it was difficult with a handsome as hell, half-naked guy hovering above her.

"You're right," he said, shocking her. Søren shifted off her, and she rolled onto her side to face him.

"I think I'm going to need you to repeat that."

Søren brushed a stray lock of hair from her cheek. "You are right. I am terrible at this. If I had any sense of self-preservation or control, I would've never bothered you in Oslo. But it seems I have neither of those things which is why I keep making stupid mistakes like letting you use my magic. You want to know the reason why I've been drinking? Because I feel like you're inside of me, ripping wounds open that I've done everything to heal. Nothing has scared me in a thousand years, not facing two armies and their gods or hunting down Darkness members, but I met you, and now I'm fucking terrified all the time."

Asta could barely breathe as he continued to stroke her jaw and trail his fingers down her neck. Her pulse thrummed under his fingertips. "Why are you terrified?"

"Because I don't know if I can keep you safe, and I can't lose anyone else. I wouldn't survive it. I wouldn't want to." The fear in his eyes was real, and she desperately tried to find the right words to say to him.

"I don't know the full story about what happened with your wife, Søren. I only know what Tirith told me. I'm not in any danger though, not yet anyway, and Tyra won't let anything happen to me. I'm okay. You don't need to worry." Asta reached out with her hand and touched his wrist.

"Tirith told you," Søren replied slowly, his tone going cold.

"Yes. I think he was trying to warn me off." Asta looked down at their bodies, almost touching. "Clearly his warnings fell on deaf ears."

The side of Søren's mouth kicked up, but his intense expression didn't change. "Tirith doesn't know the full story about what happened that night. He doesn't want to because that will mean he'll have no one to blame, and grief needs someone or something to blame."

Asta squeezed his hand. "Tell me."

"Gods, you know what? I'm actually drunk enough to do it." Søren sighed. "I never trusted Yanka, but Aramis was so in love with her that I didn't want to fight with him about it. I should have. He dismissed every warning sign—didn't even see them. When Yanka attacked the Ljósálfar in Alaska, I told Väliä to hide because she was too pregnant to run and not get caught in the cross fire. She promised me that she'd stay hidden. She told me I had a duty to help the other Álfr, not just her. She would be safe and would stay there until I came back for her, so I left her. When I found Aramis, he was so wounded he couldn't walk. I carried him to safety while the Ljósálfar warriors fought off the Darkness who were attacking us. They couldn't find Yanka, but I knew in my gut she was there for a reason. She was looking for something. I went back to check on Väliä, and when I reached her apartments, I heard her arguing with someone. I found her outside in the courtyard, blocking Yanka's escape and trying to convince her to stop the slaughter. Yanka saw me and knew that there was only one way to keep me from following her."

Tears fell down Søren's cheeks, his grief as fresh as if it had happened yesterday. "Väliä was s-so pregnant. Yanka knew and didn't care. She killed them with a blast of power that knocked me out. When I woke up, she was gone, and there was…there was so much blood everywhere. If Väliä would've stayed hidden as she'd promised, they would both still be alive. I spent the next thousand years hating Aramis, blaming him for Yanka's treachery. I let Tirith believe what he wanted, because the pain of knowing Väliä had risked herself and the baby on purpose would kill him. It was such a stupid thing for her to do. She knew what Yanka was like. The truth is I've been angry at her for so long that I haven't let anyone else get close to me, haven't been able to handle the thought of anyone touching me."

Søren wiped at his eyes with the back of his hand, brushing away the tears. "I've spent the last two years trying to get to know my brother again. I wanted to finally have *my* Aramis back like he was before that bitch destroyed our lives. He bore my anger, believing he deserved it, but the only thing he was guilty of was falling in love with a terrible woman who used him. Yanka may have dealt the killing blow, but Väliä knew better. It's her own fault that she is dead. Fuck, I can't believe I said that out loud, but it's true."

Asta's heart was breaking for him, her chest aching at the sight of this powerful, strong man broken by centuries of grief and anger. She cupped his cheek with her palm, brushing away the tears.

"Forgive her, Søren. Forgive yourself. You'll never know what drove her to risk her life that night, so don't torture yourself over it anymore. Forgive her. It's the only way you'll be able to move on. You deserve to be happy just as much as Aramis does."

Søren leaned his cheek into her palm, and his hand curved around her rib cage. "Do you understand why I'm so afraid of losing you? After a thousand years, you are the first person to make me want to believe I can move on, that I can let someone in again and be happy. This is what's breaking me every time you're near me."

"Everyone is broken in their own way. I know I am. If you can deal with my broken edges, then I can deal with yours. Just stop letting your broken edges cut you, because sooner or later, they are going to start cutting me too. Understand?"

"I'll never understand how you can be so sweet and bust my balls at the same time," he said, a gleam of humor breaking through the heaviness in the room.

"It's one of my many gifts. Ball-busting, stellar advice, ancient manuscripts, superb kissing… I could go on, but it would just bore you." The hand over her ribs tightened as he dragged her close.

"You are many things, *drékisma*, but boring is not one of them." He studied her face, his smile gentle. "Thank you for listening and for not running away screaming in the other direction."

"Thank you for finally telling me. As for running in the other direction, it's early yet." His eyes narrowed, and she bit her lip to keep from smiling.

"Keep up that attitude, Dökkálfar, and I might have to get Aramis to make another set of shackles." Asta bit his shoulder hard enough to make Søren yelp. "Gods, woman! That killed." He laughed as he rubbed at the spot.

"Don't threaten me, and I won't bite you."

"Okay, okay. I'm sorry, you feral little dragon." He was ready for it this time. When Asta moved her head to bite him again, he caught her lips with his, kissing her deep enough to rob her of her senses. When they broke apart, she couldn't remember why she'd wanted to bite him.

"I think I just figured out how to win arguments with you," he said with a grin.

"You wish," Asta replied. She reached up to trace a line of tattooed branches over his shoulder, and her fingertips tingled. "This is beautiful. What do all the symbols mean?"

Søren frowned. "What symbols? They are just lines."

"No, they aren't. The lines are made up of tiny little runes. It must've taken forever to tattoo."

"You must be drunker than I am. There are no runes." Søren shook his head. "The tattoos were done when Aramis and I became Dauði Dómr. It's a sign of who we are."

"Were they put on you with a needle or with magic?"

"Both. Why?"

Asta switched on the bedside lamp. "Roll over."

Søren moved onto his stomach, and she leaned down to study the black lines. "I think I can see the magic binding it. It's…it's beautiful."

"If you can see the magical runes in them, maybe the healers had some effect on your shields when they poked at them today."

"I don't know, but they are definitely there." She touched the tattoo again, following the runes with her finger as she admired the artwork and the contours of its canvas. Søren made a noise that sounded like a growl and a purr.

"Sorry, I didn't mean to tickle you. It's incredible though."

"Don't…don't stop," he said, and Asta was glad he couldn't see her face turn red.

"Okay," she whispered and put her hands back on him.

21

SNOW WAS FALLING IN heavy drifts when Aramis and Tyra stepped out of the front gates of Svetilo. Dressed in a long white coat lined with wolf fur, Tyra looked like an evil fairy-tale queen ready to lure men to their deaths. Aramis was beginning to think that he was one of them.

"This place is amazing," said Tyra, looking back toward the mountain fortress. In the heavy snow, it looked like a regular cold mountain except for the tall, strong gates.

"It was one of the first strongholds established here on Midgard. It's remote enough that if anyone comes looking for it, we'll see them long before they see us."

"That's a good idea when coming to a new world." Tyra's warm breath swirled around her. "Which way to the ward stones?"

"Up ahead. You'll feel them long before you see them," Aramis replied, taking the lead. When he glanced back to see if she was following, he noticed her eyes were firmly glued to his ass. "Be careful you don't trip."

"You'll catch me." She did not seem the least bit embarrassed.

Aramis shook his head. "You never turn it off, do you?"

"With an ass like yours in front of me, how could I possibly turn anything off? Besides, flirting with you is distracting me from bigger problems right now."

"Last night was your idea of flirting, was it? Tying a defenseless man down and feeling him up?"

"You really don't like losing control of a situation, do you, Starlight?" Tyra purred as she moved past him. She reached out for the long obelisk of black stone jutting out from the snow and whispered, "*Visa*." Silver-and-gray warding stretched out from the stone, linking it another two hundred meters away.

"It's incredible how you can do that."

"I'm a visual person. You should know that by now." Tyra gave him a grin that made heat creep into his face. "This is your work, isn't it?"

"Some of it. Søren and I added more after Svetilo was attacked."

"No wards against dark elves though."

"I honestly didn't think any of your people were here on Midgard. You and Asta have surprised us all." *In more ways than one.*

"I bet." Tyra laughed. "Well, let's give these wards some dark elf flavor, so if Thrynn or anyone else decides to trespass, we'll know about it." Dark purple light flowed from her hands as she whispered to the ward stones. Runes Aramis had never seen before twisted into the silvery spellwork and glowed in incredible patterns.

"I've never seen warding like that before. It's so beautiful," he whispered. He was in awe of the delicate and complex way her magic was tied into his.

"That is us. Don't we look good together?" Tyra said with a soft smile.

"We do. Will you show me more of your magic?"

The smile faltered. "You aren't talking about my warding, are you?"

"No, I'm not. That small light show in the glade was incredible. I want to see…more." Aramis didn't want to push her, but he was fascinated by new magic and by her.

"Are there any wide spaces close by?" She bit her lip.

"This way. I was going to show it to you anyway. If Bláinn really does try to bring an army here, this is the only space that will be big enough to hold them." Aramis took her hand and led her through the trees. The sun was almost gone for the day as they came to a snowy plain surrounded by tall pine trees.

"Damn, this *is* a good place to drop an army," Tyra said, looking about. "Are there any watchers out here?"

"Not this far out, but I'm going to change that now that we are going to take Asta's shields off."

"Good. Make sure they ward this place and set some traps for good measure." Tyra placed her hands on her hips while her black eyes scanned the area like a general surveying the strengths of a battlefield. "Are you sure you want to see this? You might not want me anywhere near you afterward."

"I don't see that happening, but I won't force you. I'm curious, that's all. You can always tell me to mind my own business." His words earned him the flash of a smile.

"A small demonstration then." Tyra took him by the biceps and gently maneuvered him a few meters behind her. "Stay. Don't move."

"Yes, sir," he whispered, anticipation curling through him.

She gently pulled one of the long strands of his hair. "Extra points for calling me sir." Tyra turned back to the empty field and the shadowy tree line beyond it. He heard her release a small sigh. "Don't say I didn't warn you, Starlight."

Every hair on Aramis's body stood on end as purple light streaked out of Tyra like bolts of liquid lightning. It burst across the plain in curving deadly arcs. She moved, her hands controlling the magic as it twisted in auroras of light. Then the light shot back toward her, recoiling and returning to her. It shimmered along her skin and glowed in her eyes, turning her into a goddess of war and fury. He was struggling not to fall to his knees in awe of her power. *This woman.*

"Wait for it," Tyra said. Lifting her hand up, she blew a kiss across the plain. The first line of trees crumbled, their trunks cut to pieces by her power. "I hope you didn't like those." Aramis's heart pounded, and his breath caught in his throat as he surveyed the scars in the earth and the devastated forest where her power had touched.

"You said you were only going to give me a small demonstration," he said breathlessly. Tyra turned toward him, her expression uncharacteristically sad.

"That *was* a small demonstration, wasn't it?" Aramis asked. A small nod. "How did Bláinn manage to capture you if you could do…all of this?"

"I stabbed myself in the gut, remember? I'm a warrior, Aramis. I know where to put the knife. I was almost dead when they found me, just not dead enough. Bláinn let Thrynn loose on me with his whip to keep me down. When I was finally healed enough to realize I had been sold, I had shackles around my ankles to dampen my magic and keep me tame," Tyra said, unable to meet his eyes.

"And I put you in shackles when you got here. Tyra, I'm so sorry." He was such a bastard, and he hadn't stopped long enough to consider how much psychological damage putting her in chains again could cause.

Tyra clicked her tongue. "Well, they weren't really *proper* shackles, were they? They were more like the fun and sexy kind. You know I could've broken out of them if I wanted to, but as I said then, I don't mind being chained if it's to you, Starlight."

Aramis looked back at the destroyed landscape and the incredible, ferocious woman beside him. "I pity the poor fool who tries to hunt you down or tries to hurt you again."

"You know what I am. You know a small part of why they call me *Draeimi*. You've got a good imagination and have some idea of what I've been ordered to do. If you feel repulsed or…or afraid… I'd understand." Tyra's hands clenched into fists by her side. That wild, sexy attitude she always flaunted had abandoned her. He knew there was one crude and quick way to banish all doubt from her mind, and he couldn't believe he was about to do it. Aramis got into her personal space, took her hand, and placed it over his crotch.

"Does that feel repulsed to you?" he demanded. "Don't ever assume *what* I feel when I look at you."

Tyra's lush red mouth popped open in surprise, and then she was in his arms, her legs wrapping around his waist and her arms going around his neck.

"Thank you," she said softly before her hot mouth was on his. Aramis held her tight to him. Every part of him wanted to push her up against a tree and have his way with her. Knowing Tyra, she might have been up for it, but he didn't want his first time with her to be quick and desperate.

"You are a hurricane of a woman who's probably going to destroy me, but I can't wait to see what you do next." His hands gripped her tight.

Tyra laughed delightedly. "I'm pretty sure you are going to enjoy it."

When they got back to Aramis's rooms, Tyra stuck her head into the other guest room and frowned.

"Asta isn't here. I don't know if that's a good or a bad thing," Tyra said with a frown.

"She might've been nervous and wanted the company. Her shields will hopefully be removed tomorrow, and for some unknown reason, she actually enjoys Søren's personality."

Aramis had only just gotten into his broken bed when there was a polite tap at his door.

"Should I be worried?" he asked when Tyra stuck her head in.

"I come in peace. Asta isn't the only one nervous about her shields coming off. Who knows what Tove thought was so important she needed to hide it. I need a distraction, and you're the most distracting thing around."

"Are those tiny pirate skulls?" Aramis asked, eying her pajama bottoms as she padded across the room.

"Fuck yeah, they are. Move over." She placed a bottle of wine and a laptop on the bed before climbing in beside him.

"What's this all about?" Aramis was unable to stop the smile that spread across his face.

Tyra turned on the laptop. "This is me showing you the greatest movie of all time. *Thor: Ragnarok.*"

22

ASTA WONDERED FOR THE hundredth time that morning if what she was about to do was a good idea. She'd woken up with Søren curled protectively around her, which she had liked immensely. *Should've stayed there.*

"You look like you are going to spew. Are you going to spew?" Tyra asked from where she sat beside Asta. They were in a stone room in one of the wings of the healing tower waiting for Tirith to arrive. They had decided this would be the safest space in the tower if her magic decided to flare, and she couldn't control it. The healers and Tirith had laid wards through the stone to ensure no wild magic could escape. It didn't make Asta feel the least bit better.

"You are going to be fine, *drékisma*, but you need to breathe," Søren said from the other side of the room. He was leaning against the stone wall and looking comfortable with his arms crossed. He was back to his neat, handsome, and aloof self, who was so unlike the drunk and disheveled Álfr she'd spent the night talking to. She knew something had changed between them but refused to analyze it too much. She had enough to worry about.

"Did you just call her 'little dragon'?" Tyra said with a snort. Asta narrowed her eyes at him, she had been wondering what the nickname had meant.

Søren's shrug was nonchalant. "She *is* a little dragon."

"You're giving each other nicknames? That's adorable," Aramis said.

Søren glared at him. "Like you can talk, *Starlight*. Let me guess, Tyra's nickname is Hell-beast, Destroyer of Worlds?"

Aramis glanced over at Tyra, and said, "Magnificent." Tyra's only response was a sound caught between a growl and a groan that made Aramis's eyes dance.

"Oh, please." Asta rolled her eyes. She was saved from the conversation by the arrival of Tirith and Alea, the healers' high matron.

"Good to see you are all on time. How did you sleep, Asta?" Tirith asked. She didn't dare look at Søren.

"Really well."

"And you've eaten?"

"Yes."

Alea bent down to study her face and touched her hair. "You even have wards in your eyes and hair. I would've liked to have met your mother to learn how she managed it. Do you remember her using magic at all?"

"No, but I don't really remember anything from before I was about five," Asta admitted. She had been scouring her memory ever since she learned who Tove was, but there was nothing. She couldn't remember her father's face or the house in Scotland by the sea. Tyra took her hand, a sign of solidarity and understanding that made a lump form in Asta's throat.

"Let's get on with it. This is going to be hard enough," Tyra said before looking at Asta. "You ready?"

"Do it."

Asta had spent hours with Tyra and Tirith the previous day, watching them experiment to figure out how Tove had used dark elf magic to cast light elf shields. By the end of the day, the only things they'd agreed on were that they needed to unravel the shields together and that Tove was insane.

Asta focused on Søren. His green gaze reminded her to breathe and distracted her from the warm pocket of magic Tirith and Tyra were casting over her. Tyra revealed the spellwork, and Asta saw the glittering threads layered over her body like bandages. Why would her mother do this to her?

"Look at me, Asta. Don't focus on it," said Søren, pulling her attention back to him. The healer made a small sound as Asta's pale, red-gold hair shivered, and the shield slipped off like a veil revealing a red so deep it looked like it was shot with black. Asta raised a hand to brush over the new small tips of her ears. Tyra swore but kept working. Heat was rushing through Asta's body, and it felt like she'd been submerged into a hot bath. Søren had gone pale, and when Aramis came to stand beside him, both of them wore similar expressions of shock and… something else. Asta's heart pounded. It was *fear*.

"Her magic is about to spike," Tyra warned Tirith before looking down at Asta. "It's okay, honey. We are almost done."

"It's working?"

"Yeah, it's working." Tyra frowned, and her hands hovered above Asta's forehead. "Here's hoping you don't blow me to hell." Before Asta could stop her, Tyra placed two fingers between Asta's eyes and made a twisting motion like she was turning a key.

Asta's skin tingled in warning as light and heat erupted through her, filling her veins with fire as it traveled up from her toes to her eyes and burned. Tyra, fearless of the danger, wrapped her arms around Asta and held her as she folded into herself.

"You're okay. I have you. I have you. Keep breathing," Tyra whispered, stroking Asta's hair.

"I think that's all of them," Tirith said. "Sit up, my dear. Let me have a look at you." Asta felt like she had gained a new set of lungs as she breathed in huge gulps of cool air and tried to sooth the burning in her throat. Finally, she steadied herself and sat up, pushing the bloodred hair back from her eyes.

Tyra's smile was wide. "Fuck me, you are a Drekiónd to your toes. You look exactly like them." Asta looked past her to Søren and Aramis. Both of the brothers looked like they had seen a ghost. Aramis trembled as Søren gripped his arm tight enough to bruise.

"Gods, it can't be." Tirith took a step back from her and turned to Søren. "You two get the hell out of here right now. Søren! Look at me." Søren dragged his horrified eyes from Asta to the older elf. "Get Aramis out of here. You hear me?" Without another glance in Asta's direction, Søren ripped open a gate and dragged Aramis through it.

"Tyra? What's wrong with me?" Asta's voice was tiny as she looked at her cousin in confusion.

"Nothing. You are fine. They were just surprised, that's all," Tyra said, trying to reassure her even though she looked as confused as Asta was.

"That would be an understatement," Tirith said softly.

"I will go get some elixirs that will help the magic settle." Alea backed out of the room and shut the door.

"What's going on? Why is everyone afraid of me?" Asta demanded. Tears fell from her eyes as she reached for Tyra.

"They are afraid of the past, not you," said Tirith.

"Explain," demanded Tyra.

"Those boys came from Álfheim the night their village was attacked. I don't think Aramis remembers much, but Søren does. They saw their father slaughtered and their mother—" Tirith shook his head, unable to say the words. "The general who led their attackers looked exactly like you."

Tyra went still beside Asta. "How did they get away from him?"

"I don't know. They never said," Tirith replied. "All I know is that two elfling orphans appeared here at Svetilo from a gateway. And it almost killed Søren to do it."

Søren and Aramis fell onto the snowy streets of Arkhangelsk. Aramis hurried down a side street and vomited behind a set of bins.

"It's okay," Søren mumbled to his brother, patting him on the back. Aramis righted himself, and a human glamour settled over him.

"She's one of them, Søren."

"No, she's not. She was raised on Midgard. She's got nothing to do with them," Søren replied, needing to remind himself as well as Aramis. *That hair. Those eyes.*

"I need a bar," Aramis muttered.

"We both do. Let's go before someone realizes we aren't dressed for the snow." Søren's legs felt like rubber as they stumbled through the streets and into the first dark bar they came across. After they had both taken two shots of vodka, Aramis managed to look Søren in the eye.

"I think Tyra is right—the Norns are interfering witches. How is any of this possible?" Aramis asked.

"I don't know, but we need to deal with it now. I didn't think you even remembered that night enough to—" Søren broke off when he saw Aramis's face and poured more vodka.

"Of course I remember that night. We are going to have to tell them the truth. You know that, right? Tyra will corner me the first chance she gets, and Asta looked scared."

"I don't know if I can. I only told Asta about Väliä last night. I'm man enough to admit my emotions can't take much more of this."

"How is this going to change whatever is going on between you two?"

Søren drained his vodka, hoping it would burn away the lump in the back of his throat. How was he going to explain any of it to her?

"I don't know," Søren answered truthfully. Would he be able to look at her ever again and not see the nightmare that had nearly killed them all?

"Do you think Tyra will know who the general was who attacked us?"

"Probably. Have you stopped to think Tyra might have been there?" Søren said, and Aramis flinched.

"She told me the night we brought her to Svetilo that she was never a part of the raids. She might not have even known that a Drekiónd was participating in them." Aramis sat back in the cushion of the dirty booth. "We have to go back. We can't let Asta think this is about her. She's going to be struggling with all that magic. Gods, did you feel it, Søren?"

"Tyra's magic is strange too. Maybe it's because they are Dökkálfar."

"They are both so much more than dark elves. I thought the dragon blood story was myth, but that magic was alien to me. It's no wonder Tove went to the trouble she did to hide Asta."

Guilt and worry settled in Søren's stomach. He had run out on her, and she'd looked so small and scared. *Don't let your broken pieces start to cut me.* Asta's words came back to him in a rush.

"Drink up and get your head on straight. We need to go back before they have too long to formulate their own conclusions," said Søren.

Søren's rooms were empty when they returned to Svetilo. Søren's stomach gave a hard jolt when he realized Asta's belongings were gone, and he ran to Aramis's apartments.

"Well, look who finally decided to turn up," Tyra hissed from where she sat on the arm of the couch. She was tossing one of her knives in the air and catching it over and over.

"Where is she?" Søren asked. Tyra's blade pointed toward a closed door.

Tyra answered, "Asta wants to be left alone. She's upset and overwhelmed."

"Understandable," said Aramis.

"You ran out on us. What did you expect?" Tyra replied coldly.

"It's a long story," Søren said. "It's one Aramis is going to tell you if you'll listen."

Tyra's gaze flickered to Aramis, and she let out a tense sigh. "Fine."

Søren tried to move past her, but her blade was suddenly pressed against his neck. He knew he had no chance against her in a fight, so he resorted to begging out of desperation. "Please, Tyra, let me talk to her."

"You're lucky you didn't take much longer, or we'd be having a very different conversation right now. Asta is innocent of any crimes her shit family has committed. Understand?"

"We know that. We left because we were in shock, that's all." She finally moved out of the way. "Go easy on Aramis," she added in a whisper.

Søren slipped quietly into the room, shutting the door behind him. The air smelled of burnt sugar and fire. The scent could only be Asta's new magic. He must've had a death wish to want to tangle with her when she was upset and her magic so raw. It couldn't wait.

"Asta?" he asked, edging open the bathroom door.

"Go away, Søren." Asta sniffed, and Søren saw her sitting on the floor in the corner of the room. She had curled her knees up against her chest and had hidden her face under her arms. His fierce little librarian looked so small and sad he wanted to scoop her up and hold her.

"No, I'm not going anywhere." He crouched down beside her.

"I don't want you to see me like this."

"That's going to be tricky, seeing as how I won't leave until you talk to me."

"I-I don't even recognize my own face in the mirror. I can smell and hear everything. I feel like a freak."

"You're not a freak. Aramis and I apologize for leaving the way we did. We have a lot to tell you if you want to come out and listen," he said softly. Gods, he was so bad at this. He brushed a hand over her bloodred hair, marveling at the silky texture. "If you really hate the way you look, we can teach you how to put a glamour on to make you look human. Aramis does it all the time."

"You think he'd teach me?"

"Of course he would. You'll have to get a grip on your magic first to learn it. I doubt that will take you long though. You are very clever."

"Don't suck up. It doesn't suit you." She sniffed. "You promise not to freak out again?"

"Show me, *drékisma*," Søren said, and Asta slowly lifted her head. Something shifted deep inside of him, and it wasn't surprise or fear. Big golden eyes peered out at him from a face familiar and different at the same time. Her high cheekbones and full lips were slightly larger and more defined, and her skin shimmered like it had been dusted with gold. She was so beautiful that it felt like he'd been knifed in the gut with one of Tyra's blades.

With painful clarity, Søren realized all of the emotions that had been tormenting him for the last few weeks—longing, fear, desire, dread—were all symptoms of the one big emotion he'd been doing his best to ignore since he'd first kissed Asta. He was in love with her.

With that realization came a feeling of calmness. Søren gently cupped her ears, his fingers gliding over their short tips. Yes, she had the same coloring as the general who had attacked them, but he could only see Asta. He could only see Asta from the moment he'd met her.

"Will you say something?" she said, blinking her eyes to hold back her unshed tears.

"You are perfect, my little librarian." He touched the points of her ears again. "Look at these sweet little ears. How am I supposed to resist you now?"

"Shut up," Asta said with a sniff.

"Did you grow any taller?"

"No, it is the only thing that hasn't changed," she complained.

"Good. I like you pocket-size."

"I will hurt you, Søren," Asta said before managing a smile. Her smile broke his self-control, and Søren dragged her into his lap. Her back pressed against his chest as he wrapped his arms and legs around her.

"You smell so good. Like fire and magic." He buried his nose into her hair.

"You're not worried my magic will hurt you?"

"Your magic will only hurt me if you want it to hurt me."

"You'd better be nice then." She leaned back against him. "What am I going to do now?"

"Learn how to use your new body. I can help you with that— Ow!" He laughed when she pinched him.

"I'm serious, Søren. I'm scared to know why my mother locked me up. I know I look different, but what if that's not the only reason?"

"Don't be scared of who you are. Your mother was trying to protect you, that's all. Your magic is unique, and when it started to manifest, Tove probably thought it would make it easier for Bláinn to track you."

Asta held out her hands in front of her. "I can feel my magic moving about, but I don't know how to let it out."

"What else is different? You said you can smell and hear better. Those are common Álfr traits."

"My skin is really sensitive. I can feel your heart beating through my back, and it's almost too much to have you touching me."

"That might not be a bad thing," Søren said and put his mouth around the tip of her ear, making her gasp and arch back into him. "Mmm, not a bad thing at all."

"You could've warned me," she said a little breathily, and he smiled against her hair.

"Absolutely not." Oh, he was going to have so much fun when he unraveled this little dragon. He wasn't going to do it on a bathroom floor, but he'd be tempted if they stayed there for much longer. "Do you want to come out for a bit? Listen to Aramis tell you a story? I won't gag when I see his big lovey eyes on Tyra if you don't."

"I like seeing his big lovey eyes on Tyra. Can you imagine how much trouble she'd be right now if her obsession with him was unrequited?"

"Apocalyptic." Søren laughed and helped her up.

Asta made a strange happy sound when she washed her face in the sink. "Holy gods, why does water feel so good?"

"I can't wait to see you have your first shower if you think that was amazing." In fact, he hoped to be right beside her when she did.

23

TYRA DECIDED SHE COULD forgive Søren for just about anything if he kept giving Asta reasons to wear the small smile she had on when she stepped out of her bedroom. He loomed over Tyra's tiny charge like an overprotective bear, but there was no mistaking the softness in his face whenever he looked at Asta. The poor guy was so in love Tyra almost felt bad for him. *Almost.*

Aramis still looked as if he had been kicked in the chest, so Tyra took pity on him. She poured him vodka and sat down on the couch beside him, throwing her legs over his lap. He seemed surprised at first, but then he recognized the gesture for what it was—an offer of comfort in a hard moment. The dark elf in her wouldn't allow herself to coddle him, and she strongly suspected he wouldn't welcome it anyway. He picked up the vodka with one hand and placed the other on her calf, his thumb brushing small circles on her bare skin.

"Tell me about this general," Tyra said once Asta and Søren were sitting on the seats opposite them with Søren's fingers twisted easily about hers. Tyra glanced at their hands pointedly and then met Asta's eyes.

Asta gave a micro shrug.

"What I don't remember Søren will be able to fill in. Gods, it was so long ago." Aramis pushed a hand through his silvery hair. "We would've been what? Eight summers?"

"Nine," said Søren. "Young enough that my magic was only just starting to manifest, and Aramis's hadn't even begun."

"I remember it was autumn. The village had had the harvest celebrations. Our mother was a teacher, and our father was a retired general who used to teach the new recruits in our village and the surrounding areas before sending them off to the army," continued Aramis. Tyra knew what was coming. Her mind was trying to piece together what had been happening in Svartálfaheim at the same time.

"They came in the night. The alarm didn't even sound until half the village was burning. Our father went out to help, and when they came to the house, our mother sent us out through the kitchen to hide in the woods. She was beautiful—there was no way she was going to escape the attention of the raiders. She was dragged out of the house and shoved to her knees in the blood-soaked ground. Our father lay dead only meters from her. That was when the general arrived." Aramis glanced at Asta. "I'm sorry for my reaction to you when your true face was revealed. Your hair is…is exactly like his."

"I thought he was going to try to rape her," said Søren, his tone filled with a cold fury, "but our mother was not the type to lie back and take it. When he tried to strip off her dress, she cut the bastard from one side of his face to the other with a kitchen knife she had hidden in a pocket. In the confusion she managed to reach my father's sword. She was good with a blade, but she didn't know how to fight a dark elf. He appeared behind her and cleaved her from shoulder to waist in one blow. It was then that Aramis's magic decided to manifest, and he started to glow like a star."

The hand on Tyra's leg stilled, and Aramis appeared to be unable to look at his brother. Tyra knew who the bastard was that had attacked them and had long ago added him to the list of people she wished to kill. This story only made him move closer to the top.

"Did they see you?" Asta asked gently.

"I managed to wrap my magic around the both of us, blocking the light, but it didn't help. They felt the magic being used. The general himself came to investigate the shrubs we were crouched in. I stabbed the hand that reached for us. I knew we were going to die or worse if I didn't find a way to get us out. Then a gate opened beneath us, and we were falling," said Søren with a frown. "Magic is a strange force. It lashed out to protect us and dumped us here at Svetilo. I had heard my father mention that some of the Ljósálfar had gone to Midgard, and it was like my magic knew that was where we'd be safest. I don't remember anything in between falling through the gate and waking up here in the healer towers next to Aramis."

Tyra sat up and drained her drink. Gate magic was rare and extremely hard to master. To be able to world walk at such a young age… She shook her head. These Álfr she'd fallen in with were something special in more ways than one.

Her hand dropped behind the couch to gently tangle in Aramis's hair where the others couldn't see.

"I know who attacked you," Tyra said, and Aramis tensed. "His name is Daimar. He is Tove's brother and one of the biggest bastards I know. He was the one that pushed Tove's parents for the treaty with Bláinn in the beginning."

"Do you think my grandparents knew he was raiding?" asked Asta.

"No, they wouldn't have condoned it. They are assholes, but they'd never agree to that. They are grade A snobs—dark elf purists. They would've never thought the Ljósálfar would have anything better than what the Dökkálfar already had. They certainly would've noticed if Daimar had tried to bring home some Ljósálfar slaves. No, this has freaking Bláinn written all over it. He might have offered the trip to Daimar for some adventure because the sick fuck would've seen it as entertainment," said Tyra.

"Where were you when this was happening?" Søren asked.

"I would've been at the Drekiónd stronghold, protecting the royal family. They always sent Daimar to negotiate with Bláinn. I remember him returning with that face wound. He never said how he got it, and I didn't bother to ask because he also came with the news that he'd sold Tove off to Bláinn. I don't know where he is now. He stayed with the Drekiónds, and I went with Tove," said Tyra. Old animosity was beginning to burn in her veins.

"Do you think Bláinn would've told Daimar about finding Tove and Asta?" Aramis asked.

"It all depends on if their relationship survived Tove's leaving and my betrayal. There was never any sort of affection between Daimar and me. He saw me as Drekiónd property. If they even told him I survived, he wouldn't have lost sleep over my fate." Tyra tapped her fingers against her glass. She could check the runes again, but after last time, she already knew Bláinn would find them eventually. Every pattern for the future had led to it. It was only a matter of time.

"Sticky Norn fingers," Asta said, making Tyra smile despite the tenseness in the room. Asta could always make her smile.

"I kept trying to tell you they were bitches," Tyra replied and looked at Aramis's calm, noble profile. "At least there were some good consolations this time. If Daimar comes with Bláinn, I'll give you first crack at him, boys." But only the first one. If Daimar or Bláinn came close to hurting Aramis, she was pretty sure she would turn nuclear in a way she hadn't done in three millennia.

"It's a deal," said Aramis, touching his glass to hers.

Two hours later, Søren carried a sleeping Asta to bed with Tyra watching over them the whole time. He kissed her forehead and joined Tyra by the bedroom door.

"I hope you are as good in battle as the stories say," she said to him, her eyes not moving from Asta.

"You too," he replied.

"She has no idea how terrible her family is. She's such a sweet girl—all sass but sweet. The Drekiónds would destroy her. Bláinn is bad enough, but we can't let them take her."

"I have no intention of letting anyone take her anywhere," Søren replied. "She's going to need help with her magic."

"I'm sure training is very different for dark and light elves. We aren't the nurturing sort, but for her, I'd do anything. Understand? I'm sworn to her as I was to Tove," said Tyra. She missed her old friend so badly she ached. "There is no horrible atrocity I won't commit to keep Asta safe. I love that girl more than my life."

"Me too," admitted Søren, and Tyra could hear the truth in his words.

Tyra looked sideways at him. "Have you told her?"

"No."

"Don't wait until Bláinn is here and the world is burning before you do," advised Tyra, shutting the door.

"I have your blessing?" he asked in surprise.

"Do you need it? It's not me you have to convince that your intentions are genuine." Asta could do a lot worse than someone like Søren, but because she was Tyra, she said, "Hurt her, and I'll boil your bones for glue."

"I thought he'd never leave," Tyra said to Aramis. He was still on the couch, and the vodka he was drinking made him look far more relaxed than she knew he was.

"I'm surprised he's not sleeping outside of her door. Gods, this day…"

"Has been long, emotional, draining, and uncomfortable. There's only one solution for it." Tyra offered her hand. "Come on."

Tyra was starting to know her way around Svetilo, and Aramis seemed content to walk with her. He hadn't let her hand go, which she found unusual and awkwardly pleasant at the same time.

Being amongst these Ljósálfar is making you soft, Draeimi. The words echoed through her mind as they reached the stairs leading down to the springs.

When they reached the shadows of the walkway, Tyra pounced, pushing Aramis hard against the stone wall, and pressed her lips roughly against his. It was dominant and needy and made heat burn low in her chest. He responded in kind, his arms moving around to hold her close to him.

"I've wanted you to do that all day," Aramis said, finally letting her go. Tyra grinned at him because she knew this particular Ljósálfar was never going to turn her soft.

Down at the pools, Aramis took the lead and opened a door she had never noticed before. "Let me show you the good spot."

"Where you go, I follow."

"Only because you want to look at my ass."

"It's not the *only* reason." It was a damn good one though.

The pools on the other side of the door were smaller and more spread out. Rock formations between them created natural privacy.

"Is this where all the kinky Ljósálfar come for their water orgies?" she teased, and his laughter bounced off the stone.

"Of course that is what you would think. I'm sure they have been used for those reasons, but mostly they are for Álfr who want quiet and privacy. Some Álfr have an affinity for water, so it provides a place for them to practice without disruption. Or in my case, a private place for times when I want to be left alone with a beautiful dark elf."

"Is that so? And just how many beautiful dark elves have you brought down here?"

Aramis looked over his shoulder at her. "I don't think I could survive more than one." He stopped by a pool far enough away from the lamps and candles that the water was hidden in darkness.

"There better not be any terrifying creatures in that water," Tyra said dubiously.

"Not yet there's not." Aramis dodged the boot she threw at him. "Don't worry, *Draeimi*, I'll protect you."

"Maybe you can do that glowing trick, and I can use you as a night-light."

"Keep pressing my buttons, Dökkálfar. See how far it gets you." Aramis pulled off his shirt. "Do you think you can get out of your bra on your own this time?"

"I could get out of my bra last time," she replied cheekily.

"I *knew* it." Aramis grabbed her around her skull belt buckle and dragged her to him. "You've tormented me from day one."

"It's good for you." Tyra stood up on tiptoes and took a nip at his jaw. "Just think how bored you would be without me."

Aramis unfastened the buckle with a sharp jerk. "Get in the water and stop being so cheeky."

"Don't tell me what to do." She'd killed men for using that tone with her, but she liked it when he tried to be bossy. It said he wasn't afraid of her, and she liked that most of all.

By the time Tyra got out of her clothes, he was already in the water, sitting on the other side of the pool. His head rested against a lip of rock as he watched her out of the corner of his eye.

"Enjoy the show?" she asked as she lowered herself in the steaming, dark water.

Aramis's smile flashed in the gloom. "Absolutely."

Tyra's foot brushed smooth stone, and she found the pool was deep enough to stand up in. She tilted her head back and gasped at the shimmering stalactites above her. Her heart gave a strange jerky leap as she realized exactly why Aramis had chosen this particular pool to bring her to. In the half-light, it looked like stars above them.

"I was wondering how long it would take you to see them," he said. His large calloused hand slid down her back as he came to stand behind her.

"If I didn't know better, I'd say you're trying to suck up as an apology for running out today." She rested the back of her head on the curve of his chest.

"I am sorry if I upset you and Asta." He kissed the top of her head.

"It's okay. I knew it wasn't because of us and that you'd be back. You just can't resist all this." Tyra gestured to her face.

"Are my motivations that transparent?" His arms came around her. "May I tell you something?"

"Of course," she said.

"These little stars"—he kissed the stud in the tip of her pointed ear—"drive me insane."

"Really? You're easy to please." Tyra tried to ignore the goose bumps breaking out over her arms.

"I'm really not, yet everything about you pleases me immensely, not just your heartbreakingly good looks."

"And you thought you didn't like dark elves."

"I'm changing my mind about the females, and I think we both know you're more than just a dark elf."

"Rumors abound about what I am, my dear Ljósálfar." So many rumors yet she still only had vague ideas about who—and what—her real father was.

"I'm not worried. You'll tell me when you're ready to," Aramis said, brushing his hands along her stomach.

"I don't know enough to tell you, or I probably would." Tyra twisted in his arms, lifting her legs off the bottom of the pool and wrapping them about his waist. "All I know is that I killed my mother in childbirth, and Vigdis once called me a half-bred Asgardian mongrel. Maybe my father was from there. I never pursued it because it didn't matter. Asta's family placed me in the army, and there I stayed, training every single day until I could barely move. I didn't play with other children but with blades and death. The Drekiónds did everything they could to forge me into something they could throw at their enemies that would be loyal to only them forever. And I was. I fought for them and gloried in it. I couldn't imagine wanting anything more than that from life. Then Tove was born. When I was assigned to her as a bodyguard, everything changed. I wasn't loyal to the crown anymore but to her. If they come for Asta, they will try to reclaim me as their property too."

Aramis touched his forehead gently to hers. "You are *not* their weapon or their property. This isn't Svartálfaheim. Whatever rights they think they have mean nothing here. You will never be a slave again. Do you hear me?"

Tyra's chest gave another jerky twist when she looked up into his impossibly blue eyes and saw how deadly serious he was.

"Keep talking like that, Starlight, and I'm going to think you're trying to keep me for yourself," she joked in an attempt to ease the frown from his face. He gave her a tender kiss.

"I *am* trying to keep you, but only if you choose to stay. I won't be another master. I couldn't contain you anyway. It would be like trying to bottle a thunderstorm—"

"A sexy thunderstorm."

Aramis's smile was magic, chasing her anxiety away with its intensity. "Apologies, my lady. A sexy thunderstorm."

As the stars glittered above them, Tyra rested her cheek against the hard planes of his chest and finally let his solid presence calm her raging heart.

24

ASTA HAD ALWAYS LOVED the sea. She loved it under gloomy gray skies and brilliant sunshine days. Clutching her father's hand tightly was the only way she was allowed to go anywhere near the water, so she knew she was doing something wrong when she left the house before her parents woke and walked across the road to the beach.

There had been a storm the night before, and it was always the best time to pick up new shells and frosted glass from the wet sands.

Asta didn't know what the object was that had caught her eye on the rocks, but she knew she had to get to it. Then the wave came in, fast and gray, slamming into her and dragging her under. When she finally broke free and surfaced, her father was on the beach, so far away. Another wave came over her, then her world turned to shimmering golden light. Strong arms wrapped around her, and her father pulled her free from the surf.

That night Tove's face was drawn and afraid as she spoke with Asta's father in urgent whispers. Asta had never heard her parents argue before, but they argued then and about her.

"We have to go. There's no way around it," said Tove, her hands pushing through her deep red hair.

"It was nothing—a small blip that died away as soon as I reached her," her father said.

"You don't get it, Tom. She's awakening. That blip could've been felt worlds away if someone was looking for it, and *he* will be. She's not safe. None of us are."

They hugged then, Tove clinging to him as tightly as Asta had done in the sea.

"We'll leave in the morning. Asta needs to rest. Come to bed, and tomorrow we'll go wherever you think is best."

They never reached the morning. The door to the house was blown off its hinges. Asta started to cry as Tove bundled her up. Tove's hand pressed tightly over Asta's mouth as they fled through the cellar and out of the wooden doors that led outside.

Over Tove's shoulder, Asta saw her father lying dead in the front yard with a demon standing over him. A demon with black armor and hair like the sun.

Then Tove glowed with golden light, and Asta never saw the house by the sea again.

Asta woke from the nightmare covered in sweat. *Not safe, not safe*, she thought as terror gripped her. Golden light was pouring from her skin, and her magic burned her up as it responded to her fear.

"Oh no—" she squeaked, before her magic dropped her into black nothingness. She screamed as the nothingness became a room, and she landed hard on a bed.

Angry exclamations came from beside her, and light filled the room. Søren stared at her blearily.

"Asta? Where did you come from?"

"I don't know. My magic opened up a gate under me," she said as she started to cry.

"Are you hurt?" he asked, sitting up.

"I don't think so." Asta held out her hands, and the glittery gold flared between her fingers. Søren's eyes went wide, but at that moment his door was kicked in by a pissed-off Tyra in pirate pants.

"Is she—" Tyra halted and then pulled Asta to her. "Are you *trying* to kill me? I felt magic flare, and then you were just gone."

"Clearly she didn't mean it," Søren said scathingly. He tried to straighten his blanket, and despite her fear of the dream and her magic, Asta couldn't help but ask, "Are you naked under there?"

Søren looked embarrassed, and Tyra snorted.

"Gross. Come on. We'll let grumpy get some pants on." Tyra sat Asta down on the couch and fetched her a glass of water. "What set this off?"

"A nightmare, but now that I'm awake, I think it may have been a memory. Could the shields Tove put on me hide such a thing?"

"Absolutely," said Søren, now dressed in a pair of black pajama pants that were low enough for Asta to wonder how men could get muscles in that V shape.

"Focus, Asta. What was this nightmare about?" asked Tyra.

"How my dad died," Asta said and told them everything she remembered. "When I woke, I was covered in golden light, and I was scared. Then my magic dropped me on Søren."

Tyra sniffed. "I suppose it took you to whoever makes you feel safest like it did that night in Estonia. I have to say I'm quite hurt that it keeps taking you to *him* and not me."

"Asta didn't see you kill five dark elves to rescue her. Is the magic the same as gate magic?" Søren asked.

"No. Gate magic covers long distances, like what Asta did from Estonia. This magic works differently. It's more like teleportation. I knew Tove and a few other members of her family could do it over short distances," explained Tyra.

"Awesome," Asta replied unenthusiastically. Worrying about teleporting every time she had a nightmare was just what she needed.

After spending the rest of the night curled up in bed beside Tyra, Asta had risen early and had the longest shower of her life. New waves of sensation set her skin alight under the hot water. She'd spent her whole life living in a sensory deprivation bubble, and now everything was new again. Her body had to get used to mundane things once more.

Asta stood in front of the mirror, trying to come to terms with her new face. It was still her, she reminded herself as she drew on some eyeliner that enhanced the gold in them. She pulled back her dark red hair into a high ponytail, not even attempting to hide the new tips of her ears. She touched them curiously, but it didn't cause her whole body to jerk like when Søren had done it. She'd like to think it was because he'd caught her off guard, but she knew that was a lie. He had made her old body feel weird things, and her new one was going to be no different.

Asta was halfway to the library before she felt the shadow looming behind her.

"I thought it would take you longer," she said without slowing her pace.

Søren was beside her in a second. "I thought Tyra would be with you."

"Tyra was still snoring with her mouth open when I left." Asta smiled. "I wanted to talk to Tirith. Maybe try to figure out what sets off my magic, so I know how to stop it if I wake up again like I did last night."

"Did you remember anything else?"

"No. Just Tove and I running away before Bláinn could find us. It makes sense why she put the shields over me. I'm not angry at her about it, but I wish she would've told me earlier so I wouldn't be in this position. I don't know why she didn't teach me how to use it."

"She was afraid for you, and fear can make people do stupid things. You won't be able to control it overnight, but it's nothing the Álfr haven't seen before. We all go through it, and we will all help you."

Asta took his hand. "Here's hoping I don't teleport every time I try to use it."

"I'll get you some lead boots," Søren said, and Asta laughed.

"If you think it will slow me down."

Tirith took one look at their clasped hands and frowned at Asta. "You're here early this morning."

"I teleported last night. I was hoping I could use one of your special rooms so I can try to touch my magic without damaging anything." She did not let go of Søren's hand.

"Are you going to show her how?" Tirith asked Søren.

"I'll do my best."

Tirith made a dismissive sound before taking the bunch of keys from his belt and removing a key. "Try not to blow anything up."

"Thank you, Tirith," Asta said, taking the key from him.

"I hope you know what you're doing," Tirith replied, though she couldn't be sure if he was talking to her or Søren.

The room reminded Asta of a monk's cell with bare stone floors and walls. There was nothing she could break or incinerate which eased the tightness in her chest. Was teleportation the only magic she could do?

"Now what?" she asked.

"Now you need to try to bring forth your magic," said Søren as if it were the easiest thing in the world to do.

"Yes, but *how?*"

"You said yourself that you could feel it under your skin like a tingling heat. Focus on that sensation. Remember, your magic is a part of you and you control it, not the other way around."

Asta held out her hand, focusing on the wild golden light she had seen the previous evening. When nothing happened, she closed her eyes and tried again. All she saw was her father's face, strangely peaceful despite his horrible death. Nothing happened.

"It's not working," she said.

"You've tried for a whole two seconds. Focus. Remember the seed in the pot? That is what you are right now, what your magic is. It's a little seed deep inside you that doesn't know what it's going to grow up to be."

"You were helping me in the gardens, and it was your magic that grew the seed, not mine," Asta pointed out, keeping her eyes closed. Søren's warmth came around her as he rested his hand on top of hers.

"Just focus on that seed inside of you, *drékisma*. Let it grow, so it can come out and play with me," he whispered in her ear. Asta wasn't thinking about the seed. She was thinking about his lips on her ear, and she did her best to drag her thoughts away and focus on the magic.

"You're distracting me too much," she complained.

"Life is distracting. You need to be able to grab your magic whenever you need it."

Something tickled across her hand, and Asta opened her eyes to watch the dark green shadows of Søren's magic curl around it. "You see? Even my magic wants to play with you."

Asta touched the shadows like she had in the gardens, and instead of getting a seed to grow, she focused the shadows on the magic inside of her, having them grip the magic and bring it out. Heat rippled through her body as Søren's magic seeped into her wrist.

"What are you doing, Asta?" Søren asked.

She didn't answer, only encouraged the building heat inside of her to find its way to the hooks of Søren's power. The dark green shadows pulled and tugged, and then golden ribbons of light rose out of her hand. In awe, they watched as the gold light wrapped itself around the green smoke, and suddenly, Asta was bombarded with emotions that weren't her own. Surprise, fear, joy, and…love? Asta looked up at him wide-eyed. Søren's smile was infectious.

"Look at what you are doing, *drékisma*," he said. "Why are you frowning?"

"Do you love me?" she blurted out, too surprised to have any tact.

Whatever Søren was going to say in reply was drowned out by piercing sirens echoing through the mountain fortress.

Tirith burst into the room, a sword in his hand. "Dark elves just arrived at our gates. They are flying dragon banners."

25

ARAMIS AND SØREN STOOD outside of the main doors into Svetilo, wearing their official Daudi Dómr armor of black-and-silver leather. A sigil of a tree was impressed into their chest pieces to show their rank. Aramis hadn't worn his in centuries and was surprised it still fit as well as it did.

"It's a smaller group than I expected," Søren said. His green eyes narrowed as he surveyed the crimson tent that had been constructed outside of the city's ward stones.

"I'd say it's an ambassador and maybe a few bodyguards," replied Aramis. He looked sideways at his brother and hoped he didn't look as pissed off as Søren did. It had taken a lot of cajoling on Aramis's behalf to convince Tyra to stay inside the fortress. In the end, it had taken only one look at Asta's pale face for Tyra to swear not to leave Asta's side.

"What do you think tipped the dark elves off to our location?" asked Aramis.

"They must've sensed Asta's magic somehow, or they could see where she was as soon as the shields were removed. They have the power to open gates to Midgard, so they must have a strong magic user with them who could track her." Søren made a frustrated sound at the back of his throat. "I shouldn't have pushed Asta to release her magic. As if she doesn't have enough to deal with, now she has these fucking assholes frightening her."

"Easy, brother. They are her family," Aramis said, trying to soothe.

"If they are as bad as Tyra says, I'm not letting them anywhere near Asta."

Aramis turned back to the crimson-and-gold banners that had been hammered deep into the snow. "I doubt we are going to have a say in the matter."

"Stop pretending that this isn't bothering you. Are you going to just let them take Tyra to be thrown back onto a battlefield or left in a hole?" demanded Søren.

Aramis ground his jaw together. "Tyra can protect herself, and she won't let them hurt Asta. The Drekiónds aren't going to leave without seeing Asta, so pull yourself together and let's go see what they are doing here."

Søren glared at him but managed to remove the worry from his countenance, his face settling into the cold warrior he was known as. "Fine. But they aren't stepping a foot into Svetilo until Asta says it's okay."

"Agreed. Just be quiet and let me do the talking." Aramis squared his shoulders and headed for the camp.

They waited at the ward stones until the guards outside of the crimson tent parted the curtains, and a queen appeared. She looked so much like Asta that Søren shifted uncomfortably beside him. She was dressed in black with a crimson cloak draped around her shoulders. Her deep red hair was pinned up in intricate braids that looped around the golden crown on her head. When she drew nearer, Aramis could see that the points of the crown were shaped like dragon fangs to match the necklace around her slender throat. In comparison, the king who stepped out behind her seemed less extravagant. Though tall like all Álfr, he looked less imperious and more concerned than his wife.

Aramis and Søren bowed respectfully but were careful to keep their eyes on the guards flanking the pair.

"The Ljósálfar of Svetilo and Midgard bid you good greetings, strangers," Aramis said formally. The queen lowered herself ever so slightly in reply as the king bowed.

"It has been two thousand years since our clan has had dealings with the Ljósálfar. I hope you will forgive us for not approaching you in the traditional manner, but our business is pressing," the king replied. "I am Steinar, and this is Siv of the Drekiónd clan of Svartálfaheim, my queen. We have reason to believe that you are holding one of our people captive."

"We are of Midgard and have played no part in the wars that have ravaged both of our peoples. We wouldn't hold anyone, light or dark elf, against their will," said Aramis.

"Enough. Where is my daughter? My Seiðr has sensed her power coming from this location. I want her returned to me at once," Siv demanded. Steinar placed a steadying hand on his wife's arm.

"You must excuse Siv. We have traveled many worlds seeking our lost daughter, Tove. We have been searching for her for centuries. Is she with you? Please, we don't mean any harm to you, Dauði Dómr, or the Ljósálfar," said Steinar.

Aramis shared a look with Søren, and he nodded ever so slightly. "We would like to invite you—only you—into Svetilo to discuss this matter further. We offer you protection and hospitality as a sign of good faith," Aramis said before looking at their guards. "Your men will be taken care of but understand that we are not so trusting of the Dökkálfar whose wars drove us from our homeland."

"We had nothing to do with Álfheim," Siv said indignantly.

"All the same, only you and the king may enter," Aramis replied.

"We accept your terms," Steinar answered before his wife could say anything else.

As they stepped through the wards, Tyra's magic crackled and Siv hissed. "So she survived after all. I had wondered," she muttered. Aramis tried to keep his face neutral, but there was something in Siv's tone that made the space between his shoulder blades itch.

Inside the citadel, Aramis led them to a comfortable meeting room usually used by Ruthann and Tirith. They had arranged for hot, spiced wine and other refreshments to be set out for them.

"Are we to meet with you alone, or is there a higher authority we should be talking with?" Siv asked as she accepted a goblet of wine.

"We *are* the authority," Søren replied, refusing to sit or remove his weapons.

"You must understand this is a strange situation we find ourselves in. We were unprepared for a royal visit," Aramis said.

Steinar nodded and sat down. "Especially a visit from Dökkálfar."

"Is that so? Seems to me you've already got Dökkálfar visitors. Where is Tyra?" Siv asked. When Aramis didn't reply, she made a frustrated noise at the back of her throat. "I know she's here. She's been playing with your wards. I'd know the signature of the *Draeimi* anywhere. I thought she was dead."

"Sorry to disappoint," said a cold voice from the other side of the room. Tyra appeared in a curling, purple mist. Even without armor she looked like a warrior in tight leather pants and boots with a dark purple tunic cut in the fashion of the Ljósálfar. Her hair was braided back, and she looked fierce and beautiful, forcing Aramis to look away from her before he could look at nothing else.

"Tyra, it's good to see you alive. Is she here?" Steinar asked as he hurried to her. He placed a closed fist over his chest, adding something softly in elvish that Aramis couldn't catch.

"Tove died before I could find her," Tyra said bluntly.

"You were her bodyguard, sworn to never leave her side!" Siv was on her feet, raging toward Tyra. Steinar had sunk to a chair, his face pale.

"Is that where you think I've been all this time? With Tove?" Tyra asked. The queen halted at the edge in her tone.

"We knew you had run away together," Siv said.

"Is that what your good neighbor Bláinn told you?" Tyra sat down on the arm of Aramis's chair, a sign of solidarity Siv didn't fail to notice. Her golden eyes narrowed.

"That's what we were told. That Tove had run away from her duties, and you had helped her. Do you have any idea how tenuous our alliance with Bláinn has been since then? If it weren't for Daimar's work as ambassador, Bláinn would've slaughtered us all," Siv said. Tyra's laugh was cruel and bitter, so unlike any sound Aramis had ever heard her make.

"Tell them, Tyra. They have obviously been lied to," said Søren from his place beside the door. Aramis wanted to be able to take her hand, to give her some sign that she wasn't alone as she retold the horror she and Tove had endured—how she had helped Tove escape and the price she'd paid for it. She didn't stop there. She told them of Daimar's raids with Bláinn and what they had done in Ljósálfar lands.

By the end Siv was shaking with either fury or grief, Aramis couldn't tell. Steinar was gray as he accepted more wine.

"If Tove is dead, then whose magic did Vigdis feel? That's not the kind of mistake she'd make," Steinar asked Tyra, his black eyes pleading. Tyra was quiet for so long Aramis wondered if she would tell them at all. Finally, she let out a defeated sigh.

"Tove's daughter is here."

"Is she Bláinn's?" Siv demanded.

"Of course not. Tove wasn't stupid enough to get pregnant with that prick," Tyra said viciously.

"She remarried? Please tell me it wasn't to one of these Ljósálfar," Siv said, rubbing her temple. Aramis tensed, but Tyra's hand rested against his shoulder.

"They are so pretty you could hardly blame her," Tyra said with a malicious smile. "She married a human."

"Tove *mated* with a human?" Siv spat.

"I told you she was a snob," whispered Tyra as Siv paced and fumed.

"Where is the child? Despite her tainted blood, she is a Drekiónd and belongs with the family," Siv said.

"She isn't one of your trinkets. She doesn't belong to anyone," Søren said with chilling calm. Siv raised a perfect red eyebrow at him.

"You are in no position to tell us what to do with our grandchild. I could have *Draeimi* flay you for such arrogance," Siv said.

"Not here you can't, Queen," Søren said. "Your granddaughter and Tyra are under our protection. Your crown doesn't mean a goddamn thing on Midgard and certainly not amongst the Ljósálfar. Especially as your family owes my brother and me a blood debt."

"Søren lacks tact but speaks the truth of the situation," said Aramis. "Tyra is a free woman. She may have once been sworn to serve you, but that oath was broken when you allowed her to rot in the dwarves' pit. No, don't try to protest that you thought she was dead. I doubt you even bothered to check. You have a powerful Seiðr who could have located her and seen that she was on Svartálfaheim, but you didn't seem to think she was worth looking for. You certainly didn't demand justice for her death. She owes you and your people *nothing*."

Siv leaned back in her chair, giving Aramis a long, appraising look. "So *Draeimi* has finally found herself a champion. Do you even *know* what she is, boy?"

"You mean apart from stunningly attractive?" countered Aramis, trying to stop the rage bubbling up through him.

Siv's smile turned vicious. "She's bathed in the blood of thousands. I know her true and terrible nature, and I made sure she was put to good use when she was left on my doorstep. I've seen the strongest of Dökkálfar males balk in her very presence. You're a sparkling little Ljósálfar, and what? You think you have it in you to bed my monster?"

A killing calm settled over Aramis, and Søren took a step forward to place a hand on his shoulder. Aramis's twin and battle partner had felt the change even if the horrible woman in front of them hadn't.

"Call Tyra a monster one more time, and I will make sure you never see your granddaughter or step a foot inside this fortress again," said Aramis through his teeth. Steinar silenced Siv with a glare before she could say anything else.

"Please forgive my wife. Understand that this news you have told us has been a blow, and our manners are not what they usually are," Steinar said calmly. "Our granddaughter doesn't know us or understand her heritage. It is natural that trust must be built between us before any future decisions are made. We only wish to see her, to understand what she has been through, and…and to process all of this. Don't keep her from us."

It was the tone of genuine feeling in the final sentence that pacified Aramis. Tyra was sitting in the same ramrod straight position, silent as a soldier. He hated that. He wanted her to tell them to go fuck themselves, to be that cocky loudmouth he knew. She was just sitting there, taking the abuse.

"We aren't keeping her from you. She is deciding if she wants anything to do with you or if you are just going to give her to Bláinn like you did Tove," said Søren.

"I'd like to see them try." Tyra's words were barely a whisper, but Steinar and Siv both flinched.

"My sons can deal with Bláinn for the time being, and once this matter on Midgard is resolved, I'll address these accusations you've made against Daimar," Steinar promised.

The door behind them opened, and Asta walked slowly into the room. Aramis had to admire her calm expression, knowing how anxious she was. She was dressed very neatly but in human clothes, despite their offer to provide her with something with an Álfr flair. She came to stand behind Aramis's chair with Søren. Steinar stood, his eyes darting over her features.

"Hello, granddaughter," Steinar said, his voice cracking before he gave her a low bow.

"By the gods, you look like your mother." Siv sighed. "The Drekiónd magic is strong in you, little one."

"Despite my tainted blood?" Asta said scathingly.

Score one to Asta, Aramis thought, hiding his smile.

"Siv is in shock. She didn't mean it. What's your name?" Steinar asked.

"Asta." She held his gaze.

"Asta… It means love, did you know? Tove must've loved you very much to keep you hidden for so long." Steinar's expression softened.

"Jeez, I wonder why she felt the need to do that," Asta replied.

"You even sound like Tove," grumbled Siv.

"Great, isn't it?" Tyra smiled widely.

"You have nothing to fear from us, Asta. I swear it. With the permission of the Ljósálfar, I would like the opportunity to stay, nearby if you don't trust us within the city, to discuss all of this further. Please," Steinar asked.

"It is Asta's decision," Aramis said simply.

Asta gave her grandparents a long, loaded look before giving a nod. "Okay, but if she talks about my blood being tainted again, I get to kick them out."

"I would be happy to help you," said Søren, and he and Tyra shared a feral grin.

After a long consultation with Tirith, the small group of Dökkálfar were housed in a set of chambers usually set aside for visiting dignitaries. Tyra had taken one look at Vigdis, the Seiðr, and had insisted that the rooms be carefully warded to alert herself, Aramis, and Søren of magic use.

"Siv is a bitch but is open about it. Vigdis is the one not to trust," warned Tyra as the four of them walked back to their own apartments.

"At least my grandfather seems decent," Asta said, looping her hand around Søren's. Aramis caught his brother's eye and grinned. Despite the stress of the Drekiónds' arrival and the complications that came with it, Aramis was happy to see the affection between Asta and Søren.

"Steinar has always been the saner one. Siv is the Drekiónd heir. Technically she has more authority, but he can calm her when no one else can. The poor bastard really does love her." Tyra shook her head.

"Do you think they are going to force me to go back with them?" asked Asta.

"They can try all they like. You aren't going anywhere you don't want to," Søren promised.

"They might be able to help with your magic," Aramis added.

"Oh, you mean my Drekiónd magic that is 'strong despite my tainted blood,'" Asta said, mimicking Siv's voice and making Tyra snigger despite the worry that emanated off her.

"I suppose we'll just have to see what tomorrow brings," Søren replied.

26

"THAT WENT BETTER THAN I expected," Tyra said, flopping down face-first onto Aramis's couch. "I managed to control my urge to kill them at least."

"I'm almost too afraid to ask if they are always like that."

"Unfortunately, they are. Asta seemed okay, didn't she? She would've stayed here with me if she was worried, right?"

Aramis placed a glass of vodka on the coffee table beside her, and she rolled over to take a sip.

"Søren will keep an eye on her. He makes her feel safe, and he'll keep her that way. Her magic took her to him the last time she was worried."

"Don't remind me," Tyra muttered, taking another mouthful of vodka. "You didn't have to defend me tonight either."

"Yes, I did," he said softly.

"Siv is just like that. She likes to push people's buttons. I'm no longer offended by what she says about me."

"I won't let anyone talk to you like that. I don't care who they are," said Aramis, fighting to keep the overprotective growl out of his voice. He'd always been able to control his temper, even when all of the Ljósálfar had blamed him for Yanka's betrayal and when he'd discovered he'd unknowingly been working for Baba Yaga for centuries. The moment Siv had called Tyra a monster, he'd wanted to cut the tongue out of her head.

Tyra rolled onto her side. "Do you think Vigdis knew I was enslaved? I mean, she's hated me from the moment I was born, but I didn't think she'd be that malicious."

"I don't know. If she could sense Asta as soon as she used her magic, I'm sure she could've found you if she'd looked. It would take a special kind of nasty to willingly leave someone that way."

"That's Vigdis. She's always done everything to protect the Drekiónds, and I'm their best weapon. *Was*. Gods, I don't know what I am anymore." Tyra finished her drink, and Aramis passed her his full glass. "Thanks, Starlight. All I know is I'm going to protect Asta and do everything I can to make sure I don't end up in the ground again." Her eyes flickered to the stone walls around her. It was but a second, but Aramis caught the flash of panic before she covered it.

"I've had something made for you." He got to his feet and offered her his hand. "I was waiting for a better moment than this, but after that woman talked to you so horribly today, I want to remind you that you don't have to obey anyone anymore. You are *free*."

Tyra took his hand, suspicion in the smirk on her red lips. "Okay, but I'm taking the vodka with me."

"Please do." Aramis stopped by the heavy wooden door carved with moons. "After you, Dökkálfar."

"You know I've already seen your platform."

"Don't make me carry you."

Tyra wriggled past him, reaching for the door. "Tempting, but I want my surprise."

Aramis followed her, hoping she wouldn't push him back down the curving stone staircase once she reached the top. With Tyra, he could never guess how she would react.

Aramis had asked the architects to start work on it the day after he had half-frozen while watching the stars with her. He'd had them work when Tyra was out training or with Asta. There hadn't been much time, but they had used magic to complete it quickly. Aramis nearly crashed into Tyra when she stopped on the top step.

"You made this...for me?" Her voice was small and strained.

"Yes." Aramis wished she'd turn around so he could see the look on her face and gauge her reaction. She walked slowly across the stone floor to the wall of glass that now encased the astronomer's ledge and looked out over the snow-covered mountains at the midnight sky.

The architects had enjoyed the challenge of turning the space into a bedroom and had done excellent work expanding the platform deeper into the stone of the mountain to create a bathroom and a wardrobe too. A large wooden bed and a dresser carved with stars took up most of the room, and heavy purple curtains hung on the sides of the glass wall for when she wanted privacy.

"I can't believe you did this," Tyra said, hugging herself.

"Too much?"

"Too *kind*."

"You deserve to be comfortable and have your own room. I want you in the safety of the mountain, and this was the best compromise I could think of."

Tyra let out a sigh of frustration. "You don't get it."

"Then explain it to me."

"You want the truth? After everything I've done, I deserved that dwarf pit. Why do you think I didn't try harder to escape? I only left when I found out what they were taking to Midgard—weapons that could hurt Tove. I'm never going to be good…at any of this being a lover—or whatever it is we are—stuff. You want to talk about who deserves what? You deserve someone better than I can ever be, but you still keep coming, you stubborn bastard."

"Fuck you," Aramis said, and Tyra's eyes flashed. He rarely swore, especially not at her, but he was done not getting through to her.

"What did you say?"

Aramis took a step toward her, forcing her to back up. The frustration, want, and anger that had been bubbling for weeks suddenly poured out of him.

"You heard me. You drive me insane. You know that? And that says *a lot* after I had to deal with looking after an untrained shamanitsa in the middle of a war. Even Anya wasn't as big of a pain in the ass as you. You don't get to sulk because you're some horrible fucking elf who was forced to kill for your masters. You think I haven't taken orders? Killed others because I was told to even when I didn't think they deserved it? I'm a Dauði Dómr, and I was an Enforcer for the Illumination for *centuries*. I told you when we first met, I'm *no* innocent. The Ljósálfar and my own brother turned their backs on me, and it's only in the past two years that they've allowed me to live amongst my own goddamn people! You don't get the monopoly on being a monster. You don't get to tell me what I deserve. I *know* what I deserve, and it's *you*."

Aramis glared down at her, not moving an inch as Tyra's killing magic raced out of her and sliced through his breastplate and shoulder guards. Scraps of armor and cloth fell off him onto the thick rug at his feet, but his skin remained whole.

Gods, the control she had over that immense power made him weak with reverence. He remained upright and glared, unwilling to give her any room to back out.

"Is that all you got, *Draeimi*?"

The reaction her body had every time she saw that pearly Ljósálfar skin never ceased to surprise Tyra. She wanted to rant at him for all of the emotions he made her feel, instead she just stared like an idiot. Muscles she didn't know she had clenched up in excitement the longer she let her gaze travel up his tattooed torso to the sharp angles of his face. His deep blue eyes hadn't looked away from her, and the challenge in them made her want to kick his ass and pull on the silvery strands of his perfectly braided hair. He watched her lick her bottom lip, and the air between them changed, the simple action making everything hum, hot and taut. *Fuck this.*

Aramis caught her when she sprang at him, her legs locking tightly around his waist as he gripped her hips and kissed her hard. Tyra's hands went around his shoulders, pulling the tie from his braid free and loosening the strands so she could bury her hands roughly into it.

Aramis carried her over and pinned her down on the bed, his vicious mouth never leaving hers. Tyra jolted in surprise when he took hold of her shirt and tore it in half.

"Now who is impatient?" she said as he did the same thing to the front of her bra. She didn't have time to react before he bent his head and swept a hot tongue along the curve of her breast.

"No magical restraints to stop me this time," he said against her skin.

"Not yet anyway." Tyra shuddered as he bit down hard, and she arched her back. "Okay, I promise. No restraints. But if you do that again, I might not let you walk away after only a taste this time."

"Believe me, *Draeimi*, I'm going to taste all of you before I'm through tonight." She didn't have time to process that thought as his magic curled down her thighs and her pants vanished. *Freya, save me*, she prayed as Aramis's hand gripped her thigh, pinning her to the bed as his teeth and tongue found her other breast. A sound came out of her she didn't recognize. It was vulnerable and hungry with a desire she hadn't known she was capable of.

Aramis's magic flared again, and silver shackles fastened her wrists to the headboard before she could blink.

"What the fuck! Are you serious?" she complained, giving the shackles a shake.

"At least I haven't gagged you…yet. Not so fun when you're on the receiving end, is it?" he said, his expression wicked. Tyra opened her mouth to swear at him when his hand brushed down between her legs, and she shivered.

Aramis made a satisfied sound when he found her already wet. Then those beautiful lips of his lowered over her, and Tyra let out a groan. She pulled against her restraints as his fingers and mouth worked her. Her thighs were trembling like she was some kind of ridiculous virgin all because the most savagely beautiful male she'd ever seen was between them.

Sensation and emotion flooded her until she was begging him to stop, but he kept going until an orgasm rocked her so hard she broke the chains that held her.

"I knew you could get out of them if you put your mind to it," Aramis said, pushing up on his strong arms to loom over her panting body.

Tyra couldn't form words as her magic raced out of her, turning the pants he was still wearing into confetti.

"Be careful where you wield that power," he warned.

"Don't boss me around," she said breathlessly. Her body ached with the aftershocks of her orgasm.

Aramis reached to brush off the ruined fabric, and she used the break in his concentration to flip him onto his back.

"Gods, I want you. You're just perfection," he said as his large hand ran across the scars on her stomach and gripped the curve of her hip. His smug smile vanished, and he swore as she lowered herself over the dick that was as perfect as the rest of him.

Tyra stilled, letting her body adjust as he filled her. She wanted to savor the moment, but after weeks of torment, her body was screaming for more.

Tyra lost herself in the sensation, letting her instincts take over as she rode him. It wasn't gentle or sweet; it was rough, desperate need, and pleasure so deep it brushed the edges of pain. Tyra cried out as she came again.

Aramis sat up and wrapped his arms around her, adjusting their position so he was even deeper. He didn't give her a moment of reprieve as he lowered her down onto her back and set the pace once more. Tyra wanted to tell him she had never trusted a male to be on top of her—a position that made her vulnerable—but he wasn't just any male. She trusted him, this shining one who stood up to the fucking queen for her and made her feel like she didn't deserve the darkness, like she trusted herself.

"Aramis," she whimpered against his collarbone, and he shifted so he could kiss her. She wrapped her legs tightly around his waist, her hands gripping his biceps as he somehow went deeper.

It was like being fucked by starlight, and she knew she'd never get enough of him. Maybe the Norns didn't hate her as much as she thought.

An hour later they were snoozing together. Aramis was half-draped over her, his head resting on the curve of Tyra's shoulder with her hands stroking his hair.

"I think that's the first time you have called me by my actual name," he said, his amusement a rumble in his chest that made her laugh.

"Don't get used to it. You are going to have to earn it every time."

Aramis turned his head and pressed his lips against her shoulder. "I'd be happy to. I take it this means you like the bedroom?"

Tyra used her magic to lower the lights, so the night sky in front of them blazed brighter. "I love it. I hope you do too, because I'm not moving or letting you sleep anywhere but between my thighs."

Aramis propped himself up on an elbow and brushed the tangle of hair back from her face. "I think we both know that sleep will be the last thing on my mind if I'm between your thighs."

Tyra laughed and leaned up to kiss him. "A girl can only hope, Starlight."

27

ASTA PULLED AT THE sleeve of her black cardigan for the fourth time in ten minutes. It was silly to be nervous about a meeting she had organized, but her feelings toward the Drekiónds were mixed to say the least. The tingling magic under her skin was a reminder that she wasn't fully human and that the Drekiónds were her best chance at getting answers to all of the questions she had.

Asta had sent a message to Steinar that morning to ask if he would like to go for a walk about the citadel with her, because despite her nerves and annoyance at Siv's attitude, the king had seemed like he'd be okay to talk to about Tove. She was reaching for her sleeve again when long, calloused fingers wrapped around hers.

"You are going to start making me nervous if you don't cut it out," Søren said.

"Sorry. Distract me before I chicken out of this," asked Asta. Quick as a blink, Søren's knife flashed in his hands, and the top buttons of her cardigan disappeared. For a moment Asta was back in the taxi in Oslo all those weeks ago, so hot for her new research partner she thought she was going to combust. Her pulse was in her throat as a naughty grin appeared on his face.

"I'm going to make you sew that back on later," Asta managed to say, her mouth dry. The knife flashed again, and the bottom button pinged to the floor.

"Hmm, I like this game," Søren said.

"If you keep it up, I won't have any cardigan left at all," she complained, and his green eyes lit up in delight. "Stop it. I'm meant to be seeing my grandfather! I don't need to be thinking about…all that."

"What is 'all that,' *drékisma*?" His voice dropped to a purr that made the hair on the back of her neck rise. He looped the edge of his dagger through the eye of the next button and pulled gently, so she was forced to take a step toward him or lose another one. "Are you distracted yet?"

Asta's eyes fluttered closed as the tip of his tongue touched her top lip. She forgot about her meeting, her new magic, and her own name as she rose up on her tiptoes to kiss him.

"We had better leave before I get any more ideas," Søren said when they pulled apart.

"Right. Grandfather. Dark elves. Magic." Asta was regretting setting up her meeting so early in the day. "What kind of ideas?"

"Move," Søren ordered. He went to take her hand and paused.

"What's wrong?"

"Your grandfather might not…approve." The borderline arrogance that was Søren's trademark was nowhere to be seen. Instead, he looked unsure and worried. Asta hated it.

"I don't need his approval," she snapped, grabbing his hand tightly. "Let's go."

Søren chuckled as she all but dragged him to the door. "That's my dark elf."

Asta filed *that* particularly possessive comment with the confusing things she had felt from him the day before. They joined a growing list along with her own twisted-up emotions toward him.

Søren was in a special emotional category all his own. The "Make Asta Crazy" category to be precise. Crazy in all the ways she understood the definition. He definitely knew how to make her crazy mad and crazy irritated, but somehow, he managed to make her crazy horny too. Usually all at the same time.

Asta also knew that despite the stories about him, how the other Álfr acted around him and Aramis, and what she had witnessed the night she was attacked by dark elves, Søren would never hurt her. She felt safe and secure with him in a way she had only felt once before, and that frightened her most of all. The only other person she'd felt safe with was Tove, and she had died. Asta couldn't handle the thought of losing anyone else.

Tove had made a point of drumming into her that she would never be able to trust anyone, that she would always be looking over her shoulder, that she wouldn't ever be able to belong anywhere. As she walked through the mountain city, she greeted a few of the librarians and healers she was starting to get to know. With Søren's steady presence by her side and Tyra close at hand, it was starting to feel like she did belong somewhere. The Drekiónds seemed to think her place was with them, but Asta wasn't going to be convinced easily.

"I don't like that frown," Søren said as they neared the apartments where the dark elves had been housed.

"Don't worry. It's a thinking frown, not an upset frown."

"If you don't want to do this, I'm not going to make you." He drew her to the side of the walkway so other Álfr could pass them.

"I'm a little nervous, that's all. I'm sure I'll get over it." Søren lifted her chin.

"You sure? Because my current inclination is to put you over my shoulder and take you somewhere to hide out until they go away and stop bothering us."

Asta rolled her eyes at him. "You're pretty dramatic for a caveman, aren't you?"

"You know I'll protect you from them if I need to."

"Yeah, but right now you don't need to." Asta grinned up at him. "Let's go, fierce protector. If you make me late, I'll kick your ass."

Søren flicked her nose. "You wish, pip-squeak."

"Oh, you're going to pay for that later," she promised, turning on her heel and striding off.

"Storm away all you want. It gives me a great view," Søren said behind her.

Steinar was already waiting outside of the chambers with two dark elf guards. He smiled happily when he saw Asta, and the knot of unease inside of her loosened its grip.

"Good morning, granddaughter. I was happy to receive your message this morning," Steinar greeted with an acknowledging nod at Søren who had stayed a few meters away to give them privacy.

"I wanted to have a chance to talk to you alone, without Siv. She doesn't seem to like me very much," Asta said awkwardly.

"Siv is complicated, like all women. It might not have seemed it yesterday, but she took the news of Tove's death very poorly. She had hoped we might finally find her and reconcile with her, and now that opportunity is gone," explained Steinar, his expression grim.

"I understand. Tyra once told me you like books. Is that true?" Asta didn't want to talk about Siv and Tove, not yet anyway. She needed common ground and fast.

Steinar's smile was surprised and indulgent. "I do like books, little one. I taught your mother how to read before she was four years old. Why do you ask?"

"Because I want to show you something. Bring your guards if you like," she said, but Steinar shook his head.

"They can stay and watch Siv. I don't believe I have anything to fear here, not even from your fierce Dauđi Dómr."

"He's *a* Dauđi Dómr, not *my* Dauđi Dómr." Asta felt her face turn red.

"If you say so." Steinar's black eyes sparkled with amusement. "Lead on, little one. I'm eager to see more of this incredible fortress."

Søren tried his best to keep a respectful distance between himself and the pair of Drekiónds in front of him. Asta had taken Steinar to the library, and they were bonding over old books and the Ljósálfar's illumination techniques. Steinar had been surprised to learn they had histories of peaceful times between the light and dark elves and was discussing them enthusiastically with Asta.

Søren was still close enough that if Steinar looked at Asta the wrong way, he'd be able to step in and kick that Dökkálfar's ass all the way back to Svartálfaheim. He bit the inside of his cheek as he fought the urge to barge his way into their conversation and hover over her.

Get it together. If he'd thought his overwhelming urge to protect his tiny librarian had been strong before, it was nothing compared to what he'd felt when he saw those ominous dragon banners outside Svetilo.

Søren hadn't been joking when he'd told Asta he wanted to toss her over his shoulder and run away with her. It would be so easy to just take her through a gate, far away where they would never be found. The urge to do it was growing stronger by the minute, which was ridiculous and unreasonable considering Asta and Steinar seemed to be getting along famously. That was probably why.

Gods, am I jealous? He could imagine Aramis's teasing now. Søren would never live it down if Aramis knew how flustered he was getting over Asta. His brother and Tyra had been suspiciously absent that morning, and when Søren finally saw them enter the library, he knew why.

Aramis and Tyra weren't touching, though they walked comfortably near each other, and Aramis was *glowing*. It was as if his natural Ljósálfar shimmer had been turned up high and from Tyra's wide, satisfied smirk Søren could guess why.

"Nice of you to finally join us," Søren said. Tyra came up and leaned an arm against his shoulder.

"Chill out. I knew you'd be watching her like the creepy stalker you are," she said as she eyed Asta and Steinar, whose heads were bent over a manuscript. "How long have they been like that?"

"Nearly an hour. It seems to be going well," Søren replied.

"I always said Steinar was okay. Siv is the difficult one. I knew they'd get along. This is a good thing, so stop frowning like someone pissed in your coffee."

"*Is* it a good thing? Are you not worried that he's going to try to convince her to go back with them? Where is that going to leave us?"

"You mean, where is that going to leave *you*?" Tyra flicked his ear. "Don't be daft. Of course they are going to try to convince Asta to go with them. Do you really think she'd be dumb enough to leave? You don't need to panic like a baby who's worried his favorite toy is going to be taken away. Asta can handle Steinar." Tyra straightened and headed over to talk to them, leaving Søren even more agitated.

"She's right, you know. Asta knows what Siv did to her mother. She's not going to be foolish enough to believe anything they say," said Aramis, his eyes watching Tyra talk animatedly with Steinar.

"You need to dim that glow before you burn my retinas out," Søren snapped. Aramis's smile was so delighted Søren was reminded of when they were boys and had received their first real knives. He hadn't seen that smile on Aramis since before Yanka had destroyed both of their lives.

Søren shook his head. "Pathetic."

"I didn't even notice," Aramis said, and a glamour settled over him, dimming the glow.

"Better, and a lot less obvious that you finally got laid."

"Jealousy is a curse." They stood together, watching the two dark elf females who had turned their lives so thoroughly upside down.

"Aramis, we can't let them leave." Søren sounded pathetic, and he knew it but didn't care.

"Of course we can't," said Aramis, making Søren look at him sharply. "What? You think I'm dumb enough to let Tyra go when I have only just found her? Give me some credit."

"Wow, it must've been good sex to get you this smitten."

"I was smitten before the sex, which was incredible if you want to know."

"I didn't want to know."

Aramis ignored him as he stared at the three dark elves. "We can't stop them from trying to get to know each other. They are family. They deserve to connect and see if they can get along. What we need to do is delay the Drekiónds' return to Svartálfaheim and give Asta a chance to avoid getting bulldozed by any glittering promises they make."

Søren could see the wheels in his brother's overcomplicated head turning, a plan already coming together. "What did you have in mind?"

Aramis's strange mischievous smile was back. "Diplomacy."

Søren opened his mouth to tell him he was a moron and then stopped. "It has been a *very* long time since dark elves have been welcome in a Ljósálfar court. It would be a shame to waste such an opportunity to build a bridge of understanding between our two great races."

"It would be. This is bigger than just us, brother. It affects all the Ljósálfar here on Midgard. This is a historical moment. We really need to push this up the chain of command."

The brothers shared identical, diabolical grins and said in unison, "Ruthann."

Up until two years ago, Søren would've done anything for Ruthann. As leader of the Midgardian Ljósálfar, Ruthann had ensured their anonymity and their protection since they arrived, but after Ruthann had dismissed Søren's warnings and Svetilo had nearly been destroyed, Søren had walked away from his service forever. It had only been in the past year that Aramis had gotten the two of them talking again to improve relations between Svetilo and their Alaskan Court. Despite that, Søren still sat silently for most of the video call he and Aramis had with Ruthann.

"I don't understand why I am only hearing about this now," Ruthann said, his tone unmistakably irritated through the speakers of Aramis's laptop.

"It didn't concern you until now," replied Søren.

"You found Dökkálfar here in Midgard! How does that not concern me? And now you tell me this might bring a vengeful warlord here too?" demanded Ruthann.

"They were innocent females who needed our help and protection, Ruthann. They had a book from Svetilo. We went looking for it, not them," Aramis said before Søren did something stupid like shut the laptop. "We refuse to hold on to past wars here. They haven't started any trouble—"

"Much trouble," whispered Søren too low for Ruthann to hear.

"They have been accepted by the Álfr here, and Tirith is excited to have an opportunity to not only speak with the Dökkálfar but also have a chance to harken back to older times when the races lived harmoniously together," Aramis added. "The Drekiónds are a powerful noble family with influence. If there are still wars raging between Álfheim and Svartálfaheim, this could be a way to bring peace and understanding. Don't you want to be a part of that?"

"Of course I do, and yes, I will come. The gods know you two aren't diplomats or up to such a task as polite conversation with royalty. You say they have a Seiðr with them?" asked Ruthann.

"Yes, her name is Vigdis. She's not to be trusted at this stage. We haven't been formally introduced yet—the crossing between the worlds drained her—but from what Tyra has said, Vigdis is extremely powerful. We could use someone with your abilities here in case things turn sour," answered Søren.

Aramis could see the muscle in Søren's cheek twitch at being forced to give Ruthann the compliment. It was one more thing Søren would happily do to keep his hold on Asta a little while longer. Aramis knew that feeling. His own emotions were a burning mess when it came to Tyra.

"I'll come tonight. Can I trust you to put a dinner together so we can at least welcome them properly? Something in the Winter Garden perhaps would be appropriate?" asked Ruthann imperiously.

"I will see that it's done," Aramis said before Søren could argue.

"Good. And boys? Do try to behave until then. As you said, it's a rare opportunity."

The line went dead, and Søren let out a groan. "A formal dinner? Is he serious? There are bigger things to worry about."

"Think of it as an opportunity to see Asta in a pretty dress," said Aramis. His brother's face went from annoyance to curiosity in a blink.

"Dinner it is."

"Brother, I know it's not my place to push, but have you told Asta how you feel?" Aramis tried to be tactful, but Søren's face shut like a book.

"I don't know if now is the best time."

"Søren, it could be the *only* time. Be open with her. If she feels the same, she's not going to want to leave you anytime soon. At least not until she gets to know you better and realizes how annoying you are."

"Dick. Why are you so concerned about my love life when you have your own raging hell-beast to contend with?" Søren demanded.

"I can't compete with Asta for Tyra's loyalty. Tyra won't let her go off with the Drekiónds alone, and I can't ask her to. It's up to you, brother. In the meantime, I'm going to enjoy being with her for as long as I can," Aramis said, getting to his feet. "We are going to have a training session. Do you want to join us?"

"I'd rather not watch you get all lusty-eyed as soon as Tyra brings out that sword that's bigger than Asta."

"You should see her wield it—the power she uses. She's something else."

"Something other than a dark elf with an attitude problem?"

"Yes. I'm not sure who her father is, and she doesn't know either, but something Siv said about finding her and putting her to use is irritating me. Siv knows who Tyra's father is and has never told her. Why?"

"Does it matter what she is?"

"Not to me, but it could explain why Vigdis had motive to leave her underground. Tyra said Vigdis has always hated her, and she never knew why."

Søren let out a tired sigh. "One mystery at a time, Aramis. Let's worry about getting through this dinner first."

"You're right. I'll go train, and you can get started on the preparations."

"What? Why me?"

"Because of how much Asta would like the Winter Garden and how you're a control freak who would like everything to go perfectly for her."

"I hate you so much," Søren grumbled.

28

ASTA DIDN'T KNOW WHAT to think when an Álfr delivered an invitation to a formal dinner in the Winter Garden and a dress so beautiful she was almost too afraid to touch it.

"I smell a diplomatic mission," said Tyra when she heard about it. "Those hot Álfr of ours have been scheming. I can feel it."

"What do you mean?"

"A delegation from the Alaskan Court arrived about an hour ago. Looks like the boys finally caved and told the higher-ups that dark elves were taking advantage of their hospitality." Tyra didn't look remotely worried, but the thought of meeting light elf lords made Asta's stomach drop to her feet.

"As if dealing with the Drekiónds isn't stressful enough."

"That's probably why they did it. You don't know what the court is like. It's all boring meetings and being polite to people you despise. If you are thinking about going back to Svartálfaheim, you'd better get used to it, princess."

"What do you mean go to Svartálfaheim? Why would I do that?" Tyra's shrug was maddeningly unhelpful.

"You get along with Steinar, and I'd even learn to stomach Siv and Vigdis again if it's what you wanted. It's your chance to be with family, but it's up to you."

"You're serious? You actually think I'd consider leaving?" Asta had a horrible thought. "Does Søren think that?"

"Of course he's thinking that. He's being polite and chivalrous and trying to let you make up your own mind about it. If I were in his situation, I'd be a hell of a lot less cool about it."

Asta frowned. "But you *are* in his situation. You would just leave Aramis and go back to Svartálfaheim if I wanted to? What about the relationship you guys have going on?"

"Relationship? What relationship? We've made no promises to each other. We are hanging out and enjoying each other's company. It's not like how you and Søren are." Tyra wore a genuinely confused expression like she had when she'd contemplated the concept of a Bluetooth headset.

"Oh, my sweet cousin, you're so clueless sometimes." Asta sighed.

"Whatever. Put the dress on, listen to what I said, and pay attention tonight when Vigdis and Siv start their bullshit. Svartálfaheim is like that *all* the time, but without the benefit of Søren to look at because there's no way they are going to allow a Ljósálfar in their court, much less date their granddaughter."

When a knock came at her door that evening, Asta expected to find Søren, but instead, there was only a messenger and a very dressed-up Tyra. She wore tight leather pants with laces up the front with a black jacket embroidered with silver stars and cut asymmetrically in a way the Álfr favored. Underneath the jacket was a purple silk shirt that matched her amethyst-and-silver earrings and the elaborate clips holding up her mane of black hair.

"You look amazing. Poor Søren is going to ruin his trousers when he sees you." Tyra whistled, earning a horrified look from the other Álfr.

"Thanks, I guess. You don't think this is too much?" Asta had found few opportunities in her life to really dress up for a formal event. As soon as she'd put on the black-and-gold ball gown, its long transparent sleeves covered in golden dragons, she knew she had to go bold with her makeup and elaborate with her hair.

"You look incredible. If I weren't straight, I'd be hitting on you right now. I don't think *anyone* deserves you, not even me." Tyra gave the messenger a slight shove.

"You look very beautiful, my lady. Shall we go? They will be expecting you," he said, looking out of sorts.

"Okay, let's do this. You better make sure I don't trip with these crazy skirts," Asta said, taking the arm Tyra offered her.

Asta knew she hadn't had enough time to really explore the fairy-tale mountain city she'd found herself in. She knew her way to the library and the springs, but that was really the limit of her navigational knowledge. The messenger led them across walkways, down streets, and through squares they had never visited before. As they walked, Asta noticed the air temperature begin to drop.

"I should have brought something to keep myself warm," Asta said.

"There will be no need, my lady. An enchantment has been put on the garden to keep the guests warm," their guide explained.

"Fancy light elves," Tyra whispered in her ear, and Asta bit back her laughter. Tyra had a weird fetish for the winter and the cold. Once Asta had teased her about being part frost giant, and Tyra had gone on a long rant about how frost giants were not blue nor were they half as attractive as Loki. Asta had been careful not to tease her about frost giants or winter since.

The Winter Garden was a glade of snow-laden trees lit with delicate glass globes etched with impossible patterns. A long table was covered in white linen with white porcelain settings and silver laid out for each guest. The centerpieces were made of ice and white flowers. The snowy ground had been cleared to release the lush green grass underneath it, and music drifted through the trees, played by skilled Álfr hands on instruments Asta couldn't name.

Standing in between two pines and giving instructions was Søren. He hadn't seen her yet, and it gave Asta the chance to admire his sharp and dangerous beauty. He was dressed in a black suit jacket, similar to Tyra's but with slashed sleeves to reveal the dark green fabric of his shirt, and black pants with the knee-high black boots the other Álfr usually wore. In contrast with his Álfr attire, he also wore a modern black tie with a silver pin in the exact shape of the tree tattoo that covered his body. His hair was in elaborate braids, and all Asta could think about was unraveling every single one of them.

"Breathe, honey," Tyra whispered. Asta was about to take an exaggerated inhale to express her annoyance with Tyra when Søren looked up and saw her with his impossibly green eyes. The expression on his face drove whatever breath she had left straight out of her body. As he made for her through the growing crowd of people, she felt the predator in her blood raise its head. It responded to his presence with a possessive whisper—*Mine, mine, mine, mine*—and made something sharpen and growl inside of her. She wanted to drag him off into the trees, sink her teeth into his pearly skin, and make him scream her name.

"I'm going over there because you watching him like he's dinner is making me feel awkward," Tyra said and hurried away before Søren reached them.

Søren bowed before taking Asta's hand and pressing his lips to it. To anyone observing them, it looked like a courtly gesture, but because he was Søren, he flicked the tip of his tongue on the crease of her finger and knuckle, sending a bolt of arousal straight to her lady parts.

"My lady, you are breathtaking," he said, his face a picture of civil politeness. She was going to have him tonight even if it killed her.

"Thank you, Dauði Dómr," she replied, trying to focus on where she was.

"Come, *drékisma*. There is someone I would like you to meet." Søren wrapped her hand over his arm, gently maneuvering her around several Álfr she didn't recognize.

"Asta, may I introduce Ruthann from the Alaskan Court," Søren said as they stopped in front of a tall Álfr who brought phrases like "regal bearing" and "my lord" to her mind. Not knowing the correct Ljósálfar protocol for the moment, Asta shook his hand.

"It's nice to meet you," she said. Ruthann followed up the handshake with a deep bow.

"Princess. It is an honor to finally meet you. Søren and Aramis speak of you highly," replied Ruthann. He reached into his elegant green jacket and pulled out a familiar black wallet with a note sticking out of it. "I believe you sent this to us when Søren misplaced it." He passed it to Søren while Asta wished she really could turn into a dragon and fly away in embarrassment.

"It was the only address I had," she said, unable to think of anything else to say.

"I am pleased that you found your way to Svetilo and that you are amongst your people while your new magic comes forth. It can be a difficult time, even without all the extra complications you have suffered."

"My people?" she asked.

"We are all Álfr here, so yes, we are your people, Asta Drekiónd. You will always be welcome amongst us," Ruthann said firmly but kindly. Tears pricked at the back of Asta's eyes.

"Thank you, Ruthann. Everyone here has been extremely kind to me."

"Including Søren?" There was a teasing glimmer in the Álfr's eyes.

Asta looked up at the ticking muscle in Søren's jaw, and she leaned into his warmth. "Especially Søren, my lord. I don't like to think of what state I would be in without him."

"It pleases me to hear that. I must go and mingle, but I do hope we may talk again before I leave," Ruthann said, giving her another bow.

"Do you think he read the note?" Asta asked.

"He read it aloud to me. It's how we learned you were in Estonia, and I was about to leave when you arrived." Søren gave her a small smile. "I'm surprised my hair didn't turn white when I woke up and realized you were gone. Please, don't ever leave again without saying goodbye."

"And what makes you think I'm going to leave at all?" Asta looked up just as the Drekiónds arrived with Aramis escorting them. He was dressed like Søren but with a dark blue shirt instead of green. Tyra intercepted him with an evil, mischievous smile that made her look like the Grinch.

"Whether you like it or not, you're royalty and I'm nothing. It would matter to them, even if I weren't Ljósálfar," Søren said, his grip on her tightening ever so slightly.

"They don't get a say over my life," argued Asta.

"They won't see it that way. Royalty only cares about what they want and what they think belongs to them."

"And what do you want?" She slipped her arm from his and turned her back on the dark elves moving toward her.

"Do you really need to ask?" Asta had no time to reply as Steinar greeted her, and she was pulled into the crowd.

Aramis had been searching for Tyra when he felt the kiss of her power, and he managed to turn and grab her hand just as she reached for his ass.

"Busted." He chuckled. Her smile was positively impish.

"You are delectable in that suit. How can you blame me?" Tyra said. "You seem to fit into this crowd. Are you going to get all courtly and kiss my hand?"

Aramis leaned closer so no one would overhear and whispered, "Not where I'm thinking about kissing you, Dökkálfar."

Tyra raised one black brow. "I'm starting to think we should skip out on this party."

"If only we could. It's not all bad. You look incredible all dressed up."

"Here I thought a posh guy like you would be sad I wasn't in a dress."

"And miss the opportunity to see how great you look in those leather pants? Unlikely. I do hope those laces unravel easily."

"Why? Are you thinking about trying to get into them tonight?"

"My dear *Draeimi*, I *know* I'm going to get into them tonight," Aramis said before they were interrupted by a graceful Dökkálfar with brilliant blue eyes and black hair.

"Vigdis, so nice to see you again," Tyra said with a honey-drenched smile.

"*Draeimi*. I didn't quite believe it when Siv said you were trying to court a Ljósálfar, but here you are with the most handsome one of them all. You've become rather ambitious in your old age," Vigdis replied. Her voice was a deep, sexy sound that Aramis was sure had a charm glamour on it.

"How kind of you to say I'm the most handsome," said Aramis smoothly. "I do feel the need to correct you, however. Queen Siv must have misinterpreted the situation. I am the one trying to court Tyra, not the other way around. I could use a few pointers in winning her over. Do you have any advice?"

Vigdis's smile was polite, but her eyes were cold. "My advice is to run screaming in the opposite direction like all the other males have done. I've never known *Dræimi* to love anything more than she loves bloodshed."

"Oh, I don't know if that's true. Aramis has done a few things to me that have given bloodshed some good competition," argued Tyra.

"He's willing to do a few more if you ask him nicely," said Aramis with a suggestive smile. Vigdis made a disgusted sound in the back of her throat and moved away from them.

"Thank you," Tyra said, brushing her fingers against his.

"She's charming. I can see why you like her so much."

"Don't let her fool you. She's the most dangerous one here. Don't let her corner you," warned Tyra.

"You're trying to protect me? You're adorable. You don't need to worry. I've no intention of going anywhere that you are not," Aramis reassured her even though something in his chest warmed. He couldn't remember the last time someone thought to protect him at all.

"I see you have already upset Vigdis," Siv said from behind him.

"Only by breathing," replied Tyra.

Siv ignored her. "Aramis, I'd like you to dance with me."

"It would be my honor, Queen Siv."

"You know, I wasn't entirely convinced you were serious about being friends with Tyra when I arrived," Siv said as Aramis led her to the corner of the glade where Álfr were dancing.

"Why wouldn't I be? She's an amazing female," Aramis replied. *Be polite. You used to be a diplomat, remember?* "I don't understand why you'd be so interested in my business, Queen Siv."

"Tyra is my business, Ljósálfar. Just like my granddaughter and your brother's obvious attachment to her is my business."

"They are old enough to make their own choices—ones that have nothing to do with me."

"You must understand, it's not that I don't appreciate what you have done for them. They are Dökkálfar, and they don't belong here amongst your kind. Asta has immense potential. She needs to come home."

"Asta is a child of Midgard. She *is* home. She has two uncles, so she isn't even an heir. I don't understand why you are trying so hard to force her back to Svartálfaheim."

"Her magic is deep and strong, perhaps the strongest in generations. You can't possibly train her to use it, and when it truly starts to manifest, it could kill her if she has no control," Siv said with traces of genuine concern in her voice.

"With the deepest respect, Queen Siv, I have been told such a thing before. Asta wouldn't be the first prodigy we have helped who has magic not of Ljósálfar origin. What confuses me is your insistence on making it your way or our way. Have we not opened our doors to your people despite our personal history?" Aramis gestured at the light and dark elves mingling and speaking together.

"Yes, let us not forget your accusations against my eldest son. That will further complicate our relationship with Bláinn even if it does prove to be true."

Aramis stopped dancing. "It's not a lie or a ruse to try to keep Asta as some kind of hostage. I can prove that right now."

"Then do it, Ljósálfar," Siv sneered. Aramis didn't hesitate as he forced his darkest memory into her mind, his memory of the night he and Søren fled Álfheim. Siv's grip on him tightened, and he began to lead her again, holding her up so no one noticed a change in her.

"I didn't b-believe…" Siv stammered as she came back to herself.

"I'm sorry that your son has betrayed you, but it doesn't change facts. We aren't your enemy."

"And yet you would try to keep my granddaughter and my greatest weapon from coming home."

"I'm not keeping them. I'm letting them choose for themselves. Tyra is not your weapon, so stop talking about her like she's your property."

Siv's gold gaze sharpened. "By the gods, you're not just fucking her. You really are in love with her."

Aramis kept his cool composure even if her words were like a kick in the gut. "Did Vigdis ever look for her?"

"Of course she did. I've had Vigdis scrying for Tove since Bláinn reported they were gone."

"Looking for Tove, not for Tyra."

"Tyra was never meant to leave her side. Where Tove was we thought Tyra would also be."

"For someone obviously smart, I'm surprised you took Bláinn at his word." Aramis's rage burned hotter.

"You don't know what it's like to deal with a warlord like Bláinn. You're all so safe here that you can't possibly understand what he is capable of. We need to keep Asta from him and find a way to smooth over Tyra and Tove's betrayal."

"Tyra spent two thousand years as a slave in the dwarves' pit. Thrynn almost whipped her to death. Tyra has paid enough." Aramis shook as he tried to control his horror at the thought of his Tyra alone in the darkness far from her stars. *His Tyra*. Gods, he really was in love with her.

"You surprise me, Aramis. I've been led to believe that you are the more reasonable Dauði Dómr, yet here you are reacting emotionally to a political fact. Bláinn needs to be pacified, and I'll give everything I can to keep Asta from him. I'll give whatever, and *whoever*, he wants to ensure that."

Aramis wanted to wrap his hands around her perfect pale throat. He tightened his grip on her and brought her close.

"If you even think of giving Tyra back to him or if I get even the slightest inkling that you knew she was a slave and did nothing to help her, you will learn how very unreasonable I can be. You aren't the first powerful creature to think they could hurt and bargain away what is mine. It didn't end well for them, so I suggest you consider your next words and actions very carefully."

Siv's eyes went wide in surprise, and her red lips twisted into a mirthless smile. "*There* is the God Killer I keep hearing about. I had wondered what attracted you to Tyra. Now I know."

"That's right. She's not the only monster here tonight, and you had best remember it."

"Keep that fire for the fight to come, God Killer. You're going to need it to face Bláinn. Make no mistake, he's coming for you all, and when he's done, you'll give *Draeimi* over to him just to end the slaughter he'll bring to your people."

29

IF SØREN DIDN'T KILL someone or lose his mind by the end of the night, he was going to take it as a win. He kept Asta in view at all times. Occasionally he caught Tyra's eye, and they would give each other an understanding nod. Søren couldn't fathom Asta's nerves about the evening. She was a natural, roaming seamlessly through conversations as if she had been at court for years.

This is what she was born to do, not read books with you.

There was no doubt that she was too good for him, but Søren thought she was too good for everyone else here as well. Despite her sarcastic little tongue, Asta was kind and didn't have the malicious streak she would need if she went back to the Drekiónds' court.

"You watch her like you fear that she's going to disappear any second," Steinar said as he came to stand with Søren.

"She's done it before," Søren muttered, not turning his attention away from the bloodred curls at the back of Asta's neck.

"I am grateful that you have protected her when we could not," Steinar continued. Søren tore his gaze from Asta to see if the king was mocking him.

"She doesn't deserve any of the danger she has been put in. None of it is her fault. The Ljósálfar will always be happy to give her refuge."

"Ruthann has said as much. That reassures me, but you should know that Siv won't back down from trying to get Asta to come back with us."

"And you?"

Steinar looked at his granddaughter, and his whole demeanor softened. "I made such a mistake when I allowed Tove to marry Bláinn. It pushed my daughter away, made her live in fear of us. You have no idea what that feels like. I won't do the same thing to Asta. I want her in my life in any way she will feel comfortable."

"You're the king. Can't you just command Siv to let Asta make her own decision?"

Steinar raised a black eyebrow. "Have you ever tried to command a Drekiónd female to do anything?"

Søren laughed. "Good point."

"Back off!" Asta said loudly, and Søren's attention whipped back to her. Vigdis was standing close to Asta with a surprised expression. Asta's magic had risen and wrapped protectively around her, leaving two points of power directed at the Seiðr like blades. Søren was beside her in a second.

"You heard her," he snarled.

"I didn't touch her, Dauði Dómr. Her magic tried to attack me," Vigdis said, announcing her claim loudly and drawing even more attention. Tyra appeared and gave Vigdis a hard shove.

"What part of back off don't you get, witch?" Tyra asked.

"Søren, I can't make the magic go back in," Asta whispered to him as Tyra and Vigdis started cursing at each other in the dark elf tongue.

"It's okay. Let me help." Søren's magic reached out and flowed over her, gently calming and smothering her magic until the golden daggers disappeared and his power settled over her like a deep green cloak. Asta's breath shuddered out of her, and her eyes were full of tears.

"Get me out of here, Søren," she begged.

"Take her," Tyra said midargument with Vigdis.

Søren didn't need to be asked twice. He opened a gate and pulled Asta through before anyone could stop them.

As soon as they stepped through into a room of stone, Asta bent over to clutch her knees.

"Oh shit, that went so badly," she said. Søren knelt down beside her and rested his hand on the small of her back.

"Are you hurt, *drékisma*?"

"No, but she did something or tried to. One moment we were talking okay, then she started to get an attitude about you and the Ljósálfar, and my magic went haywire like it was trying to protect me." The frightened look in her golden eyes knocked the sense from his head. He wanted to go back and rip Vigdis apart.

"It's okay. She was trying to get a reaction. She obviously has no idea how fierce my little dragon is," he said, trying to banish her fear.

"I'm bigger on the inside." Asta straightened up as much as her tiny height would allow. She gave him a poke in the shoulder and huffed. "Your little dragon, my ass."

"Good to know you still have plenty of fight even if it's only to fight me," Søren said wryly. He stood up and had a proper look at where he'd taken them. He hadn't been thinking of anywhere specific. Instead, he'd focused on being away and hidden. It took him a few seconds to recognize the lounge room of one of the Álfr hunting cabins. They were still inside the perimeter of the ward stones and would be safe enough. He took out his phone and texted their location to Aramis so that he could calm everyone down.

"We will be safe here," Søren said as he flicked out his magic, and the fireplace and lamps were lit.

"What is this place?" Asta asked as she held out her hands to the flames.

"The Álfr have a few of these cabins spread out around the forest for those who want to hunt or practice magic. It should be stocked, so we can stay here for as long as you need to."

"Good. Do you think there is anything to drink? It's freezing in here," Asta said, rubbing her hands up her arms. Søren grabbed a blanket from the lounge chair and wrapped it around her shoulders.

"I'll find you something," he said and went hunting through the kitchen. He found a few bottles of wine and vodka on a shelf in the pantry. He poured two glasses before returning to the lounge room. Asta had kicked off her shoes and curled up in an armchair near the fire.

"Here." He offered her a glass. She took it, giving him a grateful smile.

"Thank you. Did you look after your wife like this?"

Søren sat down opposite her. "I tried to. Álfr males can be a little overprotective once they find a partner."

"You don't say." Asta tried to hide her grin behind her cup, but Søren had already seen it.

"If you didn't cause so much trouble for me, I wouldn't have to be so overprotective." Then his little dragon went for his throat.

"Do you love me?" she asked bluntly. "Before the Drekiónds arrived, I felt your emotions through your magic, and I've wanted an answer since the first time I asked."

"I haven't said anything because you've had enough to worry about. What I feel shouldn't impact the decisions you make. It's about what you want, not what I want." The words were like razor blades on his tongue.

"And if I choose to go to Svartálfaheim, you are going to let me go? Just like that?"

Søren gripped the arms of his chair so hard his hands ached. He forced himself to say, "I'm not your prison guard, Asta. If you want to go, I will respect your decision and won't stop you."

Asta's eyes flashed, reflecting the firelight. "Even though you love me?"

"Yes."

"Say it."

Søren stared at a golden dragon on her dress, unable to look her in the eye and keep his calm. "If you want to go to Svartálfaheim, I will let you go even though I love you."

There was a rustle of fabric as she came to stand in front of him. A sharp nail glided down the edge of his jaw and forced him to lift his head and look at her. She wore an expression he'd never seen before. There was a sharp, predatory gleam in her eye and in the set of her viciously red smile. His whole body went tight with danger and arousal.

"*Say it*," she growled.

"I love you," he whispered. Her hands tightened on his face, and she bent her lips close to his.

"Again."

"I love you." Her fingers gripped his tie as she pulled him forward. "I love you, I love you, I love you."

"That wasn't so hard now, was it?" she said and put her hot lips on his. It was all bite, possessive to the point of violence, and he fucking *loved* it.

Asta tossed his tie aside before her clever little fingers unhooked the buttons of his shirt, and her sharp nails found skin. She made a sexy purr in the back of her throat, and Søren lost it. He dropped his cup to the floor, grabbed her hips with both hands, and pulled her onto his lap. Her long skirt was tangled around her, but she still managed to get a leg on either side of him and grind her hot little core against him. Søren's lips broke from hers as he swore.

"Hmm, there he is," she whispered and thrust against him in a way that almost made him lose all control. That good part of him that had been buried for so long forced him to pull back from her.

"Asta, if you don't want me to fuck you senseless, you need to stop that right now."

Her head cocked to one side, and her brows drew together in confusion. "And why wouldn't I want you to do that?"

"Say it." He threw her words back at her. Asta bunched her hand in his hair and pulled it, exposing his throat to her. She raked her teeth up the sensitive, lifted vein, and he groaned.

"I want you to fuck me senseless, Søren. I want to see you lose all of your perfect control. I want you to take what you want for once and stop fucking teasing me and making us both miserable. I want you to take your fill of me and trust that I'm going to do the same." He tightened his grip on her.

"Who would've thought that a sweet, cardigan-wearing librarian would have such a naughty tongue?" Søren said breathlessly.

Asta raised her head. "That goes to show what you know about librarians." She yelped as he stood up quickly and carried her into the bedroom. He set her down on her feet before turning her and pulling down the fine zipper that ran the length of her back. He kissed the curve of her spine, his hands moving underneath the opening of the dress so that he could cup and knead her breasts.

Asta turned and gave him a gentle shove, so he was forced to sit down on the bed. She shifted her hips, and the heavily embroidered dress fell to the floor with a soft hiss. Søren's gaze zeroed in on the tiny red scrap of underwear she still wore as she reached for his shoulders and pulled off his jacket and shirt. Søren lost his ability to think straight when her soft warm breasts pressed into the hard curves of his chest. He pulled her down and rolled her onto her back. He was kissing her roughly, one hand on her breasts and the other unclipping his belt so he could kick his pants free.

"I should've known you weren't an underwear guy," Asta said, running a hand down his back and grabbing his ass. "Hmm, good to know it's as firm as it looks."

"How attached are you to these?" Søren tugged at the side of her panties.

"Not at all." As soon as the words were out of her mouth, Søren's magic cut the sides of her panties, and he pulled the offending scrap of lace away.

"Nice move." Asta's laugh turned into a gasp as he stroked her gently. Søren kissed the sweet sounds from her mouth as he teased her with his fingers. He finally had her where he'd wanted her since the night he had kissed her in Oslo.

His reaction to her at the time had confused the shit out of him with its intensity. Now he knew he would always have that reaction to his dragon.

Asta's skin grew hot as the pressure inside of her built, and she neared her breaking point. She'd had lovers before, but she'd never felt comfortable with anyone touching her so intimately and had usually glossed over foreplay and gone straight to sex. True to his word, Søren was going to unravel her every way he could.

"I-I can't come this way," she whispered even as she moved against him.

"Trust me, you really can, Asta." Søren's smile was sly and sure as he kissed her. "Come for me."

"You're so bossy—" He slipped a finger inside her, and she almost levitated.

"Don't fight it, *drékisma*. Take it." Søren's finger hooked inside of her, and she had no way to fight the orgasm that roared through her. Light and magic exploded out of her skin, her body unable to handle the release that rocked her. Søren's smug expression was gone, only surprise remained as he stared at the power shimmering on her skin.

"Are you okay?" he asked uncertainly.

Asta laughed helplessly. "I'm a bit more than okay, Søren."

He trailed his hand over her breast in a languid stroke. "More?"

"Gods, yes." Asta wrapped her legs around his waist. Lost in the emotions and sensations of Søren's glorious body on top of her, Asta promised herself that she was going to learn elvish, because as soon as he moved inside of her, Søren seemed to lose his ability to speak English.

"I don't know what you're saying, but whatever it is, the answer is yes," she said as she arched into him.

"I said that we fit together so perfectly that it is as if you were made for me," Søren whispered as he moved, "and the feeling of being inside of you is going to kill me before the night is over."

Asta raked her nails down his back, and he groaned and thrust into her hard enough that she came a second time. She kissed him with trembling lips. "I love you, Søren."

He stroked her cheek tenderly. "I love you too. Anything else?"

Asta reached up to grip his shoulder. "More." Søren was only too happy to oblige.

30

TYRA PACED OUTSIDE OF Søren's apartment door, wondering if Asta was back yet and if she really wanted to walk in on what she hoped Asta and Søren were doing. She was about to go back to her own room when the door opened and Asta was there, dressed and glowing. Tyra started to giggle and Asta flushed.

"Shut up," Asta said, and Tyra's giggle turned to bawdy, loud laughter.

"Looks like someone has been thoroughly fucked."

"Shut up. I do not," Asta retorted.

"Tell that to the bite mark on your collarbone."

Asta quickly closed the top button of her shirt and grinned. "Damn it."

Tyra pulled her over and kissed her cheek. "Well done, little cousin. Want some coffee?"

"Desperately," Asta said, following Tyra to Aramis's apartments.

"Thanks for leaving me in the shitstorm so you could go shag Søren." Tyra made coffee as Asta sat down at the table.

"Were they really mad?"

"I was. Vigdis was out of line."

"I think she was doing it to get a rise out of me and see what I'd do if she started talking trash about you, Søren, and the Ljósálfar." Asta frowned. "Sorry for leaving you there."

"Don't be. They squawked a lot, but it was amusing for me to watch them attempt to salvage the situation. I felt a bit sorry for Ruthann. He did okay against Siv and held his ground about Vigdis provoking a fight in the middle of what was meant to be a peaceful event. Aramis was pure magic."

Asta accepted her cup of her coffee. "Why? What did he do?"

"Existed." Asta rolled her eyes.

"Where is he?"

"Caught up in a meeting with Ruthann. Speaking of which, Siv wants to have tea with you today and make Vigdis apologize for being a bitch."

"Do I have to?" Asta groaned.

"Well, it can't hurt. I'll be right outside the door if you need me, and it's only tea. You only have to stay as long as you want to."

"I should have stayed in bed with Søren."

"I hear you. There's something about these Ljósálfar. They are like crack." Tyra sat down beside her. "You know Siv won't like you two together."

Asta stiffened. "I don't need her permission."

"You will if we go with them. She'll already be hatching some plan to sell your vagina off to the highest bidder. Anything to get an alliance or whatever the fuck else she wants," Tyra replied. She had seen what Siv had done when Tove came of age. Her treatment of Asta would be no different. Steinar might be able to hold Siv back for a year or so, but sooner or later, Asta would be meat on a butcher block.

"Tyra, I don't want to go to Svartálfaheim. If you really want to go back though, do it."

Tyra let out a bitter laugh. "What makes you think I'd want to go back?"

"It's your home."

"No, it's not. It hasn't been for a long time. That's like saying the dwarves' pit was home. My home is where you are and where—" Tyra broke off, biting her lip to keep from saying it.

"Where Aramis is," Asta finished gently. "It's not like you have to explain yourself to me. I'd never separate you. He's kind of perfect for you."

Tyra's throat started to close from the unexpected emotion lodged there. "I just wanted you to feel free to make your own choice, Asta. Tove didn't get that. *I* didn't get that. If you wanted to go with the Drekiónds, I'd have gone with you and kept my mouth shut. I didn't want whatever I'm doing with Aramis to affect your decision, you know?"

"Did you and Søren start a club behind my back? He said nearly the exact same thing to me last night. You're both fucking mental if you think I'm going with Siv."

"It's because we both love you too much to take your choices away for selfish-ass reasons."

Asta wrapped her arms around Tyra. "I love you, my tempestuous cousin. I'm not going to leave you, and I'm not going to drag you back to that place where Bláinn is. You and I are going to stay here and drive our beautiful males crazy, and if anyone tries to stop us, we are going to destroy them. Understand?"

There was a firm certainty and steel in her voice that Tyra hadn't heard before, and she hugged Asta back. "No matter what happens, I won't let them take you," she swore, and she meant it like she'd meant few things in her life.

"I suppose this means we should go and politely tell Siv that she can leave. Steinar can stay if he wants to, but yeah, I think Siv and Vigdis should definitely go away," Asta said, and Tyra gave her forehead a kiss.

"Let's do it."

After making sure Asta's makeup was neat, and any sneaky bite marks were covered, Asta and Tyra made their way through Svetilo. The amount of information Asta's senses now took in still overwhelmed her. With her shields off, she could even feel the massive amount of power the stronghold contained.

"You're getting all dreamy-eyed. Thinking of Søren naked?" asked Tyra.

"I am now! Actually, I was thinking about how much I like this place."

"It's dramatically improved since Aramis made me a room."

"He made you a room? When? Why didn't you tell me?"

"You had other things on your mind." Tyra described the meta experience that was "fucking Starlight amongst the starlight" as they wended their way to the rooms of the dark elves. Tyra was distracting enough that Asta didn't start to get nervous until the guards let her through to the room where Siv and Vigdis waited with tea already served.

"Thank you, Tyra. You may leave," said Siv. Asta pressed her lips together in frustration as Tyra became the strange silent guard that she didn't recognize.

"I'll be right outside," Tyra said calmly before closing the door. Asta wished Tove was there to tell her how to deal with Siv, but something told her Tove hadn't figured that out herself.

"Where is Steinar?" Asta asked as she sat down.

Siv made an elegant, dismissive gesture. "Oh, out and about. Ruthann and that sour Dauði Dómr you like so much came to get him about an hour ago."

"*Søren*," Asta said through gritted teeth. "His name is Søren."

"Yes, yes. I never thought I'd see the day when one of my blood would be so attached to a Ljósálfar."

"I never thought I'd see the day when I'd have a racist grandmother, but life is full of surprises," Asta countered.

"It's not about race. It's about class," Vigdis replied haughtily.

"And that's supposed to be better?" Asta took a deep, steadying breath. "Tove was one of the most accepting and generous people I've ever known, and if this is your attitude, I can understand why she never wanted to return to Svartálfaheim."

"Accepting and generous enough to nearly plunge our people back into a war when she left. I know you think I'm some kind of monster, and perhaps I am according to Midgardian standards, but everything I've done has been to ensure the survival of our people. Bláinn wiped out most of the old families, yet the Drekiónds still survive," Siv said.

"At what cost, Grandmother? I don't know what Tove was like before Bláinn, but I saw the effect of what she went through as I grew up. I watched Bláinn kill my father. He sacrificed himself so Tove and I could get away. After that we were always moving, never settling, never belonging anywhere. We only had each other. She was my entire world, and then she was run over in the street, and I had no one until Tyra found me. Tove was scared all the time. She had nightmares about being tortured, and now I know why. She lived through that with Bláinn. Your son did nothing to help her. Instead, he left her so he could kill innocent Ljósálfar for fucking sport. Do you really think I would choose *that* kind of family over Tyra?"

"Tyra is a loyal dog. She follows her master's call," Vigdis said.

"I'm sorry, why are you here? You've done enough damage."

"Vigdis's skills got us here and kept us one step ahead of Bláinn. She even found you across the worlds," Siv explained.

"So powerful yet you couldn't find Tyra to rescue her. Interesting," said Asta.

Siv let out a pained sigh. "Can we please not fight for one moment? Have some tea at least. There is so much that you don't understand, and you won't until you come to Svartálfaheim and see it for yourself."

"You should've fought Bláinn, not pacified him," said Asta, that new, violent predator inside her raising its head. "You never should have given Tove to him and let her suffer that way."

"You think I knew he was going to torture her? Daimar went with her to make sure she was protected. I couldn't have foreseen his treachery. That is something else I have to carry as a mother and a queen. If Søren and Aramis's accusation proves correct, I'll have to order the execution of my own son." Siv sighed, and a tear slid down her cheek. "If I'm firm in my manner at the moment, it's not because I don't have a heart, Asta. It is because my heart is broken."

Asta didn't have a chance to consider whether Siv's tears were real or not, because Vigdis grabbed her and slipped a woven bracelet over her hand. It was made of hair and bone, and when Asta tried to rip it off, her hands wouldn't move.

"What the—" Asta groaned and slumped onto the floor like she had a bag of weights around her neck. Her mouth closed and refused to open again. She tried to fight and flail, but she just lay still, her body refusing to move.

"Vigdis, what do you think you are doing? I gave you no such order," Siv cried. She knelt down to help Asta, and Vigdis moved to drop a long cord around her neck.

"I'm sorry, my queen, but this was all taking far too long. I'm done waiting while you pander to the whims of this half-breed."

Through her magical gag, Siv murmured angry curses, but Vigdis only clicked her tongue sadly. "I have served you faithfully all my life, Siv. I'm tired of you ignoring my advice. I told you that Tyra would bring you all to your knees—that you should've left her in the snow, because I had *seen* that she would bring doom. You destroy your enemies, not raise them in your household, making it that much easier to betray you. She helped Tove escape when Bláinn was so close to unlocking those hidden depths of the Drekiónd power. What a waste." Vigdis looked at them with undisguised loathing before she turned away and headed for a large gilded mirror.

Asta could feel the magic in the air, a cold mix of shadows and bones and blood. She shut her eyes against it and focused on the golden core inside of her. The bracelet on her wrist was woven with hair. If she could get her magic to break a single strand, it might be enough to loosen the bracelet's hold. Her magic had helped her the night she'd been attacked in Tallin while still buried under all of the protections Tove had layered over her. Surely Vigdis's ugly bracelet wouldn't be so strong.

"Vigdis, you summoned me early," a voice said from the mirror. Ice and fear raced through Asta's veins. She opened her eyes and saw only smoke on the mirror's surface, but she would *never* forget that voice. It haunted the nightmares of her father lying bloody on the new grass and the monster standing over her.

"Lord Bláinn, circumstances have changed, and I've had to accelerate our plans. I have Siv and Tove's daughter in holding and ready for you. The girl has guardians, Ljósálfars of skill, but from what I can tell, the Ljósálfars have no army. They are ripe for your warriors to conquer. Bring them, and let's be done with this."

"Vigdis, you never fail me. I will come." The mirror cleared, and the heavy tension in the room lifted. As it did, Asta felt a faint tingling heat in her right hand.

Focus on the seed. The memory of Søren's words came back to her. Asta shut her eyes again and focused on the sharp points of power that had spiked from her skin the night before. *Come on, I just need a tiny point.* Asta bit her tongue to stop herself from crying out as a hot, sharp blade pushed out of her skin and cut through the bracelet. Instantly, the pressure in her body lifted, and she scanned the room. Vigdis still had her back to Asta and Siv as she tipped runes out onto a dining table. Asta rolled silently to her feet, picked up the heavy porcelain teapot, and hit Vigdis hard across the back of her head. Porcelain shattered and hot tea splashed across them both, and Asta dragged a wounded and still-struggling Vigdis to the ground.

"Tyra!" Asta shouted as loud as she could. The door to the room shattered as Tyra's magic tore it apart.

"You little bit—" Asta's fist slammed into Vigdis's nose, and Tyra was beside Asta, the tip of her sword at Vigdis's throat.

"Off her now, Asta. You've done enough. Go help Siv," Tyra instructed. Asta got up on wobbly feet and stumbled to Siv's side.

"It's okay, Grandmother," she said soothingly, pulling the loop of hair from around Siv's neck and tossing the foul thing to the other side of the room. Siv inhaled deeply and clung to Asta.

"I'm so sorry," Siv said, sobbing. Asta gave her back an awkward pat.

"It'll be okay. We're fine," Asta said. Vigdis made a garbled sound that could've been a laugh.

"You'll all be burning by tomorrow morning. Enjoy the moment," Vigdis spat. Tyra's dark purple power flowed out over the witch and wrapped around her mouth and nose. Vigdis tried to struggle, but Tyra's fierce expression didn't change until Vigdis had passed out.

"That shut her up," Tyra muttered.

"Siv?" Steinar's voice was panicked as he climbed past the ruined door and hurried to his weeping wife. He took her from Asta, holding her close as Siv clung to him.

"What happened here?" he asked, looking to Tyra. Asta was about to reply when Søren came into the room with an expression that would've made her run in fear if she didn't know him. He spotted her on the ground, and the rage barely shifted from his face.

"Are you hurt?" Søren asked.

"No, not really," Asta said and lifted her hand. "Just a scratch."

Søren looked at Vigdis on the floor. "Is she dead?"

"Not yet," Tyra snarled softly.

"Let's get her in a cell where she can't do any more damage, and we can get to the bottom of this," Søren said, helping Asta to her feet. She wanted to press into him, the way Siv had done with Steinar, but she didn't want to appear weak in front of the dark elves. When she was sure no one could see, she gave his hand a reassuring squeeze before letting it go.

"We don't have much time. That bitch summoned Bláinn. He'll be here by dawn if not sooner," said Asta.

31

AN HOUR BEFORE DAWN the wards sounded throughout Svetilo, announcing Bláinn's arrival. Aramis and Tyra had only been in bed for a few hours. They had listened to Asta explain Vigdis's betrayal, and Tyra had beamed with pride when Asta had described how she had clobbered the witch.

Tyra had taken Aramis to bed as soon as she could. She wasn't good with words, so she held him and let him know how she felt in other ways. She had never gone into battle with a lover before and hated the feeling. He'd never ask her to stay behind, so she didn't insult him by suggesting the same.

The modified Ljósálfar armor she strapped on felt good, and Aramis helped adjust the positioning of her shoulder guards to free up her movement.

"You look like a beautiful angel of death," Aramis said, grabbing the top of her breastplate so he could pull her close and kiss her.

"Do you want to come kill some dark elves with me?"

"My sword is your sword, *Draeimi*." Words hung heavy in his sapphire eyes, but they didn't have time for them. They headed for the door.

Søren and Asta were waiting with the Drekiónds at the main entrance to Svetilo. Ruthann and every warrior they could bring through a gate from Alaska the previous evening stood ready for instructions.

"I wish you would stay, Asta. Let us deal with Bláinn," Steinar said.

Good luck, buddy, Tyra thought as Asta raised her stubborn little chin.

"No. We face him together. Bláinn killed my father, and I am looking forward to spitting on his corpse," Asta said firmly. Despite her bravado, she gripped Søren's hand.

"I hope you are well rested and ready to show off those skills of yours, *Draeimi*," Søren said as Tyra and Aramis came to stand with them.

"Try not to run away like a little girl when I do," Tyra replied, and they shared a grin.

Tyra should've put money on where Bláinn would drop his army. The watchers had reported to Aramis as soon as the gates had opened and the warriors had started marching through. Sure enough, the plain Aramis had shown Tyra was where rank upon rank of Bláinn's finest now stood.

Tyra's old rage rushed to the surface as she stared at the gray-and-black standards on their tall poles. It wasn't his entire army, just enough to threaten them into surrendering Asta. She couldn't see them, but Tyra knew that he had at least three mages on standby, ready to open gates to bring in reinforcements if it did come to a fight. She voiced her concerns to Aramis.

"Then we focus on taking the mages out first. We make it so Bláinn is stranded with no hope of escape," Aramis said, sharing a look with Søren.

"If you and Tyra can keep the army distracted, I'll focus on the mages," Søren replied. His eyes scanned the army. "I hope you're as good as the legends claim, Tyra."

"I've defeated bigger armies than this on my own, elfling." Tyra laughed. "Try not to pee those tight leather pants once I get started."

"We have movement," Aramis said, interrupting their banter.

Bláinn had finally appeared from his war tent. He was unmistakable with golden hair and intricate black-and-silver armor as he towered above the other warriors around him. He was the only male Tyra had ever feared—not that she didn't think she could take him in combat, but for the darkness that seemed to emanate from him.

"The bastard," Asta whispered angrily beside her. "I remember him killing my father. He has to die today."

"Easy, cousin. We will both have our revenge before this day is through." Tyra didn't need Asta losing her temper and rushing out of the protection of their ranks. Thrynn followed Bláinn and then Daimar appeared. Siv made a small sound of anger and despair.

"How could he betray us like this?" Siv said.

"I suppose we will find out," replied Steinar, the grief of the father buried under the rage of the king.

The three dark elves halted at a halfway point between their army and the Ljósálfar. Tyra schooled her features and stepped forward with Aramis, Søren, Asta, the Drekiónds, and Ruthann following closely.

"*Draeimi*, your ability to survive never fails to impress me," said Bláinn. His black eyes scanned the group. "Siding with the Ljósálfar. You must be desperate."

"Not particularly. What are you doing here?" Tyra asked in a bored tone.

"I've come to finally get my revenge on those who betrayed me. Tove is dead, but perhaps her daughter will make for a better wife," said Bláinn. He stared at Asta, a cruel smile appearing on his lips. "Tovesdóttir, at last we meet."

"Go fuck yourself," replied Asta, and Bláinn's smile widened at the defiance.

"More fight and fire than your mother. That's a good sign. This negotiation is between us, no one else. You love these elves who have sided with you, I understand. You can save them from painful, horrible deaths right now if you come to me willingly."

"You think I'm stupid enough to believe that? You will burn and pillage just like your generals did in Álfheim," Asta said, stepping forward.

"I always keep my word, Asta. I promise you, if you come and take my hand, we will leave together. Midgard will be left intact, and I won't seek retribution on the Drekiónds for siding with the enemy instead of their allies," Bláinn replied. "Whatever they have promised you, I will give it to you and so much more. We could rule the Nine Worlds if we choose to."

Tyra wanted to cut off the hand he stretched out toward Asta. Asta reached out her hand like she would take his and then flipped it over, lifting her middle finger at him instead.

Tyra choked on her laughter. *The little shit.*

"I'll pass, thanks," Asta replied.

Bláinn's face was priceless in his confusion. "*Draeimi*, this child has no idea of the terror my army can unleash, but you do. Try to reason with her."

"You clearly don't know her if you think my advice will change anything." Tyra laughed. "We all know you will destroy us as soon as you have Asta, so let's not play pretend anymore."

"And what about you, my son?" Siv demanded, looking across the ice at Daimar. "You would be happy to stand back and watch your own kin be killed?"

"You have had thousands of years to come to your senses and side with King Bláinn. He is my family now," Daimar replied coldly.

"Don't waste your breath, Siv. Daimar has always been a grasping little bastard, and it would hardly be the first time he's sat back and let Bláinn do whatever he wanted to a Drekiónd. I'm going to enjoy killing you for what you did to Tove," Tyra said with a wide smile.

"Your threats do not frighten me," Daimar replied, though the twitch in his left eye suggested otherwise.

Bláinn's attention turned to Søren with a cold, assessing look. "You must be the Ljósálfar protector Vigdis mentioned. You don't seem like much."

"Neither do you. I suppose we will find out who is the better warrior by the end of the day," replied Søren.

"You choose battle? So be it," Bláinn said with one last smile at Asta. "I am going to enjoy killing your lover and then making you scream as I take you in front of his bleeding corpse."

"With your tiny dick? Doubt it. Tove said it was a wee little thing," Tyra said with a snort.

Bláinn glared at her before he moved back behind the ranks of his warriors.

"Asta, Siv, get back to the safety of the ranks. Aramis and Søren, with me. Steinar and Ruthann, be ready to lead the march," Tyra instructed as they went back to their own warriors.

"*Draeimi*, I look forward to taking my whip to you again before this day is out!" Thrynn shouted across the battlefield.

Before Tyra could reply, a soft *swish* swept past her ear, and Thrynn fell, an arrow buried in the eye slot of his helm. Tyra turned as Aramis lowered his bow. He looked furious and unapologetic as warriors dragged Thrynn's corpse out of the way.

Bláinn pointed to his eye and then at Aramis. A promise of retribution. Aramis didn't even flinch.

"That bastard won't be taking his whip to anyone ever again," said Aramis, his voice as cold as the ice under his feet. Tyra grabbed him, kissing him hard on his grim mouth.

"I love you so damn much right now. Stay behind me once the fighting starts, and I'll protect you," she promised.

Aramis stroked her cheek. "I love you too, but your timing for telling me this is terrible, you know that?"

"I know. Just do as I say and argue with me later. Søren, get ready. I'm about to clear a path for you to the mages," Tyra said.

"I'll be ready." Søren nodded, before turning to Asta. "Go to safety now, beloved. We will see you afterward."

"You better," Asta replied, following Siv to a safe place behind their warriors.

Tyra rolled her neck and let go of all the barriers she used to keep her power locked up. Her power was an endless well of battle magic that could rival a god's.

Tyra pushed aside everything that wasn't Bláinn or his army—her fear for Asta, Aramis, and Søren, her tentative hope for a future with them, and the love and family she'd thought she would never have. She would fight with every bit of her strength to protect them. She could feel Aramis behind her, watching her back. His power glowed like a star in the back of her mind.

Tyra settled into that deep, cold place inside of her that she hadn't visited in two millennia. The killing place where there was only rage and battle and the taste of blood in her mouth. Magic poured out of her, curling around her in dark purple smoke.

Bláinn's battle horns sounded, but Tyra was already moving. Her laughter was high and wild as she became *Draeimi* once more. She raced across the ice, her power whipping out with a life of its own. It struck the first line of warriors, cutting through armor and shields, flesh and bone.

Tyra charged on, her power shooting back toward her and rising up as a shield to stop a volley of arrows from raining down on her. She vanished and reappeared in the center of the enemy army. Shouts of alarm were cut off as she detonated her power like a bomb, turning Bláinn's warriors around her into red mist. Tyra saw his furious face and spotted a mage placing shields around Bláinn to protect him from her. She felt two other magical signatures near Bláinn's tent where the other mages must've been readying an attack of battle magic.

Tyra waved at Bláinn and vanished again, appearing near where Aramis and Søren were engaged with the enemy attacking their right flank. She pulled the sword from her back and infused her magic with the black blade. Tyra relished the feel of steel meeting steel, the enemy falling before her as she made her way to Søren's side.

"Bláinn has a mage keeping him protected, and there's two others near his tent. They are battle magic efficient. The only way we are going to get him out on the field is if we provoke him," Tyra said.

"With an ego that big, it won't take much to provoke him into some one-on-one combat," Søren said. He and Aramis shared a smile, looking like the twins they were. "And he really didn't like you killing his general."

Tyra turned back to the battle raging around them. "Whatever you have planned, do it now. I'll draw the warriors away to the left-hand side. It will open you up to get closer to Bláinn. And don't die."

"You hear that? I think she's starting to like me, brother," Søren said.

"You wish. I just don't want to have to deal with Asta's tears." Tyra blew a kiss to Aramis and charged back into the fray.

Søren had seen literal gods fight before, but nothing compared to the carnage Tyra unleashed. She had joked about him pissing himself, and he now realized that it had been a warning.

"And that's the woman you've fallen in love with," Søren said to Aramis, as Tyra released herself once more on Bláinn's army.

Aramis's smile was dopey. "She is magnificent, isn't she?"

Søren didn't have time to tell Aramis that he was insane. Tyra was drawing the army toward her, and Bláinn instantly commanded his warriors to overwhelm her. He didn't seem to realize that she was purposely staying in one place to bait him.

"The fucking ego on that male is astounding," Aramis commented.

"Let's go," Søren replied. He unleashed a blast of power that had Bláinn's warriors flying backward, creating a path for Aramis to race ahead of him. Aramis's blades cut down the dazed warriors on either side of them.

"Bláinn!" Søren shouted, his magic amplifying his voice. "If you want Asta, you'll have to go through me!"

The dark elf's attention flew to Søren right as he and Aramis released the charring spell Anya had taught them. Warriors screamed as they were cooked alive in their armor before collapsing into ash. The Svetilo army pushed forward toward Søren and Aramis, keeping them from being surrounded.

Bláinn shouted for his warriors to get out of his way. "You wish to die so badly today, light elf? Very well."

Søren lifted his sword and blocked the axe Bláinn swung at him. The impact reverberated up his arm.

"Finish this, brother. I have your back," Aramis shouted. His battle magic surged, and he focused it on anyone coming up behind them.

"Asta is mine, Bláinn. I will not let you take her," Søren snarled, spinning his sword as a distraction while he tried to find a weak spot in Bláinn's armor.

"That girl has no idea of her power. Give her to me, and I will give you Álfheim. Don't you want to go home?" Bláinn said, stepping back as Søren's blade cut the plume off his helm.

"Asta is my home."

Bláinn laughed. "Lovesick fool. She will be the death of you all."

Bláinn's next blow shattered Søren's shield, forcing him to dodge and roll across the slick ice to give himself time to toss the ruined metal aside.

"It is good to see the Ljósálfar still train their young in combat," Bláinn said as he maneuvered to follow Søren, "though it won't save Álfheim from what I plan to do with it."

"You will die today. That I can promise you," Søren replied, meeting Bláinn's attack head-on. Bláinn was stronger than anyone he'd encountered since his fight with Vasilli—a fight he'd barely survived.

Bláinn's heavy axe came down, and the blow forced Søren to his knees. Søren swung his body, knocking Bláinn off-balance. Søren rolled, got back to his feet, and was readying for another attack when a roar echoed across the plain. Both armies seemed to freeze in collective fear, and a gold-and-red dragon the size of a semitrailer charged toward them.

Asta's heart was in her throat as the armies clashed again and again. She had promised she wouldn't interfere, that she would obey every order once the fighting started. She wished she could fight alongside them, but she knew she'd just be in the way.

"This is the worst part of being a queen," said Siv beside her. "You watch those you love go off to die to protect you, because they believe you are worth saving. Tyra loves you like she's never loved anyone except for Tove. She will give everything she has today, and when you see what she really is, you might not be able to love her the same way. I have seen her take down armies, giants, and beasts you can only dream about."

Dread, fear, and magic rippled through Asta as Tyra appeared beside Søren and Aramis and then disappeared again. A minute later she appeared on the other side of the battlefield, and the whole of Bláinn's army descended upon her.

Asta couldn't make sense of what she was seeing. There was a flash of light, then screams echoed and blood sprayed as Bláinn's army was shredded by Tyra's magic. Bláinn didn't hesitate. He sent another wave of warriors toward Tyra in his desperation to take her down.

The smell of blood reached Asta, and she tried not to gag even as the predator rippled under her skin. She needed to get out there. She needed to help. Siv's hand tightened on her arm.

"Asta, what are you doing? I can feel your power rising," Siv said. "Calm yourself, granddaughter. This is hardly the first battle Tyra and your Dauđi Dómr have been in."

Despite Siv's efforts to calm her, Asta's magic rolled inside of her, building until she couldn't hear anything but the roar of the clashing armies in front of her.

Bláinn finally joined the battle, and Asta's focus didn't move from him as he ducked and wove and slaughtered. She thought he would go to stop Tyra, but he was heading in the opposite direction. Toward Søren.

A part of Asta was crying out in alarm and panic, but the other part—the one that had only begun to surface once her shields had been removed—was taking over.

"Asta, you need to calm down and listen to me. I can't lose you too!" Siv shouted, shaking her.

Asta pushed her aside in time to see Søren's shield shatter. He went down. Asta gave herself over to her magic, and the beast tore free. The well of power inside of her exploded, and Asta fell forward as her bones began to crack and her skin stretched. A cry burst out of her, but instead of a scream of anger, it was a roar.

All other thoughts disappeared until only one remained. *My treasure, my love.*

Asta charged, racing across the field toward the battling armies. Aramis's magic snapped against her snout to get her attention.

"The mages! Get the mages! I'll protect Søren!" he shouted.

Asta managed to gain control of her beast instincts, and she launched herself in the air with one powerful flap of her wings. She cleared the armies and landed on the edge of the forest behind Bláinn's forces.

Warriors screamed and scattered as she swiped at them with teeth and claws. Magic she didn't recognize hit her side, and she whipped her head toward it. Three dark elves were getting ready to cast at her again. Boiling heat and rage rolled up from her chest, and she roared, unleashing a stream of dragon fire toward them. Their screams lasted only a second before they, and the tents behind them, were reduced to ash. What remained of Bláinn's decimated force stopped fighting and dropped their weapons.

Asta didn't pay them any attention as her golden eyes looked back to where Søren was still fighting Bláinn. Søren's attention was fixed on her, so he didn't see as Bláinn's axe came down on his shoulder. His scream of pain made Asta's vision go white. Ice and earth and bodies churned under her feet as she raced toward him. Bláinn stared up at her and dropped the bloody axe.

"True heir of Alvida of Múspellsheim, I offer you my crown and my army in fealty to your greatness," Bláinn declared. "My magnificent queen, be—" Asta's claws swiped the air, cleaving him in two and scattering the pieces on the ice around them.

"Asta…" Søren said, his hot blood spilling onto the snow. Her head swiveled around, and with care, sharp bloody claws picked him up. "*Drékisma*, you saved me."

"*Treasure*," Asta growled through her fangs and cradled him close to her chest. No one would be taking him from her again.

32

ASTA COULDN'T REMEMBER HOW she'd gotten from the battlefield to a warm bed, but she became aware of Søren's body cradling hers. She wriggled back into him with a satisfied sigh. She could get used to this feeling.

"Are you awake, *drékisma*?" Søren asked, and there was an edge in his tone that made Asta open her eyes.

"I am now," she complained, but when she rolled over and saw the bandages wrapped tightly around his shoulder and torso, she stilled. "Are you okay?"

"Are *you*?"

Asta sat up, pushing her hair back. "I don't know. How did I get here?"

"What do you last remember?"

"Blood…" Asta looked at her clean hands. They were so small and odd looking. What had happened to her claws? *Wait, what claws?* Images bombarded her of the battle, the stench of blood, and the burning heat of her magic. She stared at her hands. She had torn Bláinn into pieces. "I-I think I was a dragon."

Søren sat up beside her and wrapped his good arm around her shoulders. "Asta, you *were* a dragon." She covered her mouth with her hands, staring into his green eyes as her memories came back to her. She touched his cheek. "Treasure."

"I'm glad you think so." Søren's eyes shone with love.

"Søren, I can turn into a dragon." Asta started to laugh in awe and amazement. The door to Søren's room opened, and Tyra was there, dressed in leather leggings and a Led Zeppelin shirt.

"I thought I heard a crazy person." Tyra raised a brow at Asta. "What the actual fuck, cousin?"

"What? You think you're the only one who can save the day?" Asta frowned. Her memories after killing Bláinn were too blurry to make out. "We *did* save the day, right?"

Tyra wrapped her arms around Asta, squeezing her so hard her shoulders ached. "Yes, Asta. We saved the day. Or you did by turning into a big freaking dragon."

"What happened?"

"Ruthann sent the rest of Bláinn's army home after they surrendered to the Drekiónds," Tyra explained.

"And Daimar?"

"I got him in the fight," said Aramis. He was leaning against the door with his arms folded. He had a healing cut on one cheek but otherwise looked whole.

Asta breathed out a shaky breath. "Good. Have my grandparents left?"

"No, they've been waiting for you to wake up, though something tells me they aren't going to push you to go back with them anymore," Tyra said with a delightfully wicked smile.

In the end, the Drekiónds *did* try to get Asta to return to Svartálfaheim with them. Steinar held Asta's hand very gently as they walked through the Winter Garden later that day.

"Of course we want you with us. We want to get to know you better," he said.

"So it has nothing to do with how I can turn into a dragon?" Asta asked.

"Not *all* to do with that. Though I wouldn't mind if you could teach me how you did it," said Siv from the other side of Steinar.

"No offense, Grandmother, but I think you breathe enough fire already. I want to know you both better too, but Midgard is my home. Ruthann has said you both will be welcome anytime. I would like to meet Uncle Hagen at some point and even see Svartálfaheim. I'm just not ready yet," Asta said as honestly as she could.

"At least we know you have enough guardians watching over you," Siv said, and Asta stole a glance at Søren, Tyra, and Aramis walking at a respectful distance behind them.

"You turned into a dragon to save your Dauði Dómr, so we know it's pointless to try to separate you. He's welcome to come to Svartálfaheim too when you feel you want to see it," said Steinar with a smile.

"Thank you, Grandfather," Asta replied.

Ruthann was waiting for them in a clearing with two guards, watching Vigdis. She had been chained, shackled, and gagged with magic-infused metal to ensure she couldn't use her power to escape.

"Are you sure you don't want me to just kill her right now? I'd be happy to do it," offered Tyra.

"No, she could still have useful information, and now that Bláinn is gone, we will need full details of his operations so we can ensure we uproot his influence in every corner of Svartálfaheim. Something tells me she knows all about it, and Hagen will be more than happy to get it out of her," said Siv. The queen embraced Tyra and whispered something in her ear that Asta couldn't catch.

"Thank you, my queen," said Tyra when they parted.

"It has been too long, and I'm sorry for much when it comes to you, Tyra." Siv gave Asta a long look. "Stay in contact, granddaughter." Ruthann opened a gate, and through it, Asta caught glimpses of a green land and a palace of stone. Siv and Steinar both bowed deeply, said their farewells, and thanked Ruthann in elvish before he closed the gate behind them.

Søren's warm arm came around Asta's waist, and he kissed the top of her head. "Now that you are finally free of both Bláinn and your grandparents, what would you like to do?" Asta smiled widely as the dragon inside twitched.

"We are going to need a big space," Aramis said, as if reading her mind.

"This can't be a good idea, can it?" asked Søren nervously, looking to where Asta stood in the snow at the edge of a cliff. "You don't have to do this. You have nothing to prove, Asta."

"Will you shut up and let her do her thing?" Tyra said, leaning her arm against Aramis's shoulder. Søren made a frustrated sound in the back of his throat and went to his little dragon's side. "Are all Ljósálfar males mother hens like he is?"

"Søren has always been protective. I'm not like that with you, am I?" Aramis said. His hand crept under her jacket and rested on the curve of her back. "Are you going to tell me what Siv said?"

"I don't think it'll matter much. She told me who my real father is," Tyra replied. She wanted to sound like she didn't care, but Aramis always seemed to know when there was a hidden worry buried amongst the bravado.

"You can tell me when you're ready. I love you, so it hardly matters who created you," said Aramis, drawing her close.

"You might care if you found out that he might be considered a god." Tyra bit her lip, her brows drawn.

"He wouldn't be the first god I encountered, and it would make sense after seeing what you can really do," said Aramis.

"What if it was, maybe, a god of war who had come to Svartálfaheim on a diplomatic mission and has no idea I exist?"

Aramis kissed her forehead. "I told you, it doesn't matter to me, only *you* do. I'll support whatever you want to do with the information."

"And if I wanted to go to Asgard?"

"Then I'll be right by your side."

Tyra wrapped her hands around his neck. "You are something else, Starlight. No wonder I love you so much." She was losing herself in their kiss when Søren made a startled yelp, and Tyra looked up to see her little Asta turn into a dragon.

"I told her not to try to fly just yet. You don't think she will, do you? She barely has control over the shift," said Søren, hurrying to join them.

"I think wherever she flies, she'll always find her way back," said Tyra as Asta unfurled her wings.

"Yeah, *treasure*, you have nothing to worry about," Aramis teased, and Søren glared at him. "Trust you to fall in love with a dragon."

Tyra laughed, but her heart was warmed at the worry and love in Søren's eyes as he watched the monstrous creature in front of them. Asta turned her big body around so she could sniff them. Søren rested his head against her snout.

"Go. Just make sure you come back," Søren said, all the fight leaving him. Asta snuffled at him before she turned quickly, ran for the cliff's edge, and launched herself off it. The three of them raced forward as the dragon opened its wings and soared upward.

"She's going to kill me," said Tyra and Søren at the same time.

"You both need to relax. Asta will come back when she's ready," Aramis said as they watched Asta soar higher.

"You're right. Every dragon needs a mountain, and we have her hoard after all." Tyra took their hands in hers, her heart dangerously full of love and hope as she watched the dragon dance on the wind. "You know, maybe the Norns aren't bitches after all."

ABOUT THE AUTHOR

Amy Kuivalainen is the bestselling author of *The Exorcist and the Demon Hunter*, the Magicians of Venice series (*The Immortal City, The Sea of the Dead, The King's Seal*) and the Firebird Faerie Tales (*Cry of the Firebird, Ashes of the Firebird, Rise of the Firebird*).

A Finnish-Australian writer who is obsessed with magical wardrobes, doors, auroras, and burial mounds that might offer her a way into another realm, she enjoys mashing up mythology and lore into unique retellings about monsters and magic.

Printed in the USA
CPSIA information can be obtained
at www.ICGtesting.com
LVHW090937210224
772370LV00017B/103/J